Mills & Boon Classics

A chance to read and collect some of the best-loved novels from Mills & Boon—the world's largest publisher of romantic fiction.

Every month, four titles by favourite Mills & Boon authors will be re-published in the *Classics* series.

A list of other titles in the *Classics* series can be found at the end of this book.

Lilian Peake

MAN IN CHARGE

MILLS & BOON LIMITED
LONDON · TORONTO

First published 1973
Australian copyright 1980
Philippine copyright 1980
This edition 1980

© Lilian Peake 1973

ISBN 0 263 73356 4

Set in 10 pt. Linotype Plantin

Made and printed in Great Britain by Richard Clay (The Chaucer Press) Ltd, Bungay, Suffolk

CHAPTER ONE

Cynthia Bourne suppressed a shudder and said to her daughter, 'If they don't answer the bell soon, I'm sure we'll be eaten alive by those two horribly pretentious predators sitting there staring at us. They look ravenous and I'm sure they're getting ready to spring!'

Juliet laughed. 'Now you mention it, they do look hungry.'

The sphinx-like stone lions to which her mother referred stood guard over the entrance like two formidable and socially selective butlers. Their petrified scowls, forever fixed, were plainly intended to impress on would-be visitors that only the most favoured were allowed to go unmolested past their watchful eyes and escape injury from their outspread, sculptured claws.

The Major residence was a rambling, two-storeyed building which had been constructed probably two hundred years before in the manner of the great country houses of the day.

Its dusky red brick was time-mellowed and soothing to the town-tired eye. The white-pillared front entrance, in common with the lions, seemed to convey the impression that it was decidedly fastidious about the people it allowed to cross its threshold. No irreverent feet, it seemed to say, would be allowed to tread on the sacred pile of the deeply luxurious carpet which was revealed as the door came open at last, and which seemed to grow like blue grass from the entrance hall floor.

Warren Major, in his fifties, eyes alert and questing, passed lightly over the girl on the doorstep to rest with ill-disguised eagerness on the face of the woman at her side.

His hand came out. 'Cynthia! Thirty years, isn't it?'

'Must be,' Cynthia Bourne replied, stepping into the hall and putting her hand in his.

'Unbelievable,' said their host. 'You've hardly changed.'

Cynthia laughed. 'Nor you, although,' she eyed him, 'there's a little more of you now than there used to be!' With some pride she added, 'This is my daughter, Juliet.' Her eyes grew serious. 'It was good of you to see us, Warren. I hate having to ask favours of you, but in the circumstances . . .'

'Think nothing of it.' He took Juliet's hand. 'Looking at you, my dear, takes me back thirty years.' He led them into the main drawing-room. Juliet rose to the occasion and gazed around with the admiration that was obviously expected of all visitors to the house.

There was a nebulous impression of gold and gilt, velvet and satin, the kind of comfort – if such a word could be applied to such an atmosphere – which only genuine affluence could achieve. Her gaze adjusted and she found herself caught unawares, like the click of a camera shutter, by two quizzical eyes belonging to a man standing in the doorway.

'My son,' Warren said. 'Drew, Cynthia Bourne, my very old friend. Her daughter, Juliet.'

With studied politeness the son's hand rested first in the mother's, then in the daughter's. He seemed aloof, but, Juliet decided, charitably trying to find excuses, it could have been his height which gave a false impression.

'My wife.' Warren's voice was abrupt and his hand moved towards the woman on the settee. 'Mildred.'

Mildred Major stretched her thin lips so far but no farther, as though a broader smile might crack the parchment-like material of which her cheeks seemed to be made. She lifted her right hand a few inches in greeting, but did not proffer it to be shaken.

'Good of you to ask us,' Cynthia said, to break the awkward silence.

'Not at all,' said Mildred in a high bird-like voice. 'It was Warren's idea, not mine.'

'Yes, well,' said Warren, over-hearty, 'what shall we do first?'

'Show them round,' his wife advised, rising from the settee, 'while I supervise the tea.'

'Drew,' his father moved his hand with a flourish towards Juliet, 'be this young lady's guide. I'll be her mother's.'

So Drew Major, tall, black-haired, in his early thirties, strolled beside Juliet, his good looks sharpened into arrogance by the aristocratic way he held his head. His manner was nonchalant, his air slightly bored, as if he could have

6

thought of many better things to do than show a wide-eyed young woman round his father's residence, as though it were a stately home, and she an over-eager visitor determined to get her money's worth.

His eyes were a little derisive as he raised first his right hand, then his left, to indicate the elegance and luxury of one bedroom after another, the elaborate furnishings of the small drawing-room, the equally imposing living-room and the long and austerely gracious dining-hall.

He smiled slightly. 'I'm sorry to inflict all this on you, but I trust you're suitably impressed? My father intends you to be. He never tires of showing his visitors the concrete evidence of the fruits of his lifetime of effort, the rich rewards of his self-taught business acumen. You're his guest, so you must show the appropriate appreciation. You mustn't let him down!'

He was being cynical, but Juliet replied with sincerity, 'Of course I'm impressed. I think the whole place is beautiful, the building as well as its contents.'

He looked into her face. 'I do believe you mean it. Tell my father that and he'll give you anything you ask for – even the job you seem to be after in the family business.'

She flushed. 'You've heard about that?'

'Of course I have. I'm the company manager, in other words the man in charge. My father's the chairman of the company, but his desk is as innocent of work as the tray of a baby's high-chair. He sits – metaphorically – with his feet up all day. I do the work. I hold the reins and occasionally, but only when necesssary,' his voice altered subtly, 'I wield the whip.'

'I see.' She was silent for a few moments. 'In that case, Mr. Major, I'm sorry.'

'What about?' He looked surprised.

'My mother's request. You don't have to give me a job in your firm just because she asked you to. I don't believe in nepotism and this is really a form of it.'

'And of course,' his eyes were mocking, 'you wouldn't go against your principles, even when you would be the beneficiary, would you?'

'I – I –' She squirmed at his sarcasm and knew he had caught her out. Of course she would take any job he offered her. In the circumstances she had to.

He knew it, too. He smiled with satisfaction. 'Don't worry about your principles. We'll find room for you somewhere and I promise you, the job won't be a sinecure. If you're employed in a Major department store, you have to work. I'll make damned sure you earn your money, like all the others. You'll have me to reckon with if you don't come up to expectations.'

He smiled, and it was then that she realized how much this man irritated her. Something in his manner made her prickle like the bristles of a brush rubbed against the skin. He was plainly tiring of her unadulterated company, because he slowed down to allow her mother and his father to catch up with them.

They returned to the main drawing-room and tea was wheeled in on a glass and gilt trolley by a large-boned grey-haired woman, who smiled with trained subservience – Mildred Major had obviously proved herself an excellent tutor in teaching the woman her place. The woman withdrew and Cynthia complimented Mildred on the scones and pastries and savoury delicacies with which Warren was insisting they fill their plates.

'I didn't cook them,' Mildred said, in her harsh, unfeminine voice. She added smugly, 'Kate's a cook as well as maid. They're her handiwork. I couldn't do without her. Warren's so particular about his food I could never rise to his standards, so I don't even try.'

'Do you still cook as well as you used to, Cynthia?' Warren's question wiped the smugness from his wife's face, as it was intended to do. 'I still remember with pleasure the meals you cooked when I used to come to your house in the old days.'

Cynthia laughed. 'Ask my husband and daughter. I find it difficult to tell since I do the cooking.'

'And like any true artist,' Warren took her up, 'you find it difficult to judge your own work?'

Mildred Major's eyes glazed at his words like ice on a pond and a pinched look crept into her face, like someone who had been out in the cold a long time.

They had barely eaten the last crumb when she gathered the used crockery together and piled it noisily on to the trolley. Juliet rose to help, but Mildred flapped her hand, urging her back to her seat. As if the mistress of the house had passed a telepathic message to the housekeeper, Kate appeared and trundled the trolley away.

There was a brief silence. Warren Major, successful businessman and more than half-way to being a millionaire, spread himself expansively across a corner of the long settee, drawing himself as far away from his wife as the limits of the piece of furniture would allow. He crossed his expensively trousered legs and, running a heavily-ringed hand over his already impeccably smooth grey hair, he said, addressing Juliet,

'If your mother had married me, she would have been mistress of all this,' his sweeping arm took in not only the elegant room but his entire estate, 'and inheritor of my considerable fortune. I say "inherit" because most wives seem to outlive their unfortunate husbands. She's sturdy enough. Look at her now, even at fifty.'

At his bidding, everyone looked – Mildred, his wife, sitting primly at the other end of the settee, folded into herself like an ageing flower closed up permanently for the night; Juliet, and Drew, with his father's controlled aggressiveness and unswerving self-assurance.

Cynthia Bourne, dressed becomingly in a deep mauve trouser suit and white polo-necked sweater, looking nearly ten years younger than her actual age, bore their scrutiny with smiling tolerance, her brown hair tinted where she had determinedly covered the grey, her smile revealing that the fact that she was not the inheritor of Warren Major's fortune and mistress of his estate did not worry her unduly.

'I've no regrets, Warren. I'm too happily married, ailing at times though my husband is, to let the thought disturb me.'

Warren smiled as though she had spoken on cue. He addressed Juliet again. 'I suppose she told you we were once engaged, but that she objected so strongly to my driving ambition and my ruthlessness, as she called it, in my dealings with others, that she cruelly and irrevocably broke off the engagement? And also that she broke my heart?' His smile flicked like a whip over his wife as though he was secretly punishing her for an unforgivable crime. Then it changed and settled challengingly on Juliet's mother.

Cynthia was unperturbed. 'My dear Warren,' her voice was gentle, 'let's face it, in those days you had no heart to

9

break. And to be honest,' the warmth in her smile was intended to soften the impact of the words, 'I rather doubt if you've ever had one. Otherwise how could you have amassed the fortune of which you're now so proud? No one does that without riding roughshod over hundreds of people.'

His laughter was hearty and he enjoyed the joke at his own expense. 'My word, she's still got the old fire! I remember the violent arguments we used to have. Have you passed on your fieriness to your daughter, Cynthia?'

He dwelt with indulgent interest on the girl sitting on the fireside chair beside him. 'She's like you were, you know. Brown hair with auburn lights, only hers is longer, roses and cream complexion, lips red and pouting and asking all the time to be kissed.'

Cynthia laughed and the lines around her eyes crinkled. 'The passage of time has certainly lent enchantment to your view of me, Warren.' She turned to his wife and her eyes held apology for the indiscretions of Warren's memory. 'I wasn't a bit like that, Mildred.'

Mildred merely turned her head away with a lifeless, disinterested gesture.

'All the same,' insisted Warren, 'Juliet's the image of what you were in the old days, no doubt about it.' He swivelled round and faced Juliet. 'Tell me, girl, do *you* think I've got a heart?'

Juliet smiled. 'Obviously you have, Mr. Major. You wouldn't be a living, breathing man without one, would you?'

'Tact. That's good. A good answer, eh, Drew? Think she's inherited her mother's fire?'

The son's eyes moved languidly over the girl in question, taking his time, dwelling on the antagonism she could not suppress, the quick but becoming flush of resentment at his scrutiny, the tightening of the lips as she awaited his verdict.

'I would say,' commented Drew at last, having looked his fill, 'although I merely hazard a guess from surface appearances, that it's not just the fire she's inherited, but the whole darned furnace. From the look of her at this moment,' he backed away with a provocative jerk, 'you'd only have to get just a little too near and you'd be set alight.'

Warren laughed loudly again. 'My word,' he looked at Cynthia, 'hearing Drew say that brings back memories. Pleasant ones, too.'

Cynthia smiled without embarrassment. Mildred's face did not flicker. She sat motionless, her body small and painfully thin, her short grey-black hair combed flat and unbecomingly from her face and doing nothing at all to enhance the pale rigidity of her features. Her clothes were in the fashion of two decades before. She seemed as incongruous beside her well-fed, immaculately dressed husband as a scarecrow sharing the settee with a fashion model. She looked at Cynthia and self-righteous disapproval pushed out her thin lips as she contemplated the other woman's bright, optimistic face and well-rounded, still-attractive figure.

'Well, Juliet.' Warren was determined, wife or no wife, to develop his theme, 'having established that I do indeed possess a heart, you've got to believe me when I tell you your mother broke it once.'

'All the same, Mr. Major,' Juliet smiled, 'I'm quite sure that, unlike Humpty Dumpty, it was soon put together again.'

The astute grey eyes, an older version of his son's, considered her. 'What makes you so sure?'

She shrugged. 'Well, it didn't stop you making a success of your life. Also, you found another woman to love,' Warren's eyes rested on his wife as a diner regards a caterpillar in his lettuce, 'and to marry. You didn't exactly pine away from unrequited love. And,' her eyes moved upwards to the younger man who was standing beside her chair, 'you had a son. All those things are positive signs of a heart well and truly mended. You also have what many men long for but never have – an heir,' she smiled at her host, 'who, unlike my mother, will one day inherit your fortune.'

The heir in question stirred and folded his arms. He asked softly, 'Since you're so articulate on the subject, not to say loquacious, Juliet, where do I stand in your estimation? Would I be rated by a woman as an excellent catch, do you think? And that no woman would break *my* heart as my father's apparently was, because of my stable financial background and the money which will one day come my way?'

She grinned up at him. 'With so much to inherit, what

11

woman could resist you?'

'Do *you* find me irresistible, Juliet?'

She shifted her eyes from his. 'Unfortunately, no.'

His father gave a short, sharp laugh. 'Her mother all over! Out she comes with it, the truth, right below the belt.'

'But,' the son persisted, apparently unaffected by the body-blow he was supposed by his father to have received, 'think of all the money, the property which will be mine one day. Doesn't that tempt you, make me irresistible, even in your jaundiced eyes?'

'No.' This time she spoke with irritation. 'And I'm not jaundiced, I'm just speaking the truth.' She recovered her good humour and shot at him, smiling, 'You aren't by any chance proposing to me, are you?'

He threw back his head and laughed, and there was grudging admiration in it.

Cynthia laughed with Warren, who said to his son, 'First she insults you, then she's cheeky. My word, Drew, if we give her a job, you'll have to keep her in her place, otherwise she'll be taking over from us and running the firm herself!' He slapped his leg and seemed to enjoy the idea. 'She's got spirit, your girl, Cynthia. She'll break a few hearts before she's finished.'

Juliet shook her head. 'I'd never break the heart of a man I loved. And I'd only marry him if I loved him. Even if he were penniless it wouldn't stop me. Look at my mother. My father was an impoverished young clerk when she married him and they've never had much money, but anyone can see how happy they are, even now.' She gave Drew a look that was by no means flattering. 'Men with money don't attract me. They repel me rather than the opposite.'

'There's no doubt,' came softly from Warren, 'she's her mother's daughter.'

Drew smiled mockingly. 'You've wounded me to the heart, Juliet.'

She smiled up at him derisively. 'I doubt if you've got a heart to break.'

He bowed. 'You flatter me.'

She was still smiling. 'Anyway, Mr. Major—'

'Oh, call him Drew,' said his father. 'After all, if things had been different, he could have been your brother.'

'Anyway, Drew,' the man she was addressing smiled

slightly at her easy use of his first name, 'men's hearts aren't made to be broken these days. Women come and go in their lives with such rapidity that their hearts are unaffected, aren't they? Now be honest!'

He hitched his elbow on to the ornate stone mantelpiece and rested a foot on the highly polished brass fender. His smile challenged her. 'You aren't by any chance inviting me to pour out the secrets of my love life? Tell you how many women—?'

'Drew!' His mother's twittering, high-pitched tones cut him off. 'You really mustn't talk like that. You know how much I dislike it.'

Her protests passed over him, and Juliet had the feeling that Mildred Major played a very insignificant part in the lives of these two men who were so alike in feature and manner. He went on, 'I will if you like, but unfortunately it would take so long . . .'

His father threw back his head and laughed. 'So many of 'em, eh, Drew? That's the stuff, boy, but take care not to get caught!'

Shocked, Juliet glanced at Mildred. That he could talk in such terms in front of his wife appalled her. But Mildred might have been deaf for all the reaction she showed. Was she perhaps used to the scarcely veiled insults which her husband seemed to take such pleasure in flinging at her?

Cynthia looked at her, too, and Juliet recognized the outrage, firmly controlled though it was, as her mother said, 'Do you know, Warren, I'm coming round to the view that I had a remarkably lucky escape when I broke off our engagement.'

Now Warren looked as though he had received a body blow, but the grimace of pain passed so swiftly it might never have been. He smiled weakly. 'Runs in the family, doesn't it? Punch drunk, they are. Below the belt every time. Watch out, boy,' he said to his son, 'don't get involved with that one,' he indicated Juliet, 'otherwise you never know where you might end up. Out stone cold on the floor of the ring, while the referee counts ten.'

Drew grinned. 'No fear of that. No woman has ever yet got me where she wants me.'

Juliet raised her eyebrows. 'The other way round, perhaps?'

Drew smiled. 'Most definitely the other way round.'

'Another of my pet hates,' Juliet murmured, 'womanizers who never take women seriously. That, plus your money—' She shook her head. 'You're simply not my type.'

'So we're completely incompatible, Juliet?'

'Absolutely.'

He pretended to mop his brow. 'My word, that was a lucky escape! Now, having got that little matter cleared up, perhaps we can talk business.'

'Excellent idea,' said Warren. 'Take her for a walk, Drew. You do the honours. You run the firm, so you ask the questions. I'm just the figurehead. There's a permanent dent in my desk where I put my feet!'

Cynthia was laughing as Drew motioned Juliet out of the room. 'I don't believe a word of it, Warren,' she was saying.

'So,' Drew said as he showed Juliet through the french windows into the gardens, 'I've been detailed by the chairman of the company to ask you a few questions.'

'Is this an interview, Mr. Major?'

'It is. Consider yourself highly honoured, Miss Bourne, that it isn't the personnel manager who is doing the interviewing, but no less a person than the company manager himself. Now, have you had any past experience in retail distribution?'

'None at all. I shall probably be quite useless to you.'

'That's the first time in my experience that an applicant has ever tried to talk herself out of a job.'

'I'm merely being honest. I am – at the moment – an art student.'

'Commercial art?'

'Graphic design.'

'M'm. Might come in useful.' He smiled. 'So you're an art student. Do you ever do any work at the college?' When she looked indignant he explained, with a smile, 'I've heard it said that all art students learn to do is how to make love and how to make trouble.'

He drew back with mock alarm at her furious expression. 'I suppose,' she said bitingly, 'you're going to ask me next whether I've seen any good sit-ins lately?'

He was unaffected by her sarcasm. He smiled again, but it faded as he asked, 'I'd like to know why – let's be blunt –

your mother had to lower her pride and ask my father, a man she had rejected years ago as a husband, to do such a favour as to come to her rescue and give her daughter a job.'

'I don't really see that it's relevant.' She frowned. 'If you haven't got a job to offer me, then would you please say so, and that will bring an end to this inquisition. Do you pry into the private lives of all your would-be employees?'

'I resent that. Every employer has a right to ask questions of any candidate, especially someone who has taken the unusual step of asking for a job to be created for them where none exists.'

She could not hide her disappointment. 'You mean you're trying to tell me politely that you haven't got a suitable job available?'

'In a sense, yes.'

She felt like crying. 'Sinecure was the word you used earlier, wasn't it? Now I see what you meant.' She sighed with resignation and turned back towards the house. 'We might as well go in.'

He caught her arm and turned her back. 'It's usually the prerogative of the potential employer to bring the interview to an end, not the applicant.'

'I'm sorry, but I wouldn't want to be a liability to anyone.'

'Stop being sarcastic, or bitter, or whatever that self-deprecating statement was meant to be.'

'I wouldn't want to be a burden—'

'I said shut up, Juliet.' His quiet, authoritative tone effectively subdued her. 'Now, whether you were an asset or a liability would depend on how much you pulled your weight. And don't worry, we shall know. We don't spy on our staff, but we have our means of checking up on the progress or otherwise of a member of the sales personnel. If you don't come up to scratch in the firm of Major and Son, you'll be out,' he clicked his fingers, 'just like that.'

'No second chance? I'm not surprised. With you at the head of it, I can well believe that the firm pursued a policy of intolerance and instant dismissal without compassion, without pity!'

He bowed his head in a mocking gesture of thanks. 'Your good opinion of me – based of course on years of an intimate knowledge of my character – flatters me inordinately. However,' his tone hardened, 'if you want a job with us, you'd better become just a little more submissive. Not to say polite.'

She wasn't quelled. Her mood switched and she grinned up at him. 'Talking of politeness, if you give me a job, would I have to call you "sir"?'

'Most of my employees do.' She glanced at him to see if he was joking, but his face was perfectly serious.

'Sorry, even if it costs me the job it's not on. I've never in my life called a man "sir", and I don't intend to start now.'

'In that case,' he smiled, 'I shall have to issue a directive to the entire staff, instructing everyone from the general manager down to the youngest, newest and most insignificant member of staff that Mr. Drew Major is henceforward to be addressed only as "sir".'

She smiled up at him. 'Yes, Drew. Of course, Drew. Sir.'

'My father,' he said, looking down at her with a faint smile, 'was so right when he warned me you would need to be kept under control.'

'Sorry. I'll try to behave.' She smiled disarmingly and he nodded, amused like someone watching the antics of a very young child.

They came to the end of the paved pathway and turned to look back at the house, and what they saw was a perfect example of perspective and symmetry. There were beds of roses on each side of the path which thrust arrow-like in a narrowing line to the very centre of the red brick mansion. Pyramid-shaped cypresses, trained and trimmed by the loving hand of the gardener into perfect replicas of each other, sprang like dark green cones from behind the rose beds, giving even greater emphasis to the feeling of perspective. With the profusion of colours, the heady scents which tantalized the nostrils like the smell of wine to a hardened drinker, the greens of the lawns and leaves and, at the end of it all, the mellow red brick and the small white-painted casement windows of the house itself, gave the scene a birthday card perfection.

'Where to now?' She looked up at him.

'Over there,' he pointed, 'is the sun lounge and there the swimming pool, but,' he looked her over, 'since you aren't appropriately dressed for swimming – no enticing bikini to tempt me—'

'I can't swim anyway,' she said, interrupting.

'Then we'll go through the rose garden to the pond.' He turned her in the right direction as if she were a robot and as they walked side by side he said, 'Tell me why you want this job.'

His voice was serious with a touch of command she could not overlook, could not escape by means of provocative remarks.

'Why, for instance,' he went on, 'are you not continuing your art training and going on to better things?'

'Domestic circumstances. In short, lack of money within the family.'

'I see.' He looked thoughtful.

'My father suffers periodically from asthma. As he gets older the attacks get more frequent and he's often forced to be absent from work, and then only his sick pay is coming in. That isn't much, so,' she sighed, 'in the circumstances, I can hardly go on being a student when I should be bringing in money to supplement my father's meagre allowance.' She hated telling this man, this rich man, so many purely private facts about her parents' and her own circumstances, and confessing to him the true state of their finances. 'In short, we're hard up. We need money desperately. Any money I earn will go into the family kitty and help us live.' She lifted a proud, pale face to his. 'So now you know our family secrets, secrets you were so determined to get out of me.'

They came to a pond, circular, lily-strewn, encircled by even more roses, scarlet, gold, white, as rich in scents as this man beside her was in money. From the centre of the pond spurted a fountain, tall, misty blue, shooting high left and right as the wind drove it.

Some of the spray pelted momentarily over Juliet's hair and dress and she stepped back, searching for a handkerchief with which to wipe herself dry. He stood watching, making no move to assist, and a lump came into her throat at the unfairness of it all. That he did not apologize for what had happened – although he had no control over the direction of the wind she felt irrationally that he was responsible because it was after all his fountain – that he and his father should be so wealthy, own so much beauty and live in such luxury while her parents had to count every penny before they parted with it, brought her to the edge of unreasonable anger.

She nearly burst out, 'I don't want your rotten job,' but with the most stringent self-control held back her temper. Of course she wanted it. She needed it, she should really be begging him for it.

'This way.' He turned her towards the house. They were nearly there, yet he still had not told her the result of their odd, unconventional interview. Should she ask him? If she had failed to convince him of her capabilities, if the answer was 'no', she would rather be told now than hear the words, 'I'll let you know. I'll ring you.'

'Drew?' He looked at her. 'Have you – will you – will there be—?' She was making a mess of it.

'A job for you? Yes. We'll push you in somewhere.' He smiled. 'Even if it's operating the lift or sweeping the floors.'

She couldn't keep the relief from her eyes. 'If it would bring in some money, I'd do even that.'

'My dear girl,' there was a hint of exasperation in his voice, 'do you really think my opinion of your potential is such that I'd direct you to those jobs? You need the money. We have it to give.'

Juliet bristled. 'I don't want charity.'

He laughed shortly. 'Charity? Never on your life! If you come to work for us, you *work*. Understand?'

Drew took them home. As they were leaving, Mildred stood on the doorstep, hands clasped primly in front of her, while Warren leaned against the lowered window of Drew's car. Cynthia was in the front seat. Mildred called a tight-lipped 'Goodbye' and went in.

As Drew prepared to drive away, Warren opened the car door, pulled Cynthia's face towards him and kissed her cheek. 'Old times' sake,' he mumbled, slamming the door shut again. 'One day I'll tell you just what you did to me.'

Cynthia seemed overcome, but recovered quickly. She reached out and squeezed his hand. 'Can't turn back the clock, Warren. To be honest, and at the risk of hurting you, I wouldn't want to.'

'She's at it again,' he said to his son, smiling ruefully. 'Slap bang, out with it. Whatever the consequences, it must

18

be the truth.'

They laughed and waved as they drove away. Juliet, staring out of the window during the drive home – they lived on the other side of the town – wished they could have returned by bus, as they had come. She hated the thought of Drew seeing the modest little terrace house they lived in. They had roses in their garden, of course, but there any resemblance to the Major residence and estate ended.

Drew didn't seem to notice the shabbiness of the street he was directed into. Juliet and her mother stood on the pavement and waved as he left them.

Cedric Bourne lowered his newspaper as they entered. 'Enjoy yourselves?' he asked with a touch of irony in his voice. 'What was it like mingling with the moneyed classes?'

His wife shrugged. 'Warren hasn't changed. I'm sorry I had to go running to him for help.'

'When a man's as knee-deep in money as he is,' her husband remarked, 'there's no need to have a conscience about asking favours of him.'

Cynthia looked at her husband with the eyes of a woman accustomed to searching a well-loved face for signs of physical suffering. Finding none, she consciously relaxed. 'Warren's not an easy person to talk to. Never was. And his wife!'

'I thought he treated her abominably,' Juliet commented. 'The things he said, not exactly to her, but with insults wrapped up like a booby-trapped parcel.'

'Perhaps he had good reason, dear,' her father said. 'You never can tell with some couples. Hasn't he got a son? I saw him in the store once. An assistant pointed him out. Tall fellow, dark hair, holds his head as if he were a member of the aristocracy.'

'A good description,' Juliet agreed. 'I can't stick the man. Unfortunately, he seems to be in charge.'

'Did he give you a job? That was the object of the exercise, wasn't it?'

Juliet shrugged. 'Don't know. He said he'd probably make one if there wasn't one available.'

Cynthia said, 'Well, that was nice of him. You must admit he was being considerate in saying that.'

'*If* he meant it. Personally, I think he'll forget all about it and I'll hear no more from him.'

Cynthia stood beside her husband, her hand resting on his shoulder. It was broad and solid, like his personality. He looked up at her and smiled, his long narrow face lighting up at her touch. He put aside his paper and pulled her on to his knee. 'Glad you married me and not Warren?'

She whispered her answer in his ear and he laughed. The phone rang and Juliet answered it.

'Am I speaking to Juliet Bourne?'

'You are.' She recognized the precise, businesslike tones immediately.

'Drew Major here. I've been thinking about your request for a position within our firm.' Good heavens, she thought, it can't be half an hour since we parted. She told herself she should be flattered. Then she reminded herself that it was without doubt the good of the firm he had in mind, not hers. Here came the refusal, polite but unarguable. 'I'm sorry, but—' Better to say it over the phone than to her face . . .

'I should like to meet you for lunch some time to discuss the matter. You must understand that I can't commit myself to anything before knowing something of your education, your past experience and so on.'

Good heavens, she thought, I only want a job as a sales-girl.

'Well, I – I'm still attending college. Term doesn't end until next week.'

'I see. So lunch would be difficult? Would you prefer us to have dinner together?'

'Oh no, thanks.' An evening spent in that man's company? 'I can manage lunch whenever you like.' If she played the subservient shop assistant in advance, perhaps that would help him to 'commit himself'.

He must have consulted his diary. 'I find I'm free the day after tomorrow.'

'So am I,' she answered, as if it were a great coin-cidence.

'Where shall I pick you up? At the college?'

'Well, yes, thanks. You know where it is?'

He said he did, only too well. She wondered what that meant. They arranged a time and rang off.

The day Drew called for her, it was pouring with rain. She was wearing her bright red trousers and multi-coloured tunic and she had left her raincoat at home. She dashed down the steps of the art school, feeling dozens of interested eyes boring into her back from the hundreds of windows behind her.

Drew threw open the door without getting out of the car and she tumbled into the front passenger seat gasping for breath and apologizing profusely for the rainwater with which her sandalled feet were dampening the luxury carpets on the floor.

Once again in his presence she tried to dry her clothes with the aid of her handkerchief, but this time, instead of looking on lazily, he reached into his left-hand pocket and produced his own.

'Sorry about this,' she apologized again as he drove out of the car park.

He smiled. 'If the colours you're wearing now ran into each other, it wouldn't even notice. They're so startling anyway you look like an artist's palette.'

'Thank you for the compliment. But if I'm not dressed in tune with your mood or for the place you have in mind to patronize for lunch, then you'd better turn round and take me back. I'll lunch as usual in the college refectory.' She wondered if she had gone too far in speaking to him so presumptuously. He was, after all – she hoped – her future employer. She made her tone a fraction more amenable. 'I think you must be out of touch with modern youth.' He gave a short, disclaiming laugh. 'This stuff,' she indicated her clothes, 'is the norm. If I dressed otherwise, as an art student, I should be regarded as decidedly odd. You're expected to express your individuality, your difference from those around you in the clothes you wear.'

He laughed loudly. '*Difference*? All around me every day in the street I see young people dressed like you. So where's the difference? It's just a uniform.'

She bit back the retort she would have made because she wanted – no, needed – to work for him. They went to a restaurant which, even in the middle of the day, was dark as an underground cave. The place was illuminated by means of candles flickering deep inside large red bowls. 'It wouldn't have mattered,' Juliet told herself, 'if I'd been wearing a nightdress, because no one would have been able to see.'

'Does this suit your artistic sensibilities?' he asked mockingly, and she nodded her appreciation.

He sat opposite her on a bench seat. His face glowed red, his white shirt had turned pink and even his expertly-cut suit had a roseate hue about it. 'In this light,' she reflected with a smile, 'even you might pass as one of "us".'

'Me, look like an arty type?' He laughed derisively. 'Heaven preserve me from such a calamity!'

She asked indignantly, 'What's wrong with artists?'

'A lot – with those I have to deal with. And a large number come from your art school. Oh yes,' at her look of surprise, 'I employ them – in the art department of the store, in display and so on.'

She grew excited. 'Is that where I might—?'

'Sorry. No vacancy.'

'Oh.' She bit her lip with disappointment.

He ordered, after consulting her wishes, and said, 'But the object of this outing is to discuss you, not artists in general. Tell me about your subject.'

If talking to him about her studies would enhance her chances of becoming an employee of his, then talk she would, and volubly.

'Graphic design covers a lot of things, like designing gift boxes, posters, packaging, even notepaper. You have to have a feeling for design to be any good at it. It teaches you the use of colour, the aesthetics of good and bad design. An object must not only be attractive to look at, but you have to ask yourself "could it be made?" And if so, would it stand up to use?'

She tried to guess what he was thinking, but the flickering scarlet glow frustrated her efforts. He seemed prepared to let her go on so she did. The food was put in front of them and she went on talking.

'You learn about printing techniques and colour printing, too. Will it, for instance, be possible for the packaging you've designed to go through the post? Can it be manufactured cheaply? You're taught lettering and photography, and about window display.'

'And all this leads to – what?'

'If you're good enough, a diploma. Then you start trudging round looking for jobs. You have a large portfolio and take it with you. Ever hopeful, you show people pictures of work you've done at the art school, colour transparencies you've taken of your stuff, and so on. You show them note-paper you've designed, boxes, book jackets, cardboard cut-outs, symbols you've thought out for firms.' She looked at him, trying to judge his response, but he merely nodded. 'Have I – have I talked myself into a job – in your art department?'

He laughed, shaking his head. 'I told you, no vacancy.' He saw her disappointment. 'Sorry. But if it's any consolation, I'll give you a job – in another department. When can you start?'

'Next Monday.'

'What about your summer holiday? I'd prefer you to have had it before you started with us.'

'I – I'm not having one.'

'But everyone needs a summer holiday.'

'You're probably right. But I couldn't afford it.'

'I see.' He was silent for a while as if trying to work something out. He must have given up, because he shrugged. As coffee was served he said, 'If you will report to the staff manager next Monday morning, she'll direct you to the department you'll be attached to.'

Juliet looked at him, gratitude lighting up her eyes. 'Thanks.'

He nodded and stirred his coffee. 'Pity,' he said, 'that you have to leave the college. Wouldn't it be better for you if you were to gain this diploma you talked about? Wouldn't it improve your career prospects and so on?'

'Of course it would, but I told you before, the money's just not there to let me do it. I can hardly exist on my grant as it is. And I certainly can't give any money to my parents to help them. I've got to start earning, and the sooner the better.'

'You realize that the pay you'll get won't be very high? With no past experience in retail selling—'

'I understand that,' she said quietly. 'But whatever I get, no matter how small, will be a help.' She paused. 'Drew.' He looked up. 'I'd like to tell you how grateful I am to you and your father—'

He shook his head, silencing her. 'Don't go on.' He smiled. 'Who knows, after a week of Major and Son, especially the "Son", you might want to hand in your notice. You haven't seen me in action yet. I've only got to appear in the store and everyone shakes with terror.' She laughed. 'You don't believe it? Wait until the other employees start talking. I know exactly what they think about my methods. But they have to admit I get results.' She laughed again, but stopped at the change in his tone as he said, 'Nor will I make any exception of you.'

She frowned. 'I wouldn't expect you to.'

'Just as well. You may not like me much now—' he looked into her eyes, 'in fact, I can see you don't – but you'll like me even less before you're finished. My father has made me in his own image. Hardened me up, he said, so that I wouldn't be fool enough as he was to fall for any girl, especially one who might discard me because of my ambitions.' She tightened at his callous reference to her mother. 'He sent me to boarding school – thought that would help the process of hardening me. He had me educated, as he never was, made me into everything he would have liked to have been. Under his tuition, I've been ruthlessly gutted of all sentiment. A sign of weakness, my father calls it. So I'm warning you.' He moved back his chair and pulled out hers as he rose.

'You mean I'm going to work for a tartar?'

He smiled. 'You'll discover that for yourself soon enough.' He settled the bill and they left the restaurant side by side. 'Tell me,' he said as they got in the car and drove away, 'has Juliet got a Romeo?'

Juliet smiled out of the window. 'Yes, she has a Romeo. His name's Malcolm. Malcolm Watling.'

'Older than you?'

'No, same age. Twenty-one.'

'Art student?'

A slight pause before she answered, then, 'No.' He seemed to be waiting for more. 'He's a sales assistant.' She looked at his profile, a little forbidding as he frowned. Could he guess what was coming? Dare she tell him? How would he react? 'At Curlews.'

He reacted – violently. His head shot round. 'What? Our deadliest rivals?'

He sounded so angry she thought it was the end. 'I'm sorry,' adding wearily, 'You can withdraw your offer of a job, if you like.'

He was so long in answering she thought he must be seeking a way of softening the blow. She would make it easy for him.

'I'll look elsewhere for a job. You can be blunt. I don't mind . . .'

He said slowly, 'No, I won't withdraw my offer, I'll take you on as an employee on one condition. Let me warn you that if anything you may hear about Major and Son in the course of your work, like business deals, policy matters and anything else which might be classified as strictly confidential, is passed on by you to any member of Curlews' staff, however junior he may be and even if he seduces you to get the secrets out of you, you will be out! Have you got that?'

She flushed at his innuendo and his objectionable manner and held back a vicious retort. In the circumstances she had to be polite to the man – he held the purse strings. 'Yes, Mr. Major.' But subservience was foreign to her nature. She burst out, 'Thanks for your faith in my integrity. I *have* got the message. How could I have missed it? It was put so – so succinctly, so tactfully. And Malcolm is my boy-friend, not my lover.'

He remained maddeningly calm. 'Thanks for that little titbit of information. I shall sleep all the more soundly in my bed at night knowing that.' His sarcasm grated on her like a piece of music played out of tune. 'Are you serious about him?'

'Is this an extension of my interview for the job?' she asked, between her teeth.

'You could put it that way,' he answered blandly.

She replied grudgingly, 'My affairs – in the social as against the sensual meaning of the word – are really my own business, but if you insist on knowing, I don't even know myself.'

He nodded noncommittally as he turned left and braked outside the art school. She looked into his face, trying to judge his mood. Still smarting from his prying into her private concerns, but knowing at the same time she had no business to be questioning him on the subject, she said, 'Since you've asked me and since you're not yet my employer, and bearing in mind our families are friendly, may I ask you a similar question? Have you got a girl-friend?'

He rested his elbow on the back of his seat and turned to look at her. He raised his eyebrows, smiled and half echoed her own words, but with greater emphasis. 'My affairs – both social and sexual – are my own business. Not yours.'

She flushed with annoyance at having allowed herself to be put so firmly in her place. She thanked him coldly for the meal.

He nodded. 'Monday morning, eight-thirty prompt. Report to the staff manager, administrative section, sixth floor.' Without another word, he drove away.

CHAPTER TWO

THE day before Juliet started work at Major's department store, she went for a long cycle ride into the country with Malcolm. They hid their bicycles in a hedge and wandered through the woods hand in hand.

They were talking about Juliet's new job. 'Wonder which department you'll be in?' Malcolm said. 'One place they won't put you is the carpet department, like me. A girl wouldn't be any use there. Ever tried to lift a carpet? The really big ones weigh a ton. Then a customer comes along and wants to have a look at the one at the very bottom of the pile and you have to flip them up one by one, and in the end, after your arm feels as though it's going to fall off with the weight of the ones on top, she says,' he used unflatteringly mincing tones, ' "Thank you, I'll think about it!" '

She laughed. 'Heaven knows where I'll be working. He said there wasn't really a vacancy to suit me. I'll probably end up operating the lift!'

'I've done that before now – and let me tell you,' they were lying between the bushes and he kissed her swiftly, 'it's no laughing matter. By the end of the day you feel dead on your feet.'

She lifted a hand and pushed back a lock of his fair hair that had fallen across his eyes. 'All the same, I'd even do that if it means earning some money. I'm sick of struggling along on a miserly grant, with nothing to spend on things I want and nothing much to give my parents for my keep at the end of the week.'

'You won't earn a lot at Majors. They're rotten payers. Now if you came to work for Curlews—'

'No, thanks,' she said, grinning. 'With a certain Malcolm Watling working there, even if they offered me a fortune for my services, I wouldn't—' The rest was lost as she struggled to get away from him. Laughing, he let her go and they made their way back to retrieve their bicycles.

'Anyway,' they pedalled home side by side along the country lanes, 'I'm only being allowed to work at Majors on certain conditions. Drew said—'

'Who's Drew?' came sharply from Malcolm.

She coloured at her slip. 'Drew Major. My mother used to know his father. We went there for tea.'

'On first name terms with the top brass, are you?' He sounded none too pleased.

'Don't be silly, Malcolm, it doesn't mean anything. Anyhow, it'll be Mr. Major, *sir*, from tomorrow on, when I'm an employee. Can you imagine me calling the man in charge "Drew"? He told me everyone calls him "sir", anyway.'

'So I suppose you're going to toady to him like the rest, "Sir Drew" him every time you meet.'

'Not likely. You should know me better than that.'

All the same, next day as she joined the flow of people passing through the staff entrance at the side of the great cream-washed building, she realized just what a small component she was in the thriving business that was Major and Son. Of course she would have to toe the line, even, if necessary, addressing the company manager as 'sir', although the word would probably turn rancid in her mouth.

Up, up she went in the swift silent lift, pressed tightly between a dozen other members of staff, their faces deadpan, their eyes unwelcoming and disinterested. The number six flashed on the floor indicator and the doors slid open. Juliet breathed in deeply and contracted herself into as near a straight line as she physically could. Then she pushed and writhed her way out, to be left alone as the lift doors closed again.

She walked a few paces, hoping someone would come along. No one did. She walked on, her heart jolting at the words on a door. Drew W. Major, Company Manager, they said. She passed by, dreading that the door would open and he would come out. But, she told herself, he was probably still in bed. It was, after all, only half-past eight.

Then she heard his voice inside the room and scuttled past as fast as she could. Which was the door she wanted? She walked to the end of the corridor and back. A door opened. A man appeared, staring at her.

'I told you to see the staff manager,' said the man in charge. 'Can't you read?' He pointed and the door opposite his own told her in large black letters that the staff manager was in residence.

'Sorry, Mr. Major,' she said, colouring furiously. Did he have to be so unpleasant on her first morning – her first hour – as an employee of his? 'I must have missed it.'

He tutted irritably and watched as she raised her hand and tapped on the door. There was a mumble from inside the room, but she couldn't decipher the words. She hesitated.

'Well, go in, Miss Bourne. Are you deaf as well as blind?'

She gave him a look of concentrated fury, pulled herself together, dug up a smile from the depths of her being like a miner hewing coal, and went in.

A woman, middle-aged and bespectacled, lifted her head, eyes as blank as the people's in the lift, expression bored, and said, 'Yes?'

Her name, it appeared from the white-lettered plastic notice standing on her desk, was Mrs. Audrey Arthur.

Under the slightly hostile stare, Juliet began to wilt. 'I'm – my name is Juliet Bourne. I—'

'I was expecting you. I've been instructed to direct you to the marking-off room. Eighth floor, turn right through a swing door and you're there. They'll tell you what to do.'

Juliet thanked her, followed the woman's directions and pushed her way into a vast dimly-lit area which could not be mistaken even by a half-educated moron for a 'room'. It was a great depressing wilderness, the walls covered in peeling yellow paint, the ceiling a dirty white, the lighting resembling a guest house lounge in a poor season. There seemed to be cages everywhere, all padlocked to guard against theft, containing a great assortment of merchandise which would one day find its way to the counters and display stands of the main store. Behind the wire mesh were pillows, washing-up bowls, hardware, shopping trolleys, toy guitars, toys, prams – all entirely unrelated but gathered there for one purpose only – to be price-tagged.

There were about a dozen women at work. They were chatting and laughing, but not one of them raised her head. Juliet was not even noticed. She stood there for nearly five minutes wondering how to announce herself.

She coughed and one of the women looked up. 'Yes?' came the same flat, disinterested tone that had greeted her in the staff manager's office.

'I've just come,' said Juliet feebly. 'I'm new.'

'Come and join us,' sang one of the brighter souls standing at a large table.

'All are welcome,' said another. 'Take off your coat, dear, and get down to it.'

Juliet removed her coat and, looking in vain for a hanger, draped it across a pile of wheelbarrows, hoping it would still be there later when she needed it, and had not been wheeled down to the store to be sold.

The women at the table were pricing large gilt chandeliers. One of the women, who announced that she was called Madge, pushed a box of price tags towards Juliet and showed her how to fix them.

'Nearly finished these,' she said. 'After this there's the purses.'

'Not the purses,' said another woman called Pat. 'The buyer of hardware keeps asking us for his canteens of cutlery. Ought to do those before purses.'

Madge shook her head. 'Let him wait. They're too heavy for us to lift. After all, we've just done these chandeliers without Mr. Wilkes to help us, and they're heavy enough.'

So purses it was. They had to be priced with adhesive labels. Mr. Wilkes, it seemed, was the marking-off room supervisor, whose job it was to lift heavy objects to the table for pricing.

'He's more away than he's here,' said Madge with disgust. 'He's always taking extra long tea and coffee breaks. That's why the big things get left and the buyers come shouting for the stuff.' She laughed. 'We just let 'em shout!'

After the purses were racks of dresses, to which Juliet was told to fix swing tickets bearing price, size and code number. Piles of plates and dishes had to be marked with grease pencils, cardigans priced with special pin tickets. It was towards the end of the afternoon that Juliet began to wonder how long she could stand the job.

The incessant chatter of the women, the taped music which was constant and sickly soothing, the roar of the air conditioning which was nerve-racking and the mindless, repetitive nature of the work depressed her beyond words. It was not as though the surroundings acted as an antidote to the monotony of the work. The poor lighting, the badly-painted walls, the absence of windows providing natural light, the wire cages reminding her of a prison, played upon her imagination to such an extent that even the shadows – of which there were many – took on a grotesque shape.

At the end of the day she felt like knocking on Drew Major's door and telling him she had had enough of his department store and was leaving forthwith. She knew, however, that she would do no such thing and that she would arrive next morning and make her way to the marking-off room in common with the other women employed there.

It was while she was telling Malcolm on the phone that evening about her first day at work that an idea came to her. She was explaining how it was the surroundings above all that got her down when the artist in her whispered a solution.

She worked through the following day, pricing washing-up bowls with adhesive labels, hats with swing tickets and shoe boxes with ball-point pens. She priced and carried the articles to the shelves, unlocking the padlocks which secured the wire cages and taking out more goods for pricing. She placed merchandise on the bucket lift which moved down to the appropriate departments in the store and from which assistants removed their own goods, pressed the button and sent the bucket lift on its way again. All the time she talked and laughed with the other women she kept her secret strictly to herself.

When the day's work was over and the marking-off room staff had gone home, she would stay behind and cover the walls, those once-yellow walls with their peeling paint and ingrained dirt, with posters which she had produced while a student at the art school. She had brought them from home that morning in a large travel bag where they now lay hidden. She had decided not to ask permission. That would be courting a refusal, which she was not prepared to risk. She believed in the maxim 'act first, ask afterwards' – since childhood it had reaped dividends for her in her dealings with her parents.

When everyone had gone and she was left alone with her shadow in that dim, uncanny stillness, she brushed off the cobwebs of fear her imagination had started to spin around her and began her task.

She applied a special adhesive to the backs of the posters. Then, with joy rising in her like the sun at dawn, she decorated the walls with paintings of the British countryside which she had designed for a travel firm; with abstract patterns; with portraits of fellow students; still life, and even a self-portrait she had once painted as an exercise.

She stood back to admire the effect and considered her efforts had been well worth while. Of course the great room was still dingy and shadowed, the goods were still stacked high and the atmosphere remained one of a wasteland of man-made goods, but at least it was possible to escape for a few enchanted moments into the colour and fascination of dreamy, impressionist landscapes, bowls of fruit, flower arrangements and drawings of young people sketched from life. She went home at last, her artistic sensibilities deeply satisfied, her social conscience assuaged, experiencing not a single qualm.

Next morning she arrived early, anticipating her colleagues' gasps of astonishment and disbelief and, she hoped, just a little praise. One by one the women drifted in, and she had her share of compliments on her skill as an artist and their gratitude for her attempts to introduce colour and diversion into their working lives.

'Don't know whether you'll be able to leave 'em up, though, love,' Madge said regretfully. 'Mr. Havering – he's the general manager – can be a stubborn so-and-so when he likes. He don't hold with what he calls initiative in the staff. Says they're all paid to do what they're told, not what they want. If he comes in, don't be upset if he orders you to take 'em all down.'

'I don't see what's wrong with trying to hide these horrible walls,' Juliet complained.

'Couldn't agree with you more, dear,' Madge answered, 'but you just convince the management of that.'

They started work. It was the turn of the birthday cards to be priced discreetly with a pencil in a corner on the back page. While they were lifting teamakers from the wire cages to the marking table, the door opened.

'Watch it, love,' hissed Madge. 'Here comes Mr. Havering.'

But Juliet nearly dropped the expensive item of electrical equipment she was holding. It was not Mr. Havering.

'Gawd,' whispered Madge, 'it's the heir to the throne himself!' She murmured out of the corner of her mouth, 'To what honour,' she pronounced the 'h', 'do we owe this visitation? Can't say I've ever seen him in here before.'

The 'heir to the throne', as she called the company manager, was gazing round the room like a man who had awoken from a nightmare only to discover that his bad dreams were a reality.

He looked at Juliet. 'You'd better put that thing down, Miss Bourne, before you drop it on your foot. I'm not worried about your foot, but I am concerned about the delicate piece of equipment you're handling.'

Mutinously but with care she placed the heavy box on the table. Then she stood still, fixing her eyes on him, and waited for what she knew was coming.

'I take it,' said Drew Major tersely, 'that it's to you we owe this very exclusive exhibition of modern art. What were you trying to do – turn the place into a poor relation of the Royal Academy?'

'No, Mr. Major,' she said quietly. 'I was merely trying to introduce into the lives of the unfortunate staff who work in this – this dungeon, a little colour and brightness, to remind them in case they've forgotten by the end of the long, long day that there's a more attractive and exciting world beyond these four walls, something one is apt to forget after being closeted for hours in this half-hearted imitation of a prison.'

'Dungeons, Miss Bourne,' Drew said dryly, but there was a warning note beneath his sarcasm, 'are, for your information, usually deep in the earth, not poised on the eighth floor of a twelve-storey building. And if the people employed here have any complaints, they know where to take them – to the personnel manager.'

Juliet was conscious of the rustle and bustle of the women working at the table. They were pretending feverishly to be deaf to Juliet's exchange of pleasantries with the man in charge.

'Did you get permission to put up these works of art?'

'No, Mr. Major.'

'Not from the general manager? Not even from the supervisor of this section?'

'No, Mr. Major.'

'Then you will kindly take them down and return them where they belong – in your portfolio of similar artistic masterpieces at home.'

Forcing aside her antipathy and remembering only her desire to brighten the lives of the people who worked in that great comfortless room, she tried to talk him round.

'But *why*, Mr. Major? What harm does it do to have a few pictures on the walls to cover the cracks? I admit that as works of art they're not very good, but they're better than nothing.' She moved towards him, but he retreated as if he was afraid that she had every intention of flinging herself at his feet. '*Please*, Mr. Major,' she pleaded, 'can't I leave them up there, just for a little while?'

'I'm afraid not, Miss Bourne.'

Furious at her inability to move him, she scowled and their eyes became entangled like two boys fighting. She withdrew hers, battle-scarred. He was the victor.

She held in her anger. 'All right, Mr. Major. I'll take them down, Mr. Major. At the end of the day.'

When he had gone, the others didn't speak, but she felt their sympathy and saw in their covert glances astonished admiration for her courage in standing up to him. But the admiration seemed to be muted by the fear of what might happen to her now. It seemed they had decided that her dismissal was imminent. How could it be otherwise after her daring opposition to the wishes of the man at the top?

At the end of the day, when the others had gone home, she looked at her pictures and her anger returned, bringing with it a twisted desire for retribution. She would show Drew Major! Motivated now by a fierce mindless passion, she tore down the paintings one by one. And, one by one, with vindictive, furious fingers, she crumpled them and screwed them into tight round balls and threw them into the waste bucket.

Then she grasped the bucket, ran along the corridor, raced down two flights of stairs to the administrative section, rapped on Drew Major's door and burst in. He was alone.

She lifted the bucket and dumped it on top of the papers on his desk. She pointed at the bucket, filled to the brim with her paintings, each one destroyed beyond recall. '*Now* are you satisfied?' she cried. 'The walls in the marking-off room are back to their miserable darkness and filth, and everything is back to normal!'

He had not moved a muscle. She looked at the destruction

34

she had wrought and it came to her just what she had done. She had destroyed some of her most cherished possessions. She began to cry.

'You can have my paintings, you can take them home and unravel them. Then you can pin them up and desecrate the immaculately decorated walls of your luxury home and spend the rest of your life laughing at them till you cry!' She began to laugh herself, overwrought and hysterical, and turned for the door.

But Drew was there before her. 'You little idiot, what have you done? Why did you do it? To hurt me? Because you haven't. You've hurt yourself instead, and you know it.' He grasped her arm and shook it to bring her to her senses. 'Stop it! Pull yourself together, girl!'

He pushed her into a chair and stood over her until she quietened down, mumbling her apologies. She wished she could take every one of those pictures and smooth them flat and have them back again. They represented days of work and effort. She had spent hours perfecting them and now they were gone.

'My God,' he whispered, 'my father said your mother had fire. He didn't know when he was lucky. Compared with her you're a blazing inferno!'

He sat down and watched her until she grew calmer. Then he spoke. 'Look, Juliet, I gave you a job. Out of the kindness of my heart I found a place for you in the firm. I needn't have done. I could have said, "Sorry, no vacancy anywhere." But I didn't. I think the least I can expect from you is an observance of the rules of the firm, a respect for those above you. Initiative is fine. Normally, I welcome it, but for heaven's sake let it be after consultation with others who know better than you. If I had let you get away with that, how could I have stopped any of the others doing the same thing all over the building where there may be paint peeling off, or dirt left behind by the passing of the years?'

'I'm sorry,' was all she could say.

'You may like to know, and I'm telling you this, although there's no need for me to do so, that I'm quite aware, as is the whole of the management, that the marking-off room is in need of alteration, rearrangement and decoration. In fact, it's on the list, its price has been estimated, its cost approved. It's moving upwards gradually in the list of pri-

35

orities. Before very long, work will start. Does that satisfy you?'

'I'm sorry,' she said again, and stood up. 'Thank you for telling me.'

'Sit down.' She sat. 'Don't you like your work in the marking-off room?'

'I hate it.'

He smiled slightly. 'Right out with it, as my father would say.' He leaned back and hitched an arm over the back of the chair. 'Do you want to be moved?'

She moistened her lips. 'Yes, please.' Her voice was hoarse.

'Why? Don't you like your colleagues?'

'They're very nice. It's the monotony, the boredom, the—'

'All right, don't go on. So you want to be moved?' She nodded. 'If I moved you, once again I'd have to push you in somewhere. I'd have to create a vacancy.' She waited, holding her breath. He was thinking, drumming his fingers on the desk top. 'Fashion?'

Her eyes, red with weeping, grew bright. 'Wonderful,' she said.

He smiled and rose. 'All right. We'll try fashion, if you promise not to fling paint all over the walls of the fashion department with a view to "brightening it up".'

'I promise,' she whispered, eyes shining. 'When can I start? Tomorrow?'

He nodded. 'I'll let them know in advance just what's coming to them. Via the general manager, that is. If I were to appear in the fashion department, they'd all suffer from shock as the women in the marking-off room did this morning. They might even start salaaming – all, that is,' he smiled mockingly, 'except one. The newest assistant.'

'I'll try to – to behave, and toe the line, Mr. Major.' She grinned. 'Sir.'

He clenched his fist at her and moved his head in the direction of the door. 'Out!' Juliet grasped the waste bucket containing her paintings. 'Leave those, Miss Bourne. I'll dispose of them. The cleaners will be round soon.'

She took one long, sad look at the remains of her pictures and left him.

When Cynthia asked her daughter apprehensively – knowing her volcano-like nature – how she was getting on at Majors, Juliet was evasive. Cynthia recognized the danger signals and her heart sank.

'Trouble already, dear? Whatever job they give you to do, you must remember it was good of them—'

'I know that,' Juliet said irritably. 'It's just that I had a – a difference of opinion,' a delightful euphemism, she told herself, for a violent quarrel, 'with Mr. Major – I mean Drew.' Cynthia started to speak, but Juliet went on, 'If you want to know who won, in a sense we both did.'

When Cedric Bourne came home from work that evening, looking tired as he usually did, he brightened considerably when he heard that Juliet had had an argument with the boss.

He laughed heartily. 'Delighted to hear that my daughter is standing up to the son of my wife's objectionable ex-fiancé.'

'That's a little strong,' Cynthia protested. 'He's not objectionable, he's just—'

'A conceited bighead,' her husband finished.

Cynthia laughed and put her arms round him. 'Don't tell me you're jealous of him after all these years?'

'Jealous?' He kissed her cheek. 'Of course not. I just hate his guts. What else am I supposed to feel towards the man you thought you fancied enough to marry?'

'But, darling, that was years before I met you, when I was too young to know what I was doing.' She saw he wasn't appeased and switched the subject to safer territory. 'What,' she asked Juliet, 'did you mean when you said you had both "won"?'

'Well, in the first place, Drew got his way. Then I got mine.' Her father applauded. 'He's moving me – to fashion.'

When Juliet reported to the staff manager next morning, Mrs. Arthur sighed. 'Second floor,' she said. 'Coats. See the buyer, tell her I sent you.' She eyed Juliet's pink sleeveless dress. 'You can't wear that.'

'But,' Juliet pointed out, 'it was all right to wear it in the marking-off room.'

'Maybe, Miss Bourne,' came wearily from the staff manager, 'but you were behind the scenes in that department, hidden from the public. The House rule dictates a black dress. Take one from stock and you can have it at cost price. That's another rule.'

'A *black* dress?' Juliet wailed. 'But I hate black. Why should I spend money on something I dislike? Can't I wear—?'

'Black dresses for women staff,' Mrs. Arthur repeated slowly, 'is the policy of the management. If you object, take the matter up with Mr. Major. Although I know you won't make him change his mind.'

All right, Juliet conceded as she swept down to the second floor, black it will have to be. But it's going to be a style of my choice.

But she hadn't reckoned with the dictates of the management.

'Black dress,' said Miss Skimpton, buyer of coats, her white hair tinted mauve, her spectacle frames shaped into Machiavellian points, her manner offhand, 'regulation short sleeves, high neck, skirt length just below the knee, black belt at waist. Go to Dresses. They've got a rail of them behind the scenes. Find one to fit you. They stock all sizes.'

Controlling her outrage with difficulty, Juliet went across the fashion floor to the dress department. 'In the office,' she was told. 'Try on one or two in the fitting room.'

The full-length mirror she looked into reflected a pale, sullen sales assistant, her skin already becoming allergic to the high, close-fitting turnover collar which hugged her neck. 'Nineteen-fifties,' she thought, disgustedly. 'If my friends come and see me, they'll be helpless with laughter.'

'It goes with the atmosphere of the store,' said one of the girl assistants. 'Early nineteen hundreds.'

Still eyeing herself with loathing, Juliet said absently, 'I don't know why Majors don't alter their policy and start catering for the sort of people who go to Curlews. My boyfriend works for them and—'

The girl called Penny nudged her. 'Better go back to Coats. Miss Skimpton's looking like thunder.'

Juliet turned and looked at the buyer of coats. 'You're right,' she said.

Miss Skimpton stormed, 'Why were you away so long, Miss Bourne? It can't take half an hour to find a dress to fit a stock size like you.'

'No, Miss Skimpton,' said Juliet meekly. After all, she had promised Drew to toe the line. She ran a finger between the collar of the dress and her neck. Her skin was beginning to irritate.

Miss Skimpton introduced Juliet to the other assistants, all of whom seemed to be replicas of her in looks, bulk and manner. One or two tried to be friendly. On discovering her inexperience, a woman who introduced herself as Edna tried to teach her some sales technique.

'But don't worry, dear, we have half-hour training sessions once a week. Some of the sixth-floor admin mob lower themselves to come down and lecture us on how to increase our sales by telling the customers bigger and better lies!' She shrieked with laughter and Miss Skimpton shushed her as a customer approached.

Edna went forward. 'Watch me,' she muttered, plastering a welcoming smile on her face and asking the customer, 'Can I help you?'

Fifteen minutes later, the customer walked out, a Major's carrier bag in her hand bulging with the coat she had just bought, a satisfied smile on her face.

'That's how you do it, dear,' said Edna. 'You advise, you reason, you praise, you coax, you admire and last of all you put on a little bit of pressure. Then you take their money.' She thrust her hand, palm upwards, towards Juliet. 'Easy. I've even sold a woman a fur coat in the middle of summer – just by talking.'

Miss Skimpton enthused, eyes alight, her throaty voice full of emotion, 'Edna's our best saleswoman. Copy her, Miss Bourne, and you won't go far wrong.'

'Copy her?' thought Juliet. 'No, thanks. I'd never live peaceably with myself again if I used her tactics. That customer looked atrocious in that coat.'

'The higher our sales,' Miss Skimpton went on, 'the bigger our profits. That's the maxim we've all got written invisibly in front of our eyes in this department.'

Then I'm going to be the exception, Juliet decided. Thus it was a few days later she was reprimanded by Miss Skimpton for not having sold one coat since she started in that section.

'I'll have to have you moved, Miss Bourne, if you don't buck up your sales. Mr. Major was asking the other day how you were getting on. I'm afraid I had to tell him. "No sale," I said. "Not one?" he asked. "Not one," I had to say. I can tell you, he looked pretty fed up.'

Juliet's heart sank. In trouble again with Drew? 'But I do try, Miss Skimpton. I just don't seem to have the right touch.'

She was also finding it difficult to fit in with the other sales assistants. They all seemed to be trying to pretend she wasn't there. They were all twice her age, and more and more the generation gap hit her forcibly when she attempted to talk to them. They excluded her from their conversation and even when she tried to join in, they made her feel an interloper.

The black dress with its choking collar was reacting on the skin of her neck like an allergy. It was bringing her out in a rash. The warm weather made the heavy material intolerable. And she was beginning to hate the sight of coats. Trade was slack because the weather was so warm. Miss Skimpton was panicking because so many styles were being left unsold on her hands.

'We'll have to mark them down,' she fussed. 'Think of the loss in profits!'

Having no one else on whom she dared vent her feelings for the unexpectedly hot summer, she poured out her ire on Juliet, who seemed to be able to do nothing right.

'Tomorrow,' she said to the other assistants, picking out Juliet with gloating eyes, 'we have our weekly staff training session. It might be Mr. Havering, the general manager. Or it might be Mrs. Arthur.' She caught her breath. 'It might even be Mr. Major, Mr. Drew Major himself. Sometimes he honours us with his presence.'

Years of practice in servility had taught this woman to worship those in authority and to her Drew Major was undoubtedly a man to idolize because of his position of power within the firm. Juliet, coming of a generation who, on principle, venerated no one, was disgusted by the woman's subservient attitude.

That evening Juliet went home and phoned Malcolm, hoping to arrange to see him. But he had a meeting to attend – he was the secretary of a local youth club – and said he was sorry, darling, he couldn't make it, but wild horses wouldn't keep him from her tomorrow.

40

In a vicious, impulsive mood, she looked at her working dress which she had flung on the bed. If the scissors had not been lying on the dressing-table she probably wouldn't have done it, but there they were, challenging her. She picked them up, seized the dress and with an exquisite feeling of revenge, started chopping at the neck of it.

The high collar disappeared, the scissors cutting lower and still lower and up again the other side. There it was, a becoming rounded neckline which needed only the removal of the sleeves to balance it. The sleeves were snipped out and she held up in front of her a stylish, up-to-date dress. Another inch off the skirt, the artist in her murmured, and it would be perfect.

She went downstairs for her mother's workbox and without telling her why she wanted it, took it upstairs. An hour later the alterations were finished. She tried the dress on and was so pleased with the result she went down to show her mother.

Instead of praising her, Cynthia blanched. 'What have you done? You won't be allowed to wear that if it's against the policy of the management.'

'Then,' said Juliet, 'the management will just have to change its policy.'

Her father laughed, 'Good for you!' He turned to his wife, eyes approving. 'Where did she get her fight from, Cynthia? She's got spirit, you must admit.'

' "Fire," Warren called it,' Cynthia mused.

Her husband closed down. 'Did he?' His voice was as flat as a punctured tyre. Then, sarcastically, 'He should know, shouldn't he?'

'Darling,' Cynthia placated, 'don't be like that.'

Cedric raised his newspaper between them.

Juliet wished her defiance of the previous evening had persisted through the night. But somewhere between the hours of sleeping and waking her courage had deserted her. She felt like a swimmer on the topmost platform of a diving board suddenly taking fright at the idea of jumping. She looked with dismay upon the altered dress. She put it on and ran to the waste paper basket in a hopeless attempt to salvage the chopped-out material and replace them like pieces in a jigsaw puzzle.

As a consequence she was late. She slipped into the office attached to the fashion department and hung up her coat. She spread out guilty fingers against her neck, feeling the bareness of her skin. She felt half-dressed. Her uncovered arms prickled and her legs seemed to stretch for miles from the hem of her shortened skirt.

The mumble of voices was dying down. The speaker must have arrived. Drawing herself to her full five feet five and swallowing a deep draught of courage from the conditioned air around her, she walked out into the fashion department to find that the chairs had been arranged in a semi-circle. She searched for an empty seat. There was one left. It was in the front row.

There was nothing for it but to brave the astonished stares of the assembled staff and make for that chair. The women gasped. The men – there were less than half a dozen – gazed, and the appreciation in their eyes was unmistakable. When Juliet felt brave enough to look up and identify the member of the staff who was to address them, it was she who gasped.

Drew Major stood at the table, papers spread out in front of him. But he was staring at her, not his papers, his eyes unbelieving, his jaw square and belligerent, his lips compressed. Amongst those conventionally dressed, dowdy-looking women in their store uniform, he made her feel as unwanted and redundant as a discontinued line of merchandise.

The company manager, having allowed his gaze to lick over her and hammer her down like the flap of an envelope, removed his eyes and concentrated on the job in hand.

'You may wonder,' said the speaker, 'why I am giving the training session this morning. I'm deputizing for the general manager who is away at a meeting. I'll begin with a statement which you've probably heard before, but which I feel is worth repeating. It is that stock well looked after is stock more than half sold. Sometimes, the task of looking after stock is entrusted to the newest assistant. Without supervision, this practice could be risky, bearing in mind,' he raised his eyes and stared at Juliet, 'the dubious quality of the new assistants we have wished on to us in these days of staff shortages.'

There was an amused titter and everyone leaned forward

to stare at the girl to whom the company manager was un-mistakably referring. She flushed deeply, but her eyes stared courageously back at him. She would not be cowed into subservience by his sarcasm, nor would he reduce her to servility and grovelling by deriding her in public. She was no second Miss Skimpton.

He had returned to his subject. 'The care of stock is im-portant because markdowns due to bad stock-keeping have a tendency to eat into the profits and with good management should be completely avoidable. Such apparently trifling things as resewing on of loose buttons and repair of slight damage which may result from customers trying on gar-ments are important too. This should in the ordinary way be given to the youngest assistant to tackle, provided,' he paused, but Juliet did not dare look up this time, 'that that assistant can be trusted to carry out the work thoroughly and responsibly.

'Other things can damage existing stock – too much heat, for instance, strong sunlight, dampness in the atmosphere, soiling of the garments through too much handling by the public – all of which tend to bring down the sales value of the goods on display.'

He paused and turned over a few pages. Juliet looked up and he raised his eyes and looked through, not at, her. 'There is, of course, the unpleasant subject of loss of stock. Some way of safeguarding it is essential, which is why we have in this store a security officer and other ways in which we can detect either pilferage by staff – a rarity, but it does unfortunately happen – or shoplifting by unscrupulous cus-tomers. As you probably all know, we operate closed circuit television in this store. We use special mirrors, which are not really mirrors at all, but which are really magic eyes, being transparent from the other side. We have members of staff specially trained for purposes of detection, and we also employ outside help in this respect. This is an unpleasant subject on which to dwell, but unfortunately it is such an important one that I have been forced to do so.'

Drew continued with his lecture for a while, then shuffled his papers together, indicating that the training session was over. The audience rose stiffly, reluctant not so much to leave the meeting as to shake off the torpor that had settled on them while listening.

Juliet noted with some fear the sluggish movement of the crowd. It hampered her attempts to get out of reach of the man in charge. With as much speed as the others would allow, and abandoning any attempt at politeness, she pushed her way through them, making for the temporary sanctuary of the fashion buyer's office until all danger of pursuit had passed. But her bid for freedom was thwarted as sharply as a warning shot fired over the heads of a riotous mob.

'*Miss Bourne*!' rang out and the command in the familiar voice stopped her in her tracks and made her hold her breath.

The others, dispersing slowly, regarded her with some pity. Although not all of them were on her side. Others, older women mostly, stared at her with self-righteous disgust. After all, hadn't she asked for trouble, turning up for work dressed like that? They glared at the bare white skin of her throat, her uncovered, slightly tanned arms, with such distaste she felt she could hardly have committed a greater sin had she arrived for work in her swimsuit.

'I wish to see you,' the voice said, abrasive as a nail file. 'Come upstairs to my office, Miss Bourne.'

He went towards the swing doors and she had to follow. With cold courtesy he held the door open for her and then preceded her up four flights of stairs. She trailed him all the way like an apprentice mountaineer following an expert at the game. By the time they had reached the sixth floor, she was gasping for breath. She concluded that he had subjected her to the long climb, instead of taking the lift as any considerate employer would have done, to deprive her of the powers of speech on arrival at his office.

He unlocked his door and she followed at his heels. He rang his secretary and told her he did not wish to be interrupted for the next ten minutes. Juliet wondered dully if that was how long it would take to dismiss her from her job. She sat down without invitation. He sat too and clasped his hands, elbows resting on his blotter, while his eyes did a quick but thorough examination in depth of her person.

She winced. Any other man's gaze wandering over her she could take with equanimity – she had had a few wolf whistles directed her way in her time – but not Drew Major's. His eyes, detached and cool, were spiced with such a strong seasoning of male evaluation that she turned a deep, uncomfortable pink.

'So,' he murmured, 'you've done it again. With your customary contempt for authority, you've snapped your fingers in the face of conformity and done your own thing as dramatically and challengingly as only you know how.'

This time she did not flinch from his steady gaze. 'Yes, I admit it. But I'm not sorry. Something inside me made me do it.'

'And,' his sarcasm began to seep through, 'that "something inside you" was quite untameable, in fact it had such power over you that your reason and your common sense were hopelessly overruled? Like an unthinking child you were seized by an ungovernable impulse, disregarding all thoughts of the consequences,' she winced again at his too-near approximation to the truth, 'and grabbed some scissors and proceeded to hack your way through the material of the firm's dress—'

'I paid for it,' she interrupted, like a sulky child.

He ignored her comment. '—and, extracting a sadistic pleasure out of every snip of those scissors, (you were hitting out at authority all the time, remember – for "authority" read "Drew Major") you created out of the original design something far more suited to your artistic sensibilities, your ego and—' his eyes wandered again over her shapeliness, 'your figure, the attractiveness of which you are only too well aware.'

She lowered her eyes. 'I'm still not sorry.'

'Well,' he leaned back, 'where do we go from here?'

'That,' she said, clasping and unclasping her hands, 'is for you to decide.'

'What would you do, I wonder, if I ordered you to go away and take that dress off? Would you do to it what you did to your paintings – tear it up into tiny pieces like a truculent child and throw it in the waste paper basket? Destroy it utterly, as a substitute for destroying me – utterly, because I represent the authority you so despise?'

She whispered, defiance staring out of her eyes, 'Yes, I would.'

'I'm sure you would. And is this,' he motioned to the dress, 'what you call "toeing the line", as you promised to do the other day? Was this what you meant by "behaving"?'

She was silent. 'Suppose,' he persisted, 'I told you to discard that dress and go and buy another staff dress, making absolutely sure that this time you did not meddle with the design, but wore it as it should be worn, during working hours, like all the other women members of staff?'

'I'm sorry,' she said dully, 'I wouldn't do it.'

'And if I said the alternative was that you'd lose your job?'

Juliet touched her lips and found them wrinkled with dryness. She took a breath. 'I still wouldn't do it.'

He tapped a pencil on the desk top. 'Stupid of me to ask such a question, wasn't it? I should have anticipated such an answer. Rebellion for the sake of it.' She opened her mouth to protest, but he went on, 'Some call it "fire", some call it "spirit".' He rose. 'I, Miss Bourne, would call it rank disobedience.' He walked round the desk and faced her. 'Tell me, why the revolt against such a trivial thing as a dress?'

Now her ire was raised. 'Trivial? You call the compulsory wearing of a garment at least twenty years out of date *trivial*? Not only do I object to a rule which, as I see it, arises out of a management policy which can only be described as a form of dictatorship—'

He raised his eyebrows high. 'So we're getting political now, are we? My father was so right when he said, as a joke, that you would probably try to take over the running of the firm. You may not know it, Miss Bourne, but your anarchy is showing, an anarchy born no doubt of the teaching you received at art school, which was to make an impolite noise at all forms of law and order.'

'Just how stupid can people in your position get?' she burst out, regardless of the fact that she was insulting the man at the head of the firm. 'You and your executive brethren seem to take a delight in perpetually regarding all artists as the lowest form of animal life!'

'Well,' he smiled, provoking now, 'aren't they?'

She was scarlet with anger, goaded all the more because he was watching her with an inscrutable expression in his eyes. 'No, they are not! Without artists, the world would—'

'Spare me that, please. Don't go into touching details about the so-called virtues of your artist colleagues and how the world would be an unbearable place to live in without them. I question that, anyway.'

She said coldly, trying to ignore his goading smile which, in its complacency, gave away that he had achieved what he had set out to do – arouse her to anger, 'If you'll allow me to return to the subject under discussion—?' He inclined his head mockingly. 'I object not only to the colour and the outdated style, but most of all to the ridiculously high neck which in this hot summer weather makes me feel I'm suffocating. No doubt in winter, with the central heating going full blast, it would almost certainly have the same unfortunate effect. It also irritates my skin and brings me out in a rash.'

He lounged against the desk, crossing his legs and folding his arms. 'Why don't any of the other women members of staff suffer similar symptoms? I'll tell you why. It's your emotional state that creates the rash, your squirming dislike of having to obey the rules that are imposed on you from above. It's not the style of dress at all. It can't be, otherwise all the other women would be scratching away merrily at their necks, wouldn't they?'

'Are you trying to tell me in a roundabout way that I'm unbalanced, that I'm neurotic?'

He shrugged. 'I'm not a psychologist, so how am I to know? But, as they say, if the cap fits . . .'

'Well, it doesn't! If you must know, I *am* rebelling – against the stuffy atmosphere of the whole store – and I'm not referring to the air conditioning.' Now she had started, nothing was going to stop her, not even if he clamped his hand over her mouth to force her to be quiet. He made no such move, so she went on, 'You might say that the dress was symbolic. Its style typifies the "high class" aura this establishment has around it like the rings round Saturn. The prices you charge are enough to keep away most of the women – the ordinary women – of the town. You may not know it, but you've got a name for being expensive.'

'That may be so,' he said evenly, not seeming to resent her remarks, 'but Majors are not exactly bankrupt.'

'But, don't you see,' she persisted, wishing she possessed the verbal expertise to convert him to her point of view, 'Curlews are cashing in on your "expensive" image. In almost every case, their prices are cheaper than yours.'

'I'm more aware than you think, Miss Bourne, of the

image of cheapness that Curlews have put about. It's largely a myth, as you would have discovered if you'd gone into the whole subject of Curlew's prices from a professional stand-point as I have, instead of the – if I may say so – very amateur, "customer" angle from which you have viewed the matter. Experience has taught me to look at other people's prices with a discriminating, not to say suspicious eye, which you with your ignorance of the ways of the retail world could not do. The goods Curlews sell in every department at a low price are purchased solely for that purpose, to create the "cheap" image. Their other goods are sold at prices comparable with ours.'

She felt she was losing ground. 'All the same, Curlews have the name for being the shop where "ordinary" women go, and Majors are regarded as the "high-class" women's shop. Malcolm told me—'

'Ah yes, the inestimable boy-friend. Tell me, is he an executive of the firm?'

'You know very well he's only a junior assistant.'

'You surprise me. I thought he must at least be a director.' He watched the colour sting her cheeks.

'Well, they adopted the slogan he suggested and gave him a pay rise for it – *The Call of Curlews*.'

'And did he also suggest that they use that maddeningly repetitive sound that greets you as you enter the store – the call of the curlew itself? A beautiful, winsome, poignant sound when heard in the right place – high up on the moors – but enough to drive you mad when heard constantly above the din of the customers' chatter.'

'Yes, he did.'

'Ah, a real "ideas" man. They should put him on the advertising staff. Or even promote him to administration.'

'Well, he's not in either. He's in the carpet department.'

'*Carpet* department? What a waste of a brilliant brain! Someone should tell them what they're missing.' He grinned sarcastically.

'He may only be a carpet salesman,' she said defensively, 'but the people at the top *do* listen to him when he tells them things, and to all their assistants with ideas, however junior they may be.'

'A gentle hint, I suppose, that Majors should do the same?'

'Why not? It's the young people who've got the ideas these days.' He laughed sardonically at that. Nevertheless she continued, 'If you invented some slogans yourself, like – like,' she groped, 'like *Major reductions, Make Mine Majors*' or – or *You get more for less at Majors*, you would get the ordinary people to come here, too.'

He paced the room. 'You've done it for me, Miss Bourne. Do you want a pay rise on the strength of your commendable but slightly feeble poetic efforts?'

She stood angrily. 'I might as well hand in my notice. It's obvious I don't fit in here. I never will, wherever you try to push me in, whatever department you wish me on to. I'll relieve you of my irritating presence. I'll go to the employment exchange, I'll join the queue for jobs . . .'

He pulled her hand from the handle and held on to it. 'Don't be such an impetuous little fool, Juliet. What are you trying to do, tear yourself up into little pieces, as you did your paintings, because you consider yourself a failure? You're such a damned rebel you'd refuse to knuckle under to any kind of authority, no matter where you worked!'

She tried to remove her hand from his, but failing, let it rest there slackly. 'I can't help what I am. When I see things that are wrong, I want to put them right. Is that such a crime?'

He dropped her hand and shook his head. 'A law unto yourself, aren't you? What are we going to do about you?' His fingers closed round her bare arms and he looked her over. 'The dress suits you like that, there's no doubt about it.' Her heart leapt. There was appreciation in his eyes which he didn't even try to hide. Then they narrowed. 'The new image.' Her heart settled down. He was seeing her not as a woman, but as a new kind of Major employee.

'May I – go on wearing it like this?' He didn't answer, just looked. 'Please, Drew?'

He scanned her face, saw the appeal there, removed his hands and turned away. 'It's difficult. There are all the others to consider.' He stood at the window, his legs stiff, hands in pockets, his back rigid. 'In the circumstances, I'm afraid I'll have to say "no".'

She had lost. She bit her lip, hesitated, then ran to the door. 'Goodbye, Drew.'

He called her back, but she had gone.

CHAPTER THREE

JULIET stayed away from work next day. She asked herself, what was the use? She decided not to tell her parents. She played truant, leaving the house at the usual time but taking a bus going in the opposite direction and getting out in the heart of the countryside. She walked, fretting, worrying, trying to think, stopping only for a few sandwiches and a cup of tea at a mobile snack bar.

She walked until her legs refused to carry her, then she sat on a milestone at the roadside, ignoring the curious looks of the car drivers as they sped past. One or two slowed down, thinking she wanted a lift, but she waved them on.

With her elbows on her knees and her chin in her hands, she didn't even try to fight the depression that weighed her down like a yoke across her shoulders. If she resigned from Majors, she would have to find something else to do. No other job would fall into her lap as this one had done.

She would have to attend interviews and fight for any position in competition with other girls. And she needed the money to help her parents. The whole point of leaving art school had been to earn her living and pay her way.

Perhaps Drew had been right in saying she was too rebellious and would refuse to bow down to any authority, no matter who it was. But that was her nature and she could not alter it. She sighed, finding no solution.

Her watch told her it was safe to return home on the next bus without arousing her parents' suspicions. But she arrived to find her mother frantic with worry.

'I've been out of my mind! Where have you been all day? Drew phoned. He wanted to know why you hadn't gone to work. When I told him that was where I thought you were, he grew mad with worry, too.'

Juliet smiled. She could imagine Drew being mad — with delight at her absence!

Cynthia went on, 'If you didn't go to work then where did you go?'

She answered her mother's outburst with one word. 'Walking.'

'*Walking*? Darling,' Cynthia sounded deeply worried, 'they haven't given you the sack?'

Juliet winced at the anxiety in her mother's voice. It was too much an echo of the uneasiness which had stalked her all day like a criminal doggedly pursuing a victim. 'I don't know, Mum. If they haven't then I'll probably have to dismiss myself.' Her voice was strained and she flopped down, white-faced, into an armchair. 'Yesterday Drew called me in. I'd transgressed again, overstepped the limits beyond which the policy of Major and Son won't allow their employees to go.'

'Was it your dress?' Juliet nodded. 'Then you can hardly blame Drew for telling you off, can you? I thought you'd been far too drastic with it.'

When Cedric came in, Cynthia told him what had happened. To Juliet's surprise and chagrin he advised caution. She had thought that at least her father would be on her side.

'You've got to have a certain amount of discipline amongst the staff to run a business successfully, dear,' he said. 'You can't have employees behaving like anarchists.' Juliet flinched. Anarchy was Drew's word, and in using it her father was as good as putting her in the wrong. 'Staff can't make their own rules and flout those of the management. Be reasonable.'

But she was incapable of seeing reason. In her present mood of self-pity, brought on partly by fatigue and partly because there seemed to be no one who was prepared to give her the sympathy and support she craved, support which would vindicate her rebellious behaviour, she would admit that no one was right but herself. She chafed against the necessity to conform and thus lose her identity which she cherished because it was such a vital part of her development as an artist.

'But they're so inflexible, Dad. They won't give an inch in any direction.'

He said with a smile, 'You mean they won't give in to you. Knowing my daughter, she probably went about things in a rash, tactless way—'

The phone rang and Cedric went to answer it. Juliet called, 'It's probably Malcolm. I promised to go out with him tonight. Put him off, will you, Dad?'

51

But it wasn't Malcolm. Her father called her, handing over the receiver. 'Your boss. The "and Son" part of Majors.'

Her heart thumped as she took over. What excuse could she give for her absence? She could hardly plead illness because he knew she was perfectly fit. Tell him the truth – that she couldn't face yet another session with him of censure and reprimand?

'Juliet? Where the devil have you been all day?'

'I took a bus ride.'

'Playing truant?'

She sighed. 'If you like to put it that way.'

'People who play truant are usually afraid.'

'I *wasn't* afraid. I was—' She thought the words, 'I was fed up, miserable, depressed, hating myelf, hating you—' But they stopped short at her lips.

'I want to see you. Tonight.'

'Sorry,' she snapped. 'I've got a date.'

'Then you'll have to break it. I told you, I want to see you. Have dinner with me. I'll give you half an hour.'

He slammed down the phone and she looked at the receiver as though it was a poisonous snake. Then she dialled Malcolm's number, excusing herself from their meeting and saying she would explain tomorrow.

Dressing to go out with Drew put her in a defiant mood. She chose the most flamboyant outfit in her wardrobe – a long-sleeved heavily embroidered blouse, fringed suede waistcoat and scarlet trousers. Black dress indeed! She would show Drew Major.

Her mother frowned. Her father asked her whose country's national dress she was wearing and could she still speak the language of her motherland? She ran out to Drew's car. She didn't want him to see the inside of the house she lived in. She could imagine his disdain if he were to see the poverty of her home in comparison with the richness of his.

She watched hopefully for his shocked reaction to her clothes, but apart from the merest flicker of the eyebrows, nothing happened. Disappointed, she provoked him.

'In these things I'm wearing you can't take me to one of your high class places, can you?'

'My dear Juliet, as my guest you really have no right to

speak to me like that.' His tone was high-handed, deliberately so.

He had successfully wielded the newspaper and she had contracted, squashed, like a fly on the window pane. She stole a look at his clothes. She was shaken to discover that he was not dressed in his usual impeccable executive style. His shirt was floral, with matching tie, his jacket, tailored to perfection was suede, his trousers the most up to date in men's wear.

'I'm sorry.' Her apology was belated and just a little flat. Her provocation had misfired.

The restaurant he took her to was along a seemingly endless passage. The entrance doors bore stained glass windows depicting various aspects of modern living – aircraft, sports cars, space capsules, long-haired youth of both sexes fixed for the lifetime of the works of art – for that was what they were – in the many twisting, writhing, almost primitive attitudes adopted by modern youth at play.

The paintings round the walls which, Juliet noted as they were shown to their table, could hardly be discerned in the half-light of the long, low room, were unintelligible enough to gladden the heart of any modern artist. She looked across the table at Drew and wondered how he knew of the existence of such a place.

'Well?' he smiled. 'Are your aesthetic sensibilities pleased by the surroundings? Is your artistic temperament assuaged, your appetite for the new, the different, the *now*, satiated?'

He was laughing at her, of course, but she smiled, nevertheless. 'I was wondering how you knew about it. I suppose you regularly bring your women here.'

He raised a corrective hand. 'Singular, please. Never plural. Woman, not women. I never complicate my life by having more than one girl-friend at a time.'

'That's such a relief,' she was sarcastic back, because for some reason his admission, whether true or false – and she felt sure it was true – pained her. 'Don't let your current lady-friend know you took me out to dinner tonight, will you? She might be jealous.'

He looked at her eyes, full of spirit, her face, full of fire, her figure, which was too conspicuous to be overlooked, and murmured, 'You could well be right.'

They ordered and when they were alone, she said, 'May I ask who she is?'

'My current girl-friend? Her name's Camille Wyngard. Her father's a highly placed Civil Servant, something important in the Treasury, her mother a socialite.'

'What's she like?' Her brain felt oddly numb, enabling her to speak only in monosyllables. 'Is she rich?'

'Very. Now, let me see, what is she like?' He rubbed his chin and studied Juliet's face as if seeking inspiration there. 'Beautiful – naturally. Shapely – naturally. Brown-haired, brown-eyed, medium height. And – er—' he withdrew his eyes from hers, 'all woman.'

Juliet searched frantically for the waiter. When would he bring the food? There must be something else she could do with her hands besides clasping them like this under the table.

Failing to find him, she returned to the subject, drawn despite herself, like a murderer returning to the scene of the crime. 'Intelligent?'

'Of course. I never take out a dull-witted woman. They have nothing to talk about.'

'Does she—' she squeezed out the words like juice from a lemon, 'does she conform, unlike me? Does she do everything that's expected of her, unlike me? Does she accept everything at its face value without questioning it, as I do?'

'She gives me no trouble.' He smiled. 'She's tractable, pliable, and responsive – very.' He eyed her. 'Shall I go on?'

For a painful moment, she imprisoned her bottom lip between her teeth. 'No, thank you.'

The food arrived and as they started eating, he asked, 'Tell me, why the dramatic absence from work today?'

'I wondered when that was coming.' Juliet concentrated on her meal. 'You know very well why.'

'Unless your excuse is really watertight, you'll have to lose a day's pay, you know.' He sounded as if he was smiling, but she wouldn't raise her eyes to confirm it.

'What's the use of coming back? I'll stay away until the end of the week, then you won't have the embarrassment of calling me into your office and paying me off and telling me you have no further use for my services.'

'They're the staff manager's and cashier's jobs, not mine.'
He was being deliberately difficult.

'I've failed in everything you've given me.'

'You're beginning to tear yourself apart. I should have expected it. It's in character.'

'Everything I do is wrong. You know that.'

He put down his knife and fork. 'Are you trying to talk me into dismissing you, thus completing the process of self-destruction?'

She shrugged helplessly, finding her food difficult to swallow. 'There's no need for me to do that. You've already made up your mind to get rid of me. That's why you've asked me out tonight, to soften the blow.'

He resumed his eating. 'My dear girl, I'm a businessman. Where the interests of the firm are concerned, I never "soften the blow". Do you think I'd really be such a despicable hypocrite as to dine and wine a girl I was about to throw out of her job?' She would not look at him. 'Juliet!'

At the sharp note in his voice she looked up.

'I was going to offer you promotion.'

It couldn't be true. She searched for mockery in his face, but there was none. For a moment her spirits soared, like a lark rising joyously into a blue, limitless sky. Then, like a lark descending from the heights, they dropped like a stone, scooping out a crater in her hopes.

'You're joking.'

'I swear I'm not.'

'Then you're doing it because of who I am, because my mother was once engaged to your father.'

'What do you take me for? I told you, I'm a businessman. I know ability when I see it, latent and undeveloped though it may be.'

'And, in your opinion, I've – got it?'

'I think so. I think that embedded deep down in all that show of rebellion is something of great promise.' He paused while the waiter removed the empty plates. 'I'm convinced that you possess that priceless thing called "vision", an attribute so rare that it's misunderstood and abused by those who haven't got it. People with vision – and they're few enough – can somehow project their minds into the future and see things as they could be. They spend their time, like you, fretting because things aren't changing fast enough. Others

– usually those who are afraid of change and, by heaven, there are more than enough of those types around – exist wholly in the present, seeing things only as they are or were, and denying that the future exists.'

She looked away, not knowing whether to thank him for the compliments he was paying her, or accept what he was saying as matter-of-factly as he was saying it.

'For some time now,' he went on, 'my father and I have been toying with the idea of opening a boutique.' Her heart began to hammer unmercifully. 'We want somehow to get the younger age groups into the store – up to now they've made themselves conspicuous by their absence. You're one of them. Can you tell me why?'

'I think,' she said slowly, trying to keep the excitement out of her voice, 'it's because there's nothing there for them, nothing to bring them in.'

'Exactly. We thought a boutique, geared to their needs, might do the trick. Am I right?'

'If it were run in the right way, and by – by the right person, yes. Who—' Dare she ask? Would she be snubbed if she did? She decided to risk it. 'Who did you have in mind?'

He smiled. 'You. After all I've been saying, who else? With your artistic training, your flair for design, your impertinence – no, in the circumstances let's be kind and call it courage in the face of established custom, you should be able to make your point and your presence known amongst the age group to which you have the fortune – or some might call it misfortune – to belong.'

'You mean – I'd be in charge? Of the whole thing?'

'Yes. You'd come into the category of buyer. Compared with the very junior sales assistant you are now, it would mean a considerable increase in salary and status.'

'But,' for the life of her she couldn't think why she was raising obstacles to her promotion, except perhaps to test the sincerity of his proposition, to make quite sure, like a child being offered a longed-for present, that it was really meant for her, 'but suppose the other members of staff don't like it? Because I'm so new they might regard it as favouritism.'

'You? A favourite of mine?' He laughed loudly. 'That's rich, after all the rows we've had! Anyway, I'd soon disillusion them. If you make a mess of things or put a foot wrong, I'll be down on you like a building collapsing in an earthquake. There's no sentiment in business, my girl, nor in me, as I've told you before.'

She smiled, bold now in her elation. 'I told *you* before that I didn't think you had a heart to break. It seems I was right.'

He raised an eyebrow. 'So you have X-ray eyes. You can see through the walls of my chest and have discovered that I'm a heartless automaton, devoid of feelings and anything resembling the emotions?'

'Yes.' She grinned, pleasure at the new life just within her grasp giving her eyes the sparkle of sunlight on water. 'You've got an automatic pump where your heart should be. Even if you had one, you'd never give it in love, would you? If a girl came along who threatened to steal it, you'd lock it in a vault with walls seven feet thick and throw away the key!'

'My word,' his eyes narrowed, 'in more appropriate circumstances I'd make you pay for that colossal piece of impudence. As my father said, you need to be kept under control.'

'Sorry.' She was smiling as she said it. She was floating on air and hardly aware of what she was saying. 'Will there be papers to sign or a letter from you confirming my change of position within the firm?'

'You're taking a lot for granted. You haven't got the job yet.'

She frowned and her heart raced, this time with fear. It was like a curtain coming down in the middle of an act. 'What do you mean?' She underwent a complete change of mood. Her elation vanished, her eyes dulled over like a curtain being pulled across a lighted window. Had she talked herself out of the job?

'I've said I'm sorry,' she told him heavily, uncertain now and apprehensive. 'If it does any good, I'll say it again. And again.' She moved to stand up and leave him. It had been a long day. She was tired from her miles of aimless walking, from the strain of fretting and worrying as she had tramped miserably through the countryside. She had been given a vision of the Promised Land and had had it snatched away. She had failed again. She couldn't take any more. 'Good-night.'

He wrenched her down into her seat. 'My God, what a temperament for some poor man to have to keep up with one day! Mercurial is hardly the word. Does wonder boy Malcolm know what he's taking on when he marries you?'

'I'm sorry,' she said again, trying to disengage her wrist from his fingers.

'It's no good doing that,' he said. 'If I let you go, you'll be off again. And I'm certainly not chasing you across the restaurant and out into the street like a man after a woman he's madly in love with.'

'I'm s—' He closed her lips with his fingers, preventing her from saying the word.

'Listen to me, my girl. I'm going to ask you a question and your whole future depends on the answer. If I promote you to the status of buyer – a very responsible position – will I be able to trust you? Will you sober down and stop being so damnably impetuous?'

'I'll try.' She raised her eyes to his, but there was no elation in them now. There was nothing she could do to recapture the euphoria which had swept over her earlier. 'Really try. I promise.' She looked down. 'And you can take your hand away. I won't run off.'

'I don't know that I want to take my hand away.'

She asked bitterly, her mood changing again, 'What are you trying to do – make me one of your women? Haven't you got enough already? I told you before you're not my type. I don't like men with money. We agreed we were completely incompatible.'

He drew in his lips like a man exasperated. 'You can say that again! Is it never possible for the two of us to carry on a normal conversation without this constant backbiting and the petty, meaningless arguments you somehow get us involved in?'

She opened her mouth. 'I'm—' She stopped at the ferocious look he gave her.

'Come on.' He rose. 'We'll carry on this discussion in the car. There we can fight like cat and dog without the fear of being overheard – or interrupted.'

As they drove through the streets she asked, 'Where are we going?'

'Since it's not late, not even dark yet, out to the country.'

They did not speak again until there were green fields on both sides of them. The sun, a golden ball, hovered tantalizingly above the horizon, shedding a red-gold glow more brilliantly as the minutes passed, like a last fling before final extinction.

Juliet shivered in anticipation of the loss of the sun's warmth. 'I'd rather go home.'

'All in good time. You'll have to put up with my company just a little longer.' He drove on for a while. 'I spoke to Romeo on the phone this morning.'

'You mean Malcolm? Whatever for?'

'To find out whether you had run to him for sympathy — and to Curlews for a job. He said,' he glanced obliquely at her and in the dusk his eyes were sardonic, 'much as he loved you, he didn't keep a detailed diary of your movements and whereabouts at any given moment. He didn't think you were the sort to run off with another man. He said he'd hazard a guess that you had run off, though — away from me. Was he right?'

Was he? she wondered. It was true she'd run away, but not from her problems. She had taken them with her, trying to solve them, but had taken them home again.

'I suppose in a sense I was running away — from myself. I didn't get far.' She smiled at him. 'I soon caught up with me again.'

He laughed. 'I'm relieved I wasn't the one you were running from.'

'Oh, but you were,' she told him with disarming honesty. 'You scare me stiff.'

'Why, Juliet?' His voice sounded odd.

'Because—' Because you seem to have such power over me, and I fear you because of it. How could she tell him that? Just knowing it would increase his power, wouldn't it? She shrugged. 'I don't know.'

'I think we'd better change the subject.' He pulled off the road on to the grass verge, switched off the engine and rested his arm along the back of her seat. His hand found her shoulder, then moved under her hair to rest against the bareness of her neck. She held her breath at his touch.

Apart from the twitter of the birds, dying down now with the approach of darkness, the occasional swish of a passing car, and the hum now and then of a night insect, the silence was intense.

She looked at his profile and felt her fear of him tautening her muscles. It was fear of a different kind this time – a fear of the emotions the feel of him was awakening in her and of what those hands of his might persuade her to do if they chose to make demands.

His hand moved back to the upholstery which he stroked and moulded between restless fingers. As he began to speak, the movement stilled.

In the darkening silence his voice, though soft, sounded loud. 'By promoting you to this new position, Juliet, I'm putting a great deal of trust in you.' He looked at her. 'You realize that?'

'Curlews have a boutique,' she told him, 'but Malcolm says it's not very successful.'

'But,' he smiled, 'with your inventiveness and good ideas, ours will be.' His fingers rested momentarily on her neck again. 'Won't it?'

'I hope so. I hope – I don't let you down.'

He laughed and withdrew his arm, leaning forward and switching on the sidelights. 'So do I, considering all the capital we shall be sinking into the set-up. You realize you'll be handling a great deal of money? You'll have to buy fitments and stock. You'll be in charge of ordering, making sure deliveries arrive when promised. You'll have to cope with reps, serve customers, handle complaints with tact. It will be necessary for you to dovetail with other departments, consult with display and advertising, and deal gently with your fellow artists in the art department. Thousands of pounds will be passing through your hands. You'll be allocated certain sums of money which you, in turn, will have to allocate to the various sections of your department.' He faced her and she could only see the outline of him now. 'You realize what you're taking on? Or have I said enough to make you want to get out of the car and run a mile?'

'The prospect is daunting,' she said softly, 'but it's a challenge I'm going to accept.'

'Good,' he said, and drove on.

'Does your father know about this idea of a boutique?' she asked.

'Of course. After all, he is the chairman.'

'Did he agree to my taking charge?'

'Absolutely. He said you've got what it takes.'

She coloured in the darkness. 'That was very nice of him.' She asked playfully, 'Did you agree?'

He answered softly, 'I do believe you're provoking me. So, just to annoy you, I'll evade the question and say, it remains to be seen.'

The car moved past the dark shapes that shaded, like an artist's sketch, into trees growing beside the hedgerows. Juliet mused, out loud, 'I'm glad your father at least has faith in me. Does he,' she asked, 'play a very big part in running the firm?'

'No. He takes a back seat. What he said when you came to tea was pretty near the truth. When he's in his office – and he's more often out than in – his feet do find their way to the desk!'

'Your mother, does she—?'

'What about my mother?' His tone was hard.

She wondered what she had said to upset him. 'Does she take much interest—?'

'In the firm? None at all.'

'I'm surprised. I'd have thought she might have been a help to your father in some ways.' He was silent. 'I mean, for instance,' she stumbled on, 'on the fashion side? Or the furnishings? Giving a woman's viewpoint . . .' Her voice tailed off.

'My parents,' he said curtly, 'are barely on speaking terms.' Now Juliet was silent. 'They've hardly exchanged a polite word for months.'

She was beginning to understand Warren Major's harsh attitude towards his wife when she and her mother had gone there to tea. 'Perhaps,' she ventured, 'if your father encouraged her—'

'Don't put the blame on my father,' he interrupted curtly. 'If you knew the truth you would apportion the blame to the right quarter.'

'But surely,' she said tritely, 'it usually takes two—?'

He interrupted with violence, 'But it only takes one to wreck a marriage. My mother's son I may be, but I'm not blind. She's driven my father so far away from her that I wonder he hasn't left her long ago. If you think he's been faithful to her all these years, then you can think again.' His voice deadened. 'He's had one woman after another.' There was an anguished silence. She felt his pain, the suffering that only a child of an unsuccessful marriage can feel.

'So now I know,' she said quietly, 'the fate my mother escaped.'

Without emotion he said, 'If my father had married your mother, he would have remained faithful unto death. He was madly in love with her – a love which would have lasted through his life.'

'How do you know?'

'He's told me often enough. She broke his heart.'

'But only,' she had to defend her mother, 'because of the sort of person he was. He was crazy with ambition. That much I did gather from her when she told me about him.'

Softly he said, 'She would have changed him.'

'But,' she protested, 'at what expense to herself? Anyway,' she went on unconvinced, 'let's be realistic. He would have reverted. And then he would have broken her heart. He would still have had his women. He's the sort of man who couldn't help it. It's his way of proving, if only to himself, his virility, his continued attractiveness to the opposite sex.'

He repeated bitterly, 'If you knew the truth, you wouldn't find it so easy to blame him for what he's done with his life. Who can stand in judgement on a man who has been forced by his wife – my mother, mark you – out of his rightful place beside her, first into another bed, then into another room?' There was a poignant silence with only the hiss of the tyres passing over the surface of the road to break it. They were nearly home now.

Drew went on, 'His life with a deadly cold, completely incompatible woman has soured him completely in his relations with women. It could, I suppose, happen to any man.'

'Even you?' He turned his head briefly and she gave him a flickering half-smile which he caught through the darkness.

'Not on your life! When – if – I marry, the woman I take to bed with me will be made to measure, all a woman should be. She wouldn't fail me in any way because I would certainly not fail her. I should want my passion reciprocated in full. But,' he became cynical, 'there's little possibility of my ever marrying, of my ever legalizing any liaison I might have with a woman. I've learnt well the doctrine my father has preached to me constantly since puberty, and which by continuous repetition has made no small impression on my consciousness. It was a doctrine he formulated after losing your mother, when bitterness set in – that women exist only to satisfy a man's physical needs and for that alone. He told me to take them and pass on, to the next, and the next . . .'

The car drew up at the kerb outside Juliet's house. 'And,' she tried to smile but her lips were tight, 'did he succeed in getting his message through? Did he successfully indoctrinate you? Have you followed his illustrious example, without fail, without scruple?'

His next words came like a slap across her face with the back of his hand. 'Wouldn't you like to know?' His tone was challenging and in the light of the street lamp she could see that his eyes were diamond bright and his smile hard and cynical.

It incensed her. 'Speaking purely as a friend of the family,' she said, keeping her tone silkily soft, 'and not as an upstart employee of yours, all I can say is that if Camille Wyngard is in love with you – though how any woman could be in that condition is beyond me – then I'm sorry for her from the bottom of my heart. I wouldn't be in her shoes for a fortune!'

'Don't worry, my dear acid-tongued Juliet,' he leaned across and opened the door for her, 'you never will be.' She scrambled out. 'If Malcolm ever deserts you, and you find yourself in need of another Romeo, count me out.'

Juliet slammed the car door. He wound down the window. 'Thank you for the meal,' she forced out, the prickle of tears behind her eyes stinging her like a nettle, 'and for the enlightening lecture that followed it on the place of the female of the species in your life. But I didn't need the warning it contained. The man I marry will be as unlike you as a – as a sparrow from a vulture!'

His laughter followed her to the front door. He got out of the car and called out, 'Come to my office in the morning, nine-thirty prompt.'

To that she had no answer. He had had the last word.

Juliet had to pacify the rebel inside her when she presented herself to Drew Major next morning.

'Sit down, Miss Bourne.' His tone was offhand. The quarrel that had taken place in the car the night before might never have happened. Nor the very personal discussion they had had about the chairman of the company's private life – and lost love.

'This boutique,' he said. 'As a buyer, your salary will be increased.' He named the sum they were prepared to pay her and she was so staggered by its generosity she nearly rejected it. 'Do you really think,' she asked shakily, 'that I'm worth all that?'

He gave her a calculating look. 'Personally no, but my father insists that it is the correct amount for the job.'

She looked down. 'I shall have to thank him. As I said before, I'm extremely grateful to him for *his* faith in my abilities, at least.'

'*I* shall have faith in you, Miss Bourne, when, and only when, you prove yourself worthy of it.'

'Perhaps,' she said, smiling and knowing she was provoking him, 'your father has more vision than you, and is a better judge of character?'

'I suggest we leave the chairman of the company out of this discussion,' he responded icily, 'otherwise you might find yourself in very deep water indeed. Floundering about, in fact, in the cold outside world, without a job!'

'I'm sorry,' she said wearily. The two words were beginning to sound as monotonous as water dripping from a leaking tap.

He told her the amount of money the company was prepared to sink into the proposed boutique. It was a very large sum. When she protested that it was almost certainly far more than she would require he replied,

'Don't worry, it won't be long before you come screaming to me, like all your other buyer colleagues, that it's simply not enough. But, in your case, unless you can prove to me not only in black and white, but in the form of turnover that you really deserve more, you won't get it.'

'So I'm on trial?'

'You are. The verdict is in your hands, and yours alone.'

Somehow she would have to find the confidence to meet this challenge. She had a sudden vision of sleepless nights worrying about her job, and whether she would rise to

Warren Major's high opinion of her. She nearly turned the job down on the spot. But something in Drew Major's face, as though he was daring her to take it on, renewed her fighting spirit and she asked where they had decided to create the boutique.

'We're prepared to allocate a reasonably large area of the fashion department to the venture. We feel it fits in with the subject, being a branch of fashion itself.'

Now doubts were creeping in. 'But it's a very specialized form of fashion.'

'I'm aware of that, but the money we can devote to this project isn't limitless.'

'Can I be assured that I'll have a free hand in the design of the boutique, and in the style of clothes I stock for sale?'

'Within reason. As you're so inexperienced, you'll have a greater need for consultation than our other buyers.'

'With whom?' she asked, her heart sinking slowly like a torpedoed ship.

'The buyer of the more conventional fashions, display, the accessories buyer and so on.'

Already she felt the stirrings of rebellion. 'I don't see why.' Her own ears told her she sounded sulky.

'Look, Juliet,' he sat down at his desk opposite her, 'I'm doing my damnedest not to bring out that fighting spirit of yours. I'm keeping calm, I'm being gentle. But by heaven, if you start any of your tricks, if you rebel against the advice I'm giving you, based on years of experience, and what's more, if you start abusing me, I'll have no compunction, I'll fire you. Understand?'

She opened her mouth to protest at the unfairness of it, took a breath, opted for discretion and started to mouth the words 'I'm sorry.' But before she could get the second word out, he was round the desk with his hands round her throat.

'If you apologize to me again, woman, I swear I won't be able to stop myself, I'll *throttle* you! Then I'll put you across my knee!'

She coloured violently and tried desperately to remove his hands, but they slipped upwards until his fingers burrowed into her hair and gripped her head. He tipped it backwards and looked into her eyes.

'My word, I see your mother there,' he murmured.

Their gaze locked for a few seconds, then his hands fell away and he returned to his seat. She was left with a scarlet face and nervous hands trying to smooth down her hair.

It took her a few moments to compose herself, then she asked, 'What's the next move?'

His voice was normal and controlled when he answered, 'We've already contacted contractors to come and erect partitions. They start tomorrow. Your first job is to order stock. You understand that we always add to the wholesale price and that the price at which we actually sell the garments must represent a profit?'

'Of course. Any fool knows that.'

He raised an eyebrow at her tone. She hissed, 'S – s—' closed her lips and held her breath. But he merely smiled and went on, 'The best way to go about things in the initial stages is to contact firms by phone and ask their representatives to call. They'll show you their wares and you can make your first orders that way. I warn you that once it gets on the salesmen's grapevine that you're in business, you'll have a stampede on your hands. The queue of sales reps may well stretch all the way down the stairs to the ground floor!'

She rose and he said, 'Miss Skimpton, buyer of coats, and Mrs. Rouse of separates will be able to give you a list of wholesalers you can ring.'

He saw her to the door. His hand came out and grasped hers. 'Good luck, Juliet. You'll need it!'

She had a date with Malcolm that evening. As she put on her make-up and combed her shoulder-length hair, she recalled what had happened when, after seeing Drew, she had asked the other fashion buyers for the names and addresses of sales representatives.

First they had wanted to know why. Miss Skimpton had turned purple and had refused to believe it. Mrs. Rouse had been sceptical and had kept probing, trying to find out why it was that she, Juliet Bourne, had been chosen out of all the other members of the fashion staff to receive such promotion. 'You're new,' she had said. 'It's hardly fair to the others who've been here much longer.'

'I think,' Juliet had told her feebly, 'he wanted someone with new ideas.' But that had been the wrong thing to say. The two women had bristled and only with the greatest reluctance had they given her the information she required.

It had taken less than an hour for the whole fashion floor to hear about it. She saw whispering groups in corners, who drew apart and watched her as she passed. They looked at her as though she was something that had crawled from a piece of cheese. There was meaning in their eyes and it did occur to her to wonder if they were speculating about a possible liaison between herself and the company manager. This, to them, would have explained her sudden promotion.

'How are you making out with boss man?' Malcolm asked as they cycled side by side towards the open country. 'He sounded pretty sharp on the phone the other day when he was checking on your movements. A bit like a probation officer keeping an eye on a young offender! You'd obviously offended him.'

'Well,' she laughed, 'if you can call being threatened with the sack almost every time we have a "business chat", "making out" with him, then we're doing fine! Actually, and you won't believe me, he's promoted me.'

Malcolm wobbled and nearly fell off his bike. '*What*? You've only been there a few days! You're fooling.'

'I'm not.' She drew in behind him to allow a car to pass, then joined him again. 'Meet Miss Juliet Bourne, fashion buyer, in charge of Major's new boutique. It doesn't exist yet, but it's more than a twinkle in its father's eye. Work starts on it tomorrow.'

'You don't mean it!' He glanced across the road at a clearing in the woods. 'Over there. Let's pull in. I need a rest to assimilate that piece of information.'

They propped their bikes against a bush and sat down. 'I bet that caused a stir amongst the Major retinue. What did the old hands say?' His tone changed to that of a crotchety old man. ' "We've been here fifty years and our fathers before us. You're just an insignificant young upstart. Why shouldn't we have got promotion?" '

She laughed. 'You're dead right. Filthy looks by the dozen. They all started whispering. I'm sure they think

Drew Major's made me his mistress and that's how I got the job.'

Malcolm looked shocked at her flippant manner. 'You keep away from boss man, Juliet. I wouldn't put it past him to try even that.'

'He's not that sort,' she said, but even as she spoke she knew he was. Hadn't he told her about his attitude to women, how he regarded them as objects who existed merely to satisfy men's physical needs?

'Anyway,' Malcolm pulled her close and kissed her, 'you're my girl.' After a few minutes he said, 'So Majors are having a boutique now? Curlews have got one, did you know?' She nodded. 'Not very successful from all I hear. Too out of the way. No one seems to know it's there and the girls who do don't like patronizing it because it's tucked away in a corner of the fashion department.'

'But,' she said, concerned, 'that's where Majors are going to put theirs.'

'Then make them change their minds. It won't work. Glenda, who's in charge of Curlews' boutique, told me the reason. She said young girls run a mile from the older women on the fashion department staff. And if the boutique's placed so that they have to walk through the conventional fashion section and past all those slightly bossy ladies to get at the things they've come for, they just won't come.'

'Now you've got me worried.' Juliet, chin in hand, stared at the tangle of bushes in front of them. 'In that case, Majors have either got to give me a better site, or abandon the whole idea.' She stood up. 'I'm going straight to Drew in the morning.'

Malcolm pulled her down again. 'Are you really? Well, at the moment it's this evening, and you're with me. You say much more about that big-headed business tycoon called Drew Major and I'll begin to think things, my girl. We can't conduct a single conversation these days without your dragging his perishing name into it.'

He pulled her against him, but she struggled away. 'Don't be silly, Malcolm. He's just my boss.'

'And don't you forget it,' Malcolm said, pulling her to her feet.

'I don't know why you're so worried. Drew and I have

only got to meet and we start quarrelling.'

That pacified him a little and he kissed her as though he forgave her.

But that night in bed she realized how much Drew Major occupied her thoughts these days. She tossed and turned at first because the knowledge worried her. Why did she think about him so much? 'It's only because he's the man I work for,' she told herself as she drifted into sleep.

Next morning she arrived at the store to find the workmen assembling their materials and carrying in their equipment. Miss Skimpton fussed and tutted, afraid that their dirty overalls and their saws and their ladders would brush against the clothes on display and ruin them.

The sight of the workmen dismantling the corner which had been set aside for the new boutique made Juliet panic. She would have to see someone about it at once. She picked up the phone and dialled Drew's extension. His secretary answered.

'I'm sorry, Miss Bourne, but Mr. Major is out all day. Try Mr. Havering, the general manager.'

Juliet fretted. She didn't want Mr. Havering. She wanted to see the man in charge. But she would have to make do with second best and hope that the general manager was empowered to authorize the change of plan and stop the workmen before they did too much damage.

Mr. Havering was in and she was invited to go and see him. He was a short man, in his early forties, fair-haired, with a neatly clipped moustache and a straight-shouldered, almost military bearing which he plainly hoped would make up for his lack of height.

He heard her out with a kindly interest and she thought she had succeeded in making some impression on him.

'I understand what you're saying, Miss Bourne,' he said, 'and sympathize with your point of view.'

Her spirits lifted. She had made contact with one of the top men and now he was on her side.

'But,' her spirits fell as sharply as a shooting star, 'I disagree with you completely. The site for such a place as a – as a boutique,' he tried out the word as if it were a new food and it obviously tasted odd to him, 'concerned with fashion as it is, is in the fashion department. I can't see how

69

you can challenge the logic of that statement.'

So the military bearing was no sham, it was there, a hard core beneath that show of kindliness. Juliet was annoyed with herself for having been taken in. She should have known that, as one of the Major hierarchy, he was made of the same unmalleable, inflexible material as the others at the top.

She rose; she wouldn't waste her time there. As the 'and Son' part of the establishment was not available she would go to the man who mattered, Warren Major, the chairman himself. She knew that he, also, was hard at the core — hadn't his son told her so? — but she was willing to take the risk and confront him. Perhaps by talking persuasively to him she would be able to mould him to her own wishes, like a sculptor chipping at a piece of stone.

Yes, the secretary said, Mr. Warren Major was in. He would see Miss Bourne.

As Juliet entered his office, the chairman of the company lowered his feet to the ground. The smile with which he greeted her was genuine and warm and Juliet felt that such a gesture of friendliness from him was rare enough to be remembered and cherished.

He seemed, Juliet thought, to be a man who was buoyed up by his own success. Like a giant plane speeding high through the skies, magnificent in its remoteness, revered for its power and size, he roared through life above people's heads, revelling in his influence, his authority over others.

But, Juliet sensed as she sat down and looked at him, like an aircraft that had come crashing to earth and shattered to a pitiful stillness, so if he were to fall, through the ill turn of fortune, misjudgment or the thwarting of his plans, he would be brought down and lie scattered under the ruins of his own personality.

She glanced round the room and, lavishly decorated and richly carpeted though it was, and despite the fact that it contained all the ingredients of a well equipped office, it had an air about it of rest and refuge rather than the rhythm and bustle of a fully utilized, meaningful place of work. She eyed the desk where his feet had been.

He threw back his head and laughed, his whole body shaking. 'Looking for the dent?' He pointed. 'There it is. I told you, didn't I?'

70

She laughed, too. 'I hope you didn't mind my coming to see you.'

'Mind? My dear, I'm delighted.' He sat forward, hands clasped, the gold of his rings glinting in the reflected sunlight. He seemed prepared to enjoy himself. 'I wondered how long it would be before my son's most awkward, recalcitrant employee would have the impudence to make her way to the summit and demand the chairman's attention! After all, as I've said before, you're your mother's daughter.'

Friendly though he was, she found herself just a little intimidated by what she had done. 'You – you know about my new appointment, about the boutique?'

'Naturally. I negotiated your salary with my son, and much to his annoyance pushed the figure up and up until he wouldn't budge another penny! He said if we were going to pay that much, we might as well put someone in the job who was really worth it. I said I refused to let him talk like that about Cynthia Bourne's daughter.'

She flushed at the son's low opinion of her, having to admit that it hit her where it hurt. 'It was very good of you,' she said inadequately. 'I wouldn't have troubled you, but Drew – I mean your son – is out and the matter is urgent.'

He looked concerned and said in a kindly way – 'how different from his son,' she thought – 'Tell me about it.'

He listened sympathetically, but Juliet would not let herself be fooled by his understanding expression. 'I know these Majors,' she warned herself. 'Dig down a few inches and you come up against granite.'

'My boy-friend works for Curlews,' she told him, 'and he said their boutique is doing badly because they've placed it exactly where you have decided to put it.'

'And you, quite rightly, think we should learn from other people's mistakes, especially our rivals?'

'Well,' she said, on the defensive, 'don't you?'

He made a patting action in the air with his hand. 'It's all right, my dear, don't bristle at the least provocation.' She laughed and relaxed. 'You see,' he smiled, 'I know how to deal with you, having learnt by experience with your mother more years ago than I care to remember.'

'So, Mr. Major,' she pressed him, 'could a decision be taken now about re-siting the boutique? The only reason I'm asking is because the builders are already working on the fashion floor. The sooner they're stopped the better.'

He lifted the receiver and dialled the general manager's extension. He gave orders for the work on the new boutique to be halted at once. The builders were to be told to await further instructions.

She thanked him as he put down the phone and he asked her where, in her opinion, should the new department be sited?

'On the ground floor,' she answered at once, 'not too far from the entrance, built on a walk-in, walk-out basis, and designed so that as people pass by they can see the goods on display.'

He beckoned her to sit beside him and, looking at a plan of the store, they discussed possible positions and agreed on a site.

He leaned back and laughed. 'You know this is all highly irregular. This shouldn't be a decision arrived at by a committee of two, and one at that a young, new and very inexperienced employee.'

She said anxiously, 'I don't want to do anything unconstitutional . . .'

'*Don't* you, my dear?' he laughed. 'Well, I can assure you you've already done it! What my son will say when he returns tomorrow—!' He leaned forward and whispered, 'Shall I tell you a secret? I'm terrified of him!' She laughed, as if she knew he was joking. 'Well, perhaps I am overstating the case a little, but I can assure you on one point, I'm passing him over to you lock, stock and barrel. You've used your charm on me, now you'll have to use it on him. And my goodness, you'll need all the charm you possess to get round *him*!'

She laughed again, more to cover her apprehension than to express amusement. She rose to go, but he motioned her to remain seated. 'Tell me, Juliet,' he fiddled with a letter on his desk, 'you must promise not to take umbrage at my question?' She nodded. 'How is your mother placed for money? Is she reasonably comfortable financially? Can she manage to pay her way?'

Juliet was puzzled. Why was he referring to her mother as though she were a widow? 'She's not alone, Mr. Major,' she pointed out gently, 'she has my father.'

A flicker which might have been pain passed across his

eyes. 'I beg your pardon, my dear. Of course she has her husband. Somehow I still can't think of her as anything other than a woman alone. But the question still stands. You see, I can't ask her, so I have to ask her daughter.'

'They're – they're reasonably comfortable, thank you. Now I'm earning, I can help them.'

'It's you who's had to make the sacrifice. You gave up your studies to do that, didn't you?' She nodded.'I only wish it were within my power . . .' He shook his head. 'With my fortune—' He shrugged hopelessly and it was what he did not say that caught at her throat.

A man with his wealth, his position and his influence, helpless to aid those he most wanted to, because of etiquette, convention and the barrier of pride on the part of those to whom he wanted to offer help.

He was silent, lost apparently in a dream, and she cleared her throat and said, 'What's the next step, Mr. Major?'

He straightened his shoulders and came back to earth. 'Sorry, my dear, I was drifting. The next "step" is hardly the right word.' He smiled. ' "Obstacle" would be more appropriate, and that in the shape of my son. We tackle him next. He'll be in tomorrow.' They stood and he patted her shoulder. 'I promise to try and soften him up before I pass him on to you!'

He took her arm and pulled her gently towards him, kissing her cheek. 'I can't kiss your mother, so I kiss her daughter instead.'

She turned at the door to thank him again for his help and support, and caught him off guard. His shoulders were sagging, his body drooping, his face corrugated with misery. He was like a fish caught in the net of his own unhappiness and who knew he was doomed to stay enmeshed for the rest of his life.

CHAPTER FOUR

JULIET's father was ill in the night. He had trouble with his breathing and at one point was fighting for breath. Juliet got up, worried, unable to sleep. She sat with her mother at his bedside, and they gave him all the comfort of which they were capable.

Cynthia was torn in two about whether to phone the doctor and disturb him in the early hours or wait until morning. She decided to cope until breakfast time and then ask him to call.

Consequently Juliet, when she did crawl into bed for a couple of hours' sleep before going to work, awoke late. Her mother had let her sleep on longer than usual, thinking she was doing it for the best.

But Juliet was horrified when she saw how late it was. She skipped her breakfast, deciding to cycle to work because she had missed the bus and the next was not due for half an hour. She cycled round the back of the store where the delivery vans parked to unload, leaned her bicycle against the wall, padlocked it and raced up the stairs, terrified in case Drew had sent for her.

Miss Skimpton greeted her joyfully with the news that she was wanted at once by Mr. Drew Major, and that he was livid with anger at discovering she had not yet arrived.

'He said,' Miss Skimpton crowed, 'that you were to go up to him the moment you arrived.' She looked at her watch and beamed, 'An hour late. You *will* find him in a good mood!'

Without waiting to remove her jacket or look in a mirror, Juliet made for the stairs again – the lift would have been too slow – and sprinted two at a time up the four flights. As she reached the sixth floor, gasping for breath, Warren Major came out of his room.

He saw her dishevelled appearance and put out his hand to stop her. 'Something wrong, my dear? You don't look up to the mark.'

She shook her head, eyeing Drew's door, and breathing

heavily. 'I'm late. I was up most of the night with my mother—'

He cut in at once, 'She's ill?'

'No. My father – he had a bad attack. I'm sorry I'm late, Mr. Major.' She moved towards Drew's door, but Warren stopped her again.

'If there's anything I can do to help your mother, or,' as an afterthought, 'your father—?'

She shook her head, thanking him. 'The doctor's coming this morning. He'll prescribe something.'

Drew's door opened. '*Miss Bourne*!' he thundered, 'not only do you arrive at a disgusting late hour, but you stand there chatting to my father as if you were paying the firm a social call instead of reporting for duty.'

Warren walked towards him raising his hand as if to caution him. 'Son—' he began, but Drew interrupted.

'I'll deal with this, Father.' Warren started to speak again, but Juliet turned to him.

'Please, Mr. Major, it doesn't matter.'

Warren shrugged and walked away.

'Crawling again, Miss Bourne?' were the words that nearly knocked her sideways as she sat down.

'Crawling, Mr. Major?' She shook her head, which was beginning to throb. 'I'm sorry, I don't know what you mean.'

'Yes,' he said nastily, 'you look as though you're barely awake. Got a hangover, Miss Bourne, after a night out with the boy-friend?' Her head drooped and she let his sarcasm pass over her. 'Chatting up the chairman at every opportunity is what I mean by crawling. Running to him when you're in trouble, going to him over my head, and when I'm out of the way, in order to get exactly what you want, knowing I would oppose your ideas and your demands every inch of the way.'

'I'm sorry,' she answered wearily, 'that you think of it like that. But you were out and I tried the general manager—'

'That was exceedingly considerate of you.'

'And since immediate action was necessary, because the workmen had already begun their work, I thought the best thing to do was to go to your father. I realize what I did was unconstitutional, and I'm sorry.'

'Unconstitutional? It was outrageous! What should have

75

been a decision by the committee of management was arrived at by two people, one of whom should have known better and the other so insignificant that if she never put in an appearance in the store again no one would miss her! I've never, in all my time with this firm,' he thrust his hands into his pockets and came round to stand in front of her, 'had as an employee anyone who's given me so much trouble in so short a time. Your wilful and constant refusal to abide by the rules is such that if there were a rule against having rules, you'd rebel against that.' He walked up and down the room. 'What peculiar chemistry did your parents use to produce such a creature as you? All I can say is, heaven be praised that they don't come like you very often!'

Hoping to distract his attention from herself and longing to know his verdict on the removal of the proposed boutique to the site she and his father had chosen, she asked, 'Do you approve of your father's decision, Mr. Major? Will you allow—?'

'No, I will *not* allow! And you dare to call it my father's decision? That's rich! *Your* decision, you mean. You knew very well that if you went to see him you'd get exactly what you wanted. He'd give you the earth if you asked for it.'

She stared up at him, whispering, 'But why?'

'Because of your mother, that's why. He's still in love with her, didn't you know?'

She paled. 'You can't mean it?' She put her hand to her head as though a brick had hit her. The room had started spinning. She wondered if she was going to faint.

He paused in his walking. 'Is there something wrong?'

She closed her eyes. 'It's probably because I didn't have any breakfast. I was so late I—'

'If you're stupid enough to come to work without food, then you deserve everything you get. Don't expect any sympathy from me.'

His unkindness, his callous disregard of her feelings which, in the circumstances, amounted almost to cruelty, drove her to her limits. She felt the tension inside her snap like a rubber band being pulled beyond its strength and her anger knew no bounds.

She hammered with her fist on his desk and shrieked, 'No, I don't expect any sympathy from you! Or compassion. Or understanding. What you haven't got you can't give, can you? I don't expect anything from you in the way of feelings. I was right that day when I said you hadn't got a heart ...' The anxieties of the night, the lack of sleep and food caught up with her and she began to sob, lowering her arms on to his desk and resting her head on them.

'If you think you're going to get round me as you got round my father by putting on an act—'

Unable to stand another moment in his presence, she jerked herself off the chair and lurched to the door. It opened and Warren stood there. Unsteady as she was she fell against him, and he put his arms round her and offered her comfort and she sobbed against his shoulder.

'It's my father,' she whispered, 'it's my father,' over and over again.

'What's the matter with her father?' she heard Drew ask.

'Taken ill in the night,' Warren told him. 'She and her mother have hardly had any sleep.'

'But why the hell didn't she tell me?'

'I don't suppose you gave her a chance, son. I heard her shouting. What have you been saying to her to bring her to this state?'

She heard Drew move as if he had slumped into a chair.

Warren stuffed a handkerchief into her hand and she took it gladly. He said over her head, 'You never talk to any other member of our staff as you talk to her.' His voice softened. 'Why her, son, why her?'

There was no reply.

'Are you,' Warren's voice persisted, 'punishing me for the life I've led? Hurting me through her, knowing how I feel—?'

Juliet could not bear to hear any more. She pulled away from him and, her sobs growing less, hid her face in his handkerchief. She knew she must look a sight and she could not let Drew Major see. He thought little enough of her already.

'You'd better come to my room, my dear.' Warren turned her by the shoulders.

'She can stay here,' Drew snapped.

'No, thanks, son. I wouldn't leave her to your tender mercies now any more than I'd leave a new-born baby in your care.'

Warren led her into his office, sat her in the visitor's chair, fussed round her. 'Would you like a drink?'

She raised her head and gave him a watery smile. 'I daren't. I've had no breakfast. I overslept and I was so late I rushed straight out.'

He gave an exasperated sigh. 'It's a wonder you haven't passed out, what with one thing and another.' He went to the door. 'Will you be all right if I leave you for a few moments?'

Juliet nodded and when he had gone, rested her head on the back of the chair and closed her eyes. Her head was aching, her face felt blotchy, her eyes swollen, but she didn't care any more.

Some time later the door opened and she sensed it wasn't Warren. Drew was holding a tray of sandwiches and coffee. 'My father sent these.' He lowered the tray to the desk and stood there watching her. After a moment he said stiffly, like a man unused to apologizing, 'I'm sorry. If you'd told me about . . .'

She turned her head to one side. 'You're not really sorry. You hate me, I'm sure you do.' He had nothing to say. 'We can't go on like this. Our relationship just isn't workable. I'll have to leave – there's nothing for it. As you said the first time we met, we're incompatible. How right you were!'

'You're not leaving, Juliet.'

She opened her eyes. 'You can't stop me. I resign as from now, this minute.' She got up. Her legs felt weak, but she made for the door. His arm came out and caught her across the waist.

'You're staying right here,' he said softly, facing her. 'Your resignation has not been accepted. And, what's more, I'm prepared to reconsider the whole question of re-siting the boutique.'

She shook her head. 'It doesn't matter to me now where you put it. I won't be in charge. I'm leaving.'

His fingers round her waist tightened. 'I'll go further. I'll agree to the chairman's decision to move the boutique downstairs and putting it exactly where you want it, without insisting on referring the matter to the board of management.'

She stared. 'You don't mean it?'

He took her by the shoulders and moved her gently backwards into the chair again. He smiled. 'You've forced me into it, haven't you? Inch by inch, you're getting your own way. You're an unscrupulous little minx, do you know that?'

She shook her head again. 'But I told you, I'm leaving.'

'You're not leaving. When you've eaten that food, you can go back to work and get down to ordering the stock for your new boutique.'

He put the tray on her lap and she picked up one of the sandwiches.

'Unfortunately,' he said, watching her eat it, 'I can't promise not to shout at you again. I wish I could. But somehow you have that effect on me.'

She smiled up at him. 'And you on me!'

'At least we're aware of each other's shortcomings.'

'And that,' said Warren, coming in, 'is halfway towards a reconciliation.'

'I doubt it,' said Drew, lingering in the doorway. 'We've just decided we hate each other.'

'Well,' Warren said briskly, 'that's as good a start as any. Who knows where that might lead?'

'The road to hell,' said Drew. 'You should know.' He snapped the door shut behind him.

Juliet spent the day studying catalogues of display stands. She knew they had to be practical as well as eye-catching and it was not always easy to combine the two. Her studies at art school had taught her that it was not only the clothes she would stock in the boutique which would attract customers, it was also the manner in which they were displayed.

Men were working on the ground floor erecting the partitions which would separate the new boutique from the other departments. Their hammering could be heard even above the chatter of the customers who moved aimlessly or with purpose around the counters and came and went through the swing doors. People, Juliet thought, were the life-blood of a department store, circulating through its veins and arteries like blood round the human body, keeping it healthy and alive. Without people a store would fail and die.

When Juliet had told Miss Skimpton that the boutique would not be part of the fashion floor after all, she had been surprised and, in a grudging sort of way, pleased. She had thanked Juliet for being so considerate. It hadn't occurred to her that Juliet might have requested the boutique's removal from conventional fashions for any other reason than that of gratifying Miss Skimpton. Tactfully, Juliet did not enlighten her.

Her father was a little better when she arrived home. The doctor had called and the medicine he had prescribed had brought some relief.

In the kitchen her mother told her, 'Warren phoned. He said you'd told him about Cedric. Juliet,' she looked troubled, 'he offered his help.'

Help? He surely hadn't offered money? 'He asked,' Cynthia went on, 'if Cedric had seen a specialist. I said yes, one our own doctor had recommended. Then Warren offered to pay for Cedric to see one of the top specialists in London. I was so overwhelmed I didn't know how to thank him. He told me to ring him back when we'd talked it over.'

So that was the way Warren had calculated he could most effectively offer financial assistance without fear of offending. Surely, Juliet thought, her father would overcome his antipathy to Warren sufficiently to accept such a chance?

But Cynthia flopped into a chair. 'Cedric wouldn't hear of it.'

Juliet was dismayed. 'Why not?'

'Pride, stupid pride. He dug in his heels as only your father can. He said he didn't want help from any ex-boyfriend of mine. I asked him how idiotic could he get being jealous of a man I'd thought I was in love with thirty-odd years ago? I said it didn't matter who it was offering help – in our position it was the money that counted.'

'Then what happened?'

'We had a ridiculous argument.' Juliet was appalled to see her mother start to cry. 'He said – he said was I saying now that he didn't earn enough to please me and was I blaming him for not making himself a fortune like my ex-fiancé?' Juliet put her arm round her mother, feeling more helpless than she had ever felt in her life. She had never been the one to offer comfort before, it had always been the other way round.

'Then we had a quarrel. It didn't matter that I said I'd

80

take any steps to help him get better, even to accepting money from Warren Major. He wouldn't budge. Oh, darling!' Her mother rested against her daughter as Juliet had rested against Warren for comfort that morning.

She stroked her mother's hair and let her cry, then she said, 'You go to bed. You're tired out with your broken night. Mum, I – I cried this morning. I was in Drew's office,' she didn't tell her why, 'and I was silly and let things get on top of me. Mr. Major – Warren – was so good and offered me a shoulder to cry on.'

They hugged each other. 'You shouldn't get so involved in our troubles, darling. You've got your own life to lead.' She sighed. 'I might do as you suggest. I'm worn out. You haven't got to worry about the meal. The food's cooked.'

'I'll bring it up to both of you.'

Some time later, Juliet tapped on her parents' bedroom door and took in their trays. They sat side by side in bed, and Juliet could see that their quarrel was over and they had become reconciled. She said they looked like two turtle doves and they called her 'nurse'.

Cynthia drew her daughter down to whisper in her ear, 'Will you phone Warren? I haven't had the heart.'

Juliet agreed, at the same time dreading it. Warren answered. Stumbling over her words, she told him as tactfully as she could that her father had felt unable to accept—

He cut in, 'I know what you're going to say. I've come across stubborn pride before, and I know it when I see it.'

'It wasn't my mother,' Juliet hastened to explain. 'She would have accepted gladly.'

'I'm sure she would. No woman likes to see the man she loves struggling with an illness which might be alleviated by the expenditure of money in the right quarter.' He paused and his voice softened. 'Just as no man likes to see the woman he loves desperately worried and unhappy.'

Drew must have taken the receiver from his father because his voice said curtly – was he upset by what his father had just said? – 'There's no need for you to come in on time in the morning, Juliet. In the circumstances you have my permission to arrive late.'

Unreasonably irritated by his high-handed manner, she snapped back, 'Thanks for your concern, but as you're never tired of telling me, if you did that for me, you'd have to do it for others, wouldn't you? And that would never do, would it? In any case, I don't want your charity.'

'Charity?' He sounded puzzled.

'Yes, in the form of time off with pay.' She banged down the receiver.

Then she stared at it, conscience-stricken. Now what had she done? Snubbed the man in charge, thrown back in his face his thoughtful gesture, his consideration for her in the light of the difficult circumstances at home?

She lifted the receiver and dialled his number. He answered.

'Drew? I want to apologize for what I said. You're right when you say I'm too impetuous. I – I really will have to curb it as you say. I'm very sorry.'

'Stop grovelling,' he snapped back. 'And you can save your breath – your apologies are getting monotonous!' His receiver crashed down.

Until the boutique was ready, Juliet had been given permission to share the office belonging to Mrs. Rouse of Separates. She used her phone next morning and dialled Drew's extension. As she waited to speak to him she hoped he had forgiven her for her rudeness the previous evening.

His voice was businesslike and brisk, but there was nothing unfriendly about it, so she supposed he had. When she asked him, did he think the boutique would be finished?

'The men are making good progress, as you've probably seen for yourself. Provided you have the display equipment delivered on time, the official opening could take place in about a couple of weeks. You know you can store stock and equipment in the marking-off room for a limited period, until you're ready for it? Which means you're free to order in advance.'

She said she did know. 'I worked up there for a time, Mr. Major,' she reminded him stiffly.

'All right,' he must have been smiling, 'don't take umbrage. My memory's not that short.'

'Sorry,' she said, then wished she could have swallowed the word. 'Sorry I said "sorry".'

He laughed. 'Have you thought about publicity? We

could take some space in the local paper and give it a bit of a splash. You know, new venture and so on. Contact the advertising department.'

Malcolm called that evening. Juliet told him about the progress of the boutique. 'We're taking a couple of half columns in the local paper to advertise the opening.'

'Getting a big name to come and do the honours?'

She hadn't even thought of it, she said. 'Doubt if it's worth it. And they cost a lot in fees and expenses. To start with, until I can prove my worth, I'm on a limited budget.'

Things were back to normal at home now. Her father had recovered from his latest asthmatic attack and had returned to work. Her mother's anxiety had once more receded into the background and she was happy again – until her husband's next attack.

On the day the advertisement announcing the opening of the boutique was due to appear, Juliet seized the local newspaper and turned the pages. It was there, small but, she hoped, effective. Idly, she turned on and her eyes were caught and riveted by a half-page advertisement. Curlews' boutique, it told the world, was the finest in town. Its clothes were the trendiest, its prices the lowest, its value the best that money could buy. You can't resist, it said, the call of Curlews' boutique.

All round the edges of Curlews' advertisement were sketches of models newly arrived. Across the centre were the words in giant-sized lettering, 'S-p-l-a-s-h!' followed in smaller letters by the words 'Your money at Curlews.'

Compared with this ostentatious piece of publicity, Major's restrained promotion of their product was weak and puny.

Barely able to restrain her fury, Juliet rang Malcolm. She caught him just before he left for work. She accused him of treachery, betrayal and disloyalty. 'Why did you do it?' she demanded, adding in dramatic tones, 'And I thought you loved me!'

He swore that he had not done it intentionally. 'I happened to mention to the buyer of carpets what you'd told me about Major's announcement of their new boutique. He's in touch with the great high-ups and must have passed the information on. I wasn't to know he'd do that, was I?'

83

'You could have lost me my job,' she wailed. 'If not that, then my position as buyer. Then I'll have to take a drop in salary and be demoted . . .'

Malcolm cut her short, said he was sorry but it was just one of those things, wasn't it, and if he didn't go now he'd miss the bus. She said bitterly that she hoped he did.

On her way to work she wondered how she was going to break the news to Drew. She met him on the stairs and decided to brave his anger there and then. He was going to sweep past her, but she put out a hand and stopped him.

'What now?' he asked wearily.

'About the advertisement—' Some members of staff hurried past and Drew pulled her to one side.

'You're blocking the stairs. Don't bother to explain. I know exactly what you're going to say. The boy-friend came. Am I right? You poured out your heart to him about the boutique. Right again?'

'I'm afraid so, Mr. Major. I didn't do it on purpose, nor did he.'

'Of course you didn't. No one in their right mind would try to queer their own pitch. Nor would a girl's beloved give away her secrets and deliberately spoil things for her. But you'll have to be a damned sight more careful in future. Next time it might be much more serious. You *would* have to have a boy-friend in the enemy camp, wouldn't you?' She opened her mouth automatically to apologize, but he reached out and closed it effectively with his fingers. 'Spare me that, Miss Bourne.' He passed on his way, calling back, 'But remember, don't let it happen again.'

After tea, Malcolm called for her. He said he was sorry and kissed her on the doorstep. With a show of reluctance she let him in.

'Still love me?' he asked sheepishly.

'That assumes,' she answered, on her dignity, 'that I loved you in the first place.'

He winced, and her mother, overhearing, said, 'My goodness, Malcolm, you really are in the doghouse tonight!'

He laughed. 'If I sat up and begged, do you think she'd forgive me?'

The phone rang and Cynthia went to answer it.

'Dad's out,' Juliet said, 'so we can go in the sitting-room.'

Malcolm asked if she'd got into trouble with the boss.

'He said in a roundabout way that he understood, but it mustn't happen again.'

When Cynthia came in, her eyes were shining. She told them, 'That was Warren.'

Juliet's heart bumped. Why was her mother so happy about it?

'He asked me if I'd like a freezer. I said I'd love one, but I'd love the money to pay for it better! So he told me they were expecting a bulk purchase of deep freeze cabinets any day at a ridiculously low price and if I wanted one I could have it.'

'Did you accept?'

'On the spot. I've wanted one for years. We could re-arrange the kitchen and make room for it.'

'But what will Dad say? Won't he call it being offered charity again?'

'He'll *have* to agree. It's a chance I can't miss.'

'That was a bit of luck for Major's electrical department,' Malcolm said thoughtfully. 'I wonder which wholesaler did them that good turn?'

'Malcolm!'

He started guiltily. 'Sorry, Juliet. It's a case of keeping up, not so much with the Joneses, as the Majors. It's the employer-loyalty in me coming out. If you work for Majors long enough, it'll get you, too.'

'I doubt it. Anyway,' she said loftily, 'shouldn't loyalty to your girl-friend come first?'

'You win.' He moved nearer and took her hand. 'I promise to try to keep it to myself.'

'You must,' she wailed, 'otherwise I really will lose my job. Drew's given me two dire warnings already about passing on information to my "Romeo" as he calls you.'

The others laughed. 'A lot of encouragement I get from "Juliet",' Malcolm complained. 'The real Romeo did a lot better. Look at you this evening. Talk about turning the other cheek when I kissed you and giving me the cold shoulder!'

'When you've finished trotting out tired clichés about different parts of my anatomy, we'd better go.'

He turned up a non-existent coat collar and pretended to shiver. 'Next time I come I'll wear my winter woollies!'

Cynthia laughed and waved them off. They went to a film and when Malcolm left Juliet on the doorstep, she let him kiss her without drawing away and even condescended to kiss him back for a few moments.

Drew was on the phone to her again next morning. 'I want to have a talk with you some time. Since you're such a babe in arms when it comes to the art of buying, I feel you need a bit of tuition.'

She began to thank him, but he cut her short. 'Don't run away with the idea that it's you I'm worried about. If it were I'd let you flounder at the deep end until you learned to swim simply out of the need for self-preservation. It's Majors' financial standing that concerns me. I'd hate us to go bankrupt because of the ignorance of a very young buyer called Juliet Bourne. Some of those reps you'll be dealing with are reasonable types and only want to earn an honest living. But some are wolves – and I mean wolves – in disguise. If that sort spot your innocence of the ways of the commercial world, and with their experience they're bound to do so, they'll rob you of money right and left. So a word in your ear would, I feel, be not only advisable but absolutely essential if you're not going to be allowed to let those reps devour your profits even before the goods you order are on the display stands.'

She said dutifully. 'Yes, Mr. Major,' and waited for the pause to end.

'Now,' he said, 'looking at my desk calendar, I see tomorrow is Saturday. It's asking a lot of you – and knowing you you'll probably get on your soapbox and demand overtime – but could you come to my father's house tomorrow after lunch? That is if it isn't depriving you of the company of your Romeo.'

'Well, he was coming round, but we were only going for a cycle ride. Yes, Mr. Major, I'll do as you say.'

'My word,' came softly into her ear, 'you unnerve me. Such docility so early in the morning!'

She laughed. 'I do occasionally go against my principles and obey orders sometimes, Mr. Major!'

He laughed with her. 'That really is good news, Miss Bourne. May you long continue to break that particular principle. It would make life so much easier for me.' He rang off.

Saturday was cloudless and unbearably warm. Juliet wondered what to wear. She tussled with her longing to put on her sundress, deciding in the end on something just a little more formal. She was after all going to the Major residence for business reasons, not pleasure. She wore a thin sleeveless top and lightweight skirt and, remembering the cold splendour of Warren's house, pulled on a cardigan in case even now her outfit was too informal.

Mildred Major opened the door. Her royal blue dress was long and hung limply from the waist. The neck was conventional with collar and revers, the front fastening discreetly to the top button. It must have been a dress in vogue ten years before and, looking at her, Juliet knew that the changing fashions of the ensuing decade had passed her by.

'They're in the garden,' Mildred said in her lifeless way. 'You'll have to look for them. Go round the back.' She pointed her finger vaguely to the left and closed the door in Juliet's face.

'It's a wonder,' Juliet thought disgustedly, 'she didn't tell me to go to the tradesmen's entrance.'

Feeling as let down as someone who had had the chair snatched from under them, Juliet wandered round to the back of the house. She walked through the rose garden and was passing the fountain feathering out over the pond when a shout hailed her. She turned. Of course, the swimming pool!

Warren Major was standing and waving his arm. As she approached, he said, 'Welcome, stranger. What brings you here?'

'I did,' said a lazy voice a few yards from Juliet's feet.

Drew was lying on a large towel beside the pool, wearing only his swimming briefs. His tanned, lean body was glistening with water. He had obviously just come from the pool and had not bothered to dry himself. He was letting the heat of the sun suck up the moisture from his skin.

'Sit down, my dear,' Warren invited, taking the garden chair beside her. He too was in swimming trunks, but there was no leanness about his body, which bulged with spare flesh. Even his physique reflected his affluence and his informality seemed to drive an even bigger wedge between himself and the woman who was, in name only, his wife. 'How's your mother?' betrayed the line of his thoughts.

'Very well,' Juliet answered, adding unasked, 'my father's fine, too – at the moment.'

Warren nodded without comment, his interest waning after her first reply. Why does he keep pretending I haven't got a father? Juliet thought, fiercely resenting his attitude. But the feeling passed as she looked at the restless, unhappy eyes that raked the grounds which encompassed them as though he were searching for something he was convinced was lurking there just out of his reach. Something his money couldn't buy.

'This,' Drew addressed his father, arms raised behind his head, eyes masked by sun-glasses, 'is a business call, believe it or not. Not a social one.'

'You disappoint me, son. I thought she'd come for love of you, not the firm.'

'Love?' Drew raised his head, then lowered it again, closing his eyes behind the darkened lenses. 'There's little love lost between us, is there, Juliet? Give us a few more minutes and we'll be quarrelling again. In fact, I'm surprised we haven't started already. It's probably only your presence as an intermediary that's having a restraining effect on us both.'

Warren rose, laughing. 'I'll bow out and leave you to it. I wouldn't want to interfere. Chairman of the company I may be, but I should hate to put my nose in where it isn't wanted!'

'The only time he does interfere,' said his son idly, 'is when it's to the detriment of the firm, when the man who runs the outfit is conveniently out for the day and a rebellious young woman pushes her way into his office and makes impossible demands, to which he agrees totally and unreservedly.'

Juliet flushed, guessing his meaning.

'All right, son, point taken.' Warren raised his hand and went on his way.

'Come and sit next to me, Juliet.' Without rising or opening his eyes, Drew patted the towel.

With reluctance she moved to sit beside him, feeling the overpowering attraction of him pulling at her like a magnet.

He raised his head and looked at her disparagingly. 'My word, you're too well dressed for words! Can't you take some clothes off?' He lifted his hand and tugged not over-gently at her cardigan, removing it from her shoulders. She slipped her arms out of the sleeves and he threw it to one side.

'I may look well-dressed,' she said, 'but I'm quite cool. I haven't got much on underneath.'

He raised himself on to his elbow and looked her over. 'Now you have got me interested.' He whipped off his sun-glasses. 'Yes, I see what you mean.' He indicated her sleeve-less top. 'Isn't that what they call a see-through blouse? The name's appropriate. It doesn't leave much to the im-agination. All the same,' he replaced his sunglasses and stretched out again, 'you should have come in a two-piece swimsuit, then you could have joined me in the water.'

'What would have been the use? I told you, I can't swim.'

'You'll have to get Romeo to teach you.' He smiled pro-vocatively. 'I bet he's taught you a few things already.'

Indignantly she answered, 'It's not like that between us.'

He turned to face her, his eyes hidden. 'Are you trying to tell me you're young, innocent and unblemished? And you an ex-art student? I can hardly believe it.' His hand groped for hers and found it. 'You tempt me to find out just how experienced you are in – er – certain matters.'

She tugged her hand away. 'I came here to work, Mr. Major, not to play.'

He sighed and sat up, his skin almost dry now. 'That's Drew Major put in his place! Now, Miss Bourne, since you insist on being so formal, have you any queries, any questions you'd like me to answer?'

'Yes,' she said promptly, 'how will I know, when a sales-man shows me his stock, which clothes to choose? I imagine that at first, I'll want to buy everything I see, and I know I can't do that.'

He laughed. 'Glad you realize it. Well,' he poured a drink from the jug of lemonade which stood on a folding picnic table beside him and gave her the glass, then took one for himself, 'first you think of your most typical customer, then you think of her requirements and then you select garments which will most closely answer those requirements.' He drank deeply. 'There are really three guiding principles which govern the selection of fashion goods – the buyer must have "feel", flair and taste, all of which you should possess already as a result of your art training.' She nodded. 'All the same, even when you've decided on your typical customer, the choice could still be embarrassing. At which point you'll have to use what is called, for want of a better term, "know-how". It's something you'll develop as you become more experienced.'

'Oh dear, you make it sound a bit daunting!'

'I don't think so. As long as you've got common sense, and I think you have—'

She bowed her head graciously. 'Thanks for the compliment. I'm not used to praise from you.'

'This, Miss Bourne, is a business discussion. So you can stop being cheeky.'

She peered at him to see how serious he was, but the dark lenses were disconcertingly blank.

'First,' he went on, 'you must consider in which order you're going to examine the garments the rep shows you. You might decide, and in your case, I think it would be wise since the clothes you'll be stocking won't be in the higher price ranges, to see the cheapest articles first, going through the range until you reach the most expensive.'

He refilled her glass and an ice cube rattled into it, then he emptied the jug into his own, tossing the contents down his throat. 'Once you've made your decision, you must stick to it, no matter what the salesman says. He'll probably want to show you the most expensive lines first, because they're what he wants to sell most. But it's the buyer's requirements which matter, not his, and even if he argues, you must argue back. Salesmen are trained to take the lead in a sale, but a successful buyer sticks to his guns and wins. In other words, you must put the salesman in his place.' He smiled at her. 'That shouldn't be difficult for you. You can employ that so-called "fire" my father insists you possess, and which I call impudence. If you show a rep what you're made of from the start, he'll soon learn to respect your judgment.'

'From the way you're talking,' she put down her empty glass and hugged her knees, 'it sounds as though a buyer needs to know a certain amount about psychology. You've got to know the salesman's mind well enough to be a jump ahead of him all the time.'

He frowned into the distance. 'In a sense, that's right. You, the buyer, have a fixed budget – that is, a certain sum of money you have been allocated. He, the salesman, wants to get you to spend as much money and order as many of his goods as possible. You have to learn to recognize when he's putting on the pressure to such an extent that if you listen to him, you'll be over-spending and that can lead to all sorts of complications where your budget's concerned. Sales reps are just one side of your job, though.'

'Oh dear, what have I taken on? You're making me nervous!'

'It's about time you realized the amount of trust I've invested in you in promoting you to such a position.' His tone was almost a reprimand. 'Don't fail me, Juliet.'

She clasped her fingers round her knees, infinitely touched by the sudden appeal in his voice. More than anything she wanted to please this man, to gain his respect and admiration, to make him think of her not as an unworldly artist, but as an accomplished business woman. She wanted to justify the trust he had placed in her. Would she ever manage it?

'You'll be handling large quantities of stock and cash,' he went on. 'You'll need the courage to take risks in the form of buying fashions not yet in vogue but which you think may become popular not in the present season, but perhaps in the following spring or summer. You have to know how to deal with people. You must be patient with the complainers – and there are plenty – and receive little in the way of gratitude. You must get your sums right, otherwise your profits will be non-existent. You must realize there are seasonal fluctuations. You must not only have the right touch to keep customers, suppliers and staff happy, but know how to communicate effectively with them. You also,' he turned and smiled, 'have to keep on good terms with your superiors. You must know not only when to be aggressive – no difficulty there! – but also when to be polite and know how far you can "push" people, at the same time knowing how much you can "give".'

'So,' she smiled back at him, 'from now on I've got to be a sort of superwoman.'

'Yes,' he agreed, then softly, his eyes moving over her, 'but whatever you do, Juliet, don't lose your femininity. That way you'll not only gain a man's admiration, but his respect, too.' He lay back, closing his eyes.

The sun beat down, the breeze stirred the roses, tampered with the bushes and shrubs which edged the path around the swimming pool and rippled across the surface of the water.

'Thanks,' she said, 'for your advice. I appreciate it very much.'

He was so quiet she thought he was asleep, but he turned on to his front to let the sun tan his back. 'Lie down, Juliet,' he murmured. 'Relax. You need some rest after that prolonged lecture.'

With some hesitation and a large measure of self-consciousness, usually alien to her, she lay back beside him and turned her face away. She didn't know why, but her heart was thumping – it could have been the heat of the sun – and there was an odd tension in her limbs. She found that her hands clasped under her head were moist.

The silence, broken only by the occasional passing car in the road at the front of the house, induced sleep, but she resisted it without much trouble, as her body felt too alive, her mind too alert to relax completely. If he had touched her, merely stretched out a hand, she knew for certain that the invisible barrier between them would crumble to nothing and ... But her mind cowered from the consequences like a child being pushed alone into a dark room.

'Juliet.' The word was a whisper. She turned her head and wished she could see his eyes. 'Since you have nothing better to do, you wouldn't care to spend the rest of the afternoon here, and have a meal?'

She sat up and looked around. There was a spurt of longing inside her that made her want to do just that. The beauty all about her, the peace, the solitude, the company of the man beside her – what about the man beside her? He was her boss, he meant nothing more to her than that.

She must not let herself even begin to love him, the son of the man her mother had rejected so many years ago. It was unthinkable. She knew his views about women, his refusal ever to be tied down to one woman in his life.

Nothing better to do? It was typical of his arrogance – she

knew she was whipping herself into a state of anger towards him as a form of self-defence, or even self-preservation – to assume she was at his beck and call.

'Thanks for the invitation,' her tone was intentionally abrupt, 'but I think I'll go for that cycle ride with Malcolm after all.' She stood up, smoothing her skirt, fighting the sun-drenched lethargy of limbs and pleased with herself for her successful battle with her feelings.

He sighed, rose and pulled on his shirt. It hung loosely over his swimming briefs. As he stood, towering over her, lithe, athletic-looking, she could not believe he was the same man who, immaculately dressed, executive to the finger tips, ran the firm of Major and Son.

He folded his arms and gazed down at her. 'I've never before had dealings with a woman who disliked me.' His fingers raised her chin and his eyes, still hidden, scanned her face. 'It's a novel experience.' He put his arm across her shoulders and she had to pretend that she could only just tolerate his touch. He got the message and his arm fell away. 'I'll see you out,' he said abruptly.

'No need,' she murmured, walking at his side.

'Better still, if you wait until I've got a few more clothes on, I'll give you a lift home.'

'There's no need,' she repeated. 'I'll go back the way I came, by bus.'

'Wait in the hall.' He sprinted up the stairs. She was beginning to wonder where his parents were when he re-appeared, having added trousers to his shirt.

A car pulled up in the driveway and he frowned. 'Who the—?' he said, and answered the heavy, commanding knock.

'Darling,' said a feminine voice when the door was opened, 'I was at a loose end. Then I thought of you. I knew you wouldn't mind.' She held up her face. 'Aren't you going to kiss me?' Then she saw Juliet and her frown made a petulant pleat between her brows. She turned large, wondering eyes up to Drew's. 'Darling, been amusing yourself in my absence?'

'Juliet, Camille Wyngard. Camille, Juliet Bourne, friend of the family.'

'Only of the family? But darling,' the word grew softer every time the pouting lips uttered it, 'you've never spoken about her before.'

The eyes that ran, like mice, up Juliet, from her sandalled feet, over her flimsy blouse to the untidiness of her hair, were puzzled and disturbed. The face that refused to smile was oval-shaped and heavily made up, the figure from the shoulders downwards a temptation to any man. The fair hair curved into the hollows of her neck and the sun-dress she wore was designed to catch far more than the sun's attention.

'Go to the pool,' Drew told Camille. 'I'm running Juliet home.'

'It doesn't matter, Drew,' Juliet said, her voice coming out as dry as an autumn leaf. 'I'll make my own way home.'

'You heard what she said, darling.' Camille caught his arm.

Juliet began to move down the steps, but Drew pulled his arm from Camille and clamped his fingers on to Juliet's shoulder, swinging her round. He had an odd look in his eyes which she mistrusted.

A few seconds later her lack of trust was justified. Drew had bent down and kissed her mouth. She jerked away, scarlet. 'What do you think you're—?' He cut off her words with another kiss.

'Thanks, sweet, for your delightful company. Don't keep me waiting too long before you come again, will you?'

This time Juliet ran down the steps, quite out of reach. What game was he playing? She looked back to see his mocking grin. Camille slid her arms round his neck. 'What are you doing, darling?' she murmured against his lips. 'Giving me notice to quit?'

Out of the corner of her eye Juliet saw the two lions, enigmatic and supercilious as ever, gazing into the distance as though nothing catastrophic had happened. But it had. Two kisses from Drew, and she was wanting more.

Drew showed Camille into the house and closed the door. A last look back at the entrance, and Juliet could swear she saw the ghost of a smile on the lions' superior faces.

CHAPTER FIVE

ON Monday morning, Juliet was summoned to the company manager's office. What now? she wondered.

He was smiling as she entered and holding out her cardigan. 'You left this behind on Saturday.' He tutted. 'Forgetfulness – a bad characteristic in a buyer. One you'll have to eradicate.'

She snatched it from him, thanking him grudgingly.

'Did you enjoy your cycle ride?' he wanted to know.

'Yes, thank you.' She asked spitefully, 'Did you enjoy—?'

'My girl-friend?' he grinned. 'Yes, thank you.'

He had got the better of her. 'The next time,' she snapped, 'you want to make your girl-friend jealous, choose someone else, someone from your own social circle, not me!'

She slammed out of his room, shutting in his malicious grin.

A sales representative was waiting for her when she returned to the fashion department. She invited him into Mrs. Rouse's office.

'I thought it was usual for a rep to make an appointment before calling,' she said, acting on the old saying that attack was the best form of defence. She also did it to hide her nervousness.

The man, medium-height, thick-set, red-faced, with eyes that roved appreciatively over her slim figure, smiled. 'Point to you, Miss – er—?'

'Bourne, Juliet Bourne.' They shook hands.

'Fresco fashions.' He produced his card. 'Dermot Edmond.'

'As you probably know, Mr. Edmond,' she spoke in her most businesslike manner, 'the boutique for which I'm buying stock isn't open yet. I have nothing at all in the way of supplies—'

'Which gives me a clear field? That's heartening, for my commission as well as my firm!' He rubbed his cheek. 'Since you want so much in the way of stock, I think the best thing is for you to come to the factory with me. It's on the industrial estate on the outskirts of the town. We've got the whole range there. You know we specialize in separates?'

'That's just what I want. If you'll wait until I confirm that it's all right for me to go with you—' Immediately, she regretted the words. To a man as astute as he was, having to get permission to leave the store revealed her inexperience and gave the man the advantage.

She dialled Drew's extension. His abruptness, following on his earlier good humour, took her by surprise. 'Go out to the factory? Yes, I suppose so. But remember what I told you. Some of them are wolves, in more ways than one. They're after your money, as well as the other thing. Keep a tight hold on it – them. Your budget isn't elastic. Oh, and,' he paused, 'don't keep running to me asking permission to do what is after all your job. You don't need your hand held. You're a buyer, a big girl now!' He rang off with a slam.

Flushing, she turned back to the man. He didn't miss her high colour. He grinned, 'Had words with the boss? Rumour has it he's an awkward devil. Never met the man myself.'

As he drove her through the town, he became a little too personal. Had she got a boy-friend? he wanted to know. Did she have an evening free sometimes?

'Very rarely,' she said firmly. If he took it as a snub, well, that was all the better.

The factory was modern, freshly painted and pleasant to work in. The building, with its modern, clean-cut line, was typical of those usually found on a new industrial development. The show room was well designed with subtle lighting to enhance the firm's products.

Remembering Drew's advice, Juliet insisted on seeing the cheapest end of the range first. The salesman remonstrated with her as expected – Drew had been right again – but she won her point.

From the moment the first garments were shown to her, she worked by instinct which, with the background training she had received as an art student, carried her through her first trial as a fashion buyer.

She sorted the collection of separates into 'certainties', 'possibles' and 'rejects'. Some she found difficult to classify, and it was then that she longed for the experience she lacked. Some of the styles were so new she rejected them at once, although she wondered afterwards if she should have done. Had she failed to use that 'vision' Drew seemed to think she possessed?

As soon as she had made her final decisions on the items she wanted, she wrote them down in her official order book as Mrs. Rouse had advised her to do. 'Never rely on memory,' Mrs. Rouse had said. 'You're bound to forget something that way.'

Dermot Edmond produced a bottle of wine from a cupboard and a couple of glasses and he suggested a toast to their mutual success and future co-operation. He eyed her over the top of his glass as if sizing her up.

'I'm free this evening. Are you?' he asked. 'Would you have a meal with me somewhere?' As if to encourage her he added, his eyes ingenuous, 'I could give you a few tips on the gentle art of buying and dealing with obstreperous reps.'

The bait was too strong for her to resist. She took the offer to help at its face value and could find no harm in accepting the invitation.

She thought about Malcolm, but he couldn't be annoyed because in a way this would be a business engagement. She thought about Drew, and how contemptuously he had spoken of some of the salesmen's morals. She thought about those kisses Drew had given her and the way he had 'used' her for his own ends.

'Yes,' she said defiantly, 'I'm free.'

Dermot Edmond's eyes glistened. 'Eight o'clock. Give me your address and I'll call for you.'

She wondered what her parents' reactions would be, but she would tell them she was perfectly capable of taking care of herself. And in any case, Drew wasn't right about everything.

She told Mrs. Rouse that afternoon that she was going out with a sales representative. 'Which one?' Mrs. Rouse asked. Juliet told her. Mrs. Rouse said she didn't know him. 'I don't deal with way-out clothes like you'll be doing, only the more conventional styles. All the same, I shouldn't go out with him if I were you. It might be a bit like favouritism. If you go out with one rep, you'll be expected to go out with the lot.' She frowned. 'Might get yourself a bad name, dear. And you don't know the man, do you?'

'But I'll have to go, Mrs. Rouse. I promised. The only

trouble is I don't know what to wear. My clothes are all a bit "way-out", as you put it.'

'Borrow a dress from the racks. It's allowed, as long as you bring it back next morning. No one's said we could, on the other hand it's well known that it goes on, and no one's said we can't, so we all do it. Look,' she beckoned to Juliet to follow, 'here's one that'll suit you fine.' She took it from the hanger. It was bright red, with a low-cut neck, draped skirt and wrist-length sleeves. 'Try it on.'

Juliet took it into a fitting room. The dress transformed her into a sophisticate, and she imagined it was the style of dress which Camille Wyngard might wear.

'A bit of make-up and your hair done, and you'll look a treat,' said Mrs. Rouse.

There were voices outside the fitting room. One of the assistants said, 'Miss Bourne's in there with Mrs. Rouse.'

Drew appeared at the fitting room door. Mrs. Rouse saw his hostile expression and melted away, leaving Juliet to her fate.

'Whose dress is that? Yours?'

Embarrassment reddened her skin until it almost matched the colour of the dress. 'No, Mr. Major.'

'Are you buying it?'

'No, Mr. Major. I was just trying it on.'

'For what purpose? Are you, by any chance, training to be a model and thus augment your salary?'

It was plain that her explanation would have to be good, so she told him the truth. 'I was going to borrow it, Mr. Major. Only for this evening. I was told it was allowed. I'd – I'd meant to return it.'

She was up to the chin in guilt, and it was sucking her in like a bog. Now suspicion had crept into his eyes, like a cat on the prowl, and his frown held disbelief and dismay. Her colour deepened. Was he thinking she had intended to steal it? She wanted the floor to open, she wanted to tear the dress off and throw it at him.

His eyes narrowed. 'Who told you it was allowed?'

She couldn't give Mrs. Rouse away. 'Someone.' That sounded even more incriminating. 'I was told it was an – an unwritten rule.'

'Were you, indeed? Then it's an "unwritten rule" I shall revoke – in writing. I suppose you know what I'm thinking,

98

Miss Bourne? You may not realize that petty pilfering by the staff is one of my worst headaches, secondly only to shoplifting by a certain percentage of customers?'

She was silent. Nothing she could say would exonerate her from the blame he seemed so keen to attach to her. But she was also aware that her silence didn't help, either.

He changed the subject. 'Where are you going tonight that you feel the need to dress up?'

Sulkily she replied, 'I'm going out.'

'With whom? Malcolm? If so, he'd hardly appreciate you in that dress. It makes you look – something I have assumed up to now that you were not. Easily available. Seeing you in that makes me wonder if I'm wrong.'

She felt his sarcasm was quite unfair. She rallied, her clear conscience loosening her tongue.

'I haven't committed a crime, Mr. Major. I've only tried on a dress. Customers are doing it all the time.' Her voice wavered. 'You can't really mistrust me as much as that?'

He heard the appeal, but his voice was hard as he said, 'Don't change the subject. Where are you going this evening?'

'Out.' But she could see he was not satisfied. 'With – with a man.' That sounded terrible. 'With the rep who called this morning, the one who took me to his factory.'

He walked towards her and his hand gripped the neck of the dress as if he was about to tear it off. 'Oh no, you're not! Unless you really want to be seduced? If so, there are men much nearer home whom you know a little better and who would be only too willing to oblige.' He gave the dress a tug. 'You can take that off. Not only do you agree to go out with a man you've never met before today, but you were thinking of wearing a dress which in addition to inviting trouble, unmistakably says "Come and get me." '

'But I promised. He seems a nice enough man, Mr. Major. He said he'd give me a few hints on being a buyer.'

'Good grief,' he looked disgusted, 'were you born yesterday, girl? You fell for that line? Run back to your Romeo and ask him to tell you the facts of life.' He went to the door. 'It's no good trying to exact a promise from you that you won't go out with the man, so I'll threaten you, instead. If you keep that date tonight or any other night with any sales representative who comes to see you, I'll fire you. Understand?'

She understood, she said, and he went away. That even-ing she did run to her 'Romeo' as Drew had suggested, leaving her mother to apologize and explain her absence to Dermot Edmond.

The day the deep freeze arrived, Cynthia was as happy as a girl with a new engagement ring. Her husband was indul-gently disapproving but grudgingly pleased that she was happy.

'Now,' he said, 'you'd better ask your ex-boy-friend where we're going to get the money from to fill the perishing thing. I suppose you know you purchase in bulk when you're buying frozen food?'

She put her arms round him as winningly as a young girl and said, 'We'll fill it a bit at a time.' He held her to him for a few minutes, then left her to it.

Malcolm came and admired it and a brooding look came into his eyes. 'I'd love to know their source of supply. It's a bargain at the price.'

Juliet told him quickly, 'It was a special price to Mother, wasn't it?' she appealed to Cynthia.

'A *very* special price, darling. I think he must have knocked off far more from the price than he said he would.'

'All the same . . .' Malcolm murmured, but Juliet gave his arm a shake.

'You promised not to tell anyone at Curlews.'

'All right.' He kissed her forehead. 'I'll keep the promise, but Majors don't deserve it. If you weren't working for them—'

'Then you wouldn't have known about it, would you?'

The phone rang and Juliet answered. 'Is your mother there?' Warren's voice was eager.

With an equal eagerness, Cynthia ran to the phone. 'Warren?' Her voice was high and excited and she must have sounded to him as she had years before when he used to phone her. She thanked him twice over for the deep freeze and they chatted for a long time.

Troubled, Juliet left the house with Malcolm, waving to her mother as they went. Cynthia waved back absently as though her thoughts were back in the past too.

'My father's still in love with your mother,' Drew had said. But what of her mother's feelings? Surely she didn't reciprocate Warren's love after all these years?

Juliet was growing excited about the opening of the boutique. The special lighting effects she had asked for had delayed completion by a week or so, but she had insisted that they should be at least as good as those she had seen at the other boutiques she had patronized in the past.

Drew had argued that the money they were able to devote to the enterprise was not unlimited.

'What's the need for all this nonsense?' he asked one morning as they stood together watching the electricians fitting up the coloured lights which, when finished, would move enticingly over the clothes, subtly changing their colours and highlighting the fashion trends as conventional lighting never would.

'It's not nonsense, Mr. Major. It's as vital a part of the boutique as assistants are in the main store. It's what my customers will expect. You told me the other day that I must cater for the typical customer when I'm buying stock.'

'But this,' he raised his arm, 'isn't stock. It's like the icing on a cake. Pretty but superfluous.'

She shook her head pityingly. 'It creates goodwill, can't you understand?'

He laughed. 'Spoken like a hardened professional buyer! What do you know about goodwill?' He lowered his voice. 'Especially where I'm concerned. I suppose you'll be telling me next in your typically blunt – not to say rude – way that I'm too old to understand all these modern ideas.'

'You've said it for me,' she answered with a grin.

'Straight below the belt, as my father would say. The truth of the matter is that I find it difficult to get down to the level of your potential customers.'

'Now you're being rude,' she said, offended.

'It's my prerogative. I'm the boss, so I can be rude as I like!'

They watched the electricians for a few more minutes. She pointed. 'Why the television screen?'

'You should know why. It lets the customers know in a polite way that there's closed circuit television operating inside the store. As I told you at that morning training session, it guards against shoplifting. It's vital for security purposes.'

He left her. Later she was informed by the receiving room that there had been a delivery of her stock and where was it to go?

'The marking-off room, please, for pricing,' she told the porter. She took the lift to the eighth floor and supervised her stock being stored on hangers in the wire cages with which she had grown so familiar while working up there. The other women hailed her like an old friend and she chatted to them for a while.

Looking round the marking-off room, still dull and depressing with its unattractive bare walls, reminded her ruefully of her efforts to brighten the place when she had first joined the firm. Then a thought struck her with such force she nearly cried out. She had a place of her own now – the boutique!

She left the others with a wave of the hand and sped down eight floors to her own little corner which, deserted by the electricians, was almost ready to be filled with stock.

What couldn't she do with a paintbrush and some paint? Her pent-up artistic feelings started hammering on the walls of her mind like a prisoner crazy to get out. She would buy her own paintbrush so that Drew could not criticize her for unnecessary expenditure, then she would bring those bare, uninteresting walls to life. This evening, she promised herself, she would stay on after hours and make a start on the painting. It must be done tonight, before the display stands were fitted and clothes filled the racks.

She seized her handbag and walked swiftly through the ground floor, passing perfumery, radio and electrical and haberdashery and found the section devoted to home decoration. She bought four tins of paint and a couple of brushes, asked the assistant to wrap them so that she could not be accused of taking them without payment – she was still smarting from Drew's implied accusation over the dress – and carried them back to the boutique, stacking them away in a corner. Then she phoned her mother to tell her she would be late home.

When the last customer had gone and the doors closed for the night, she sighed with relief. The anticipation she had dammed up inside her all day had burst its banks and she could hardly wait for the last member of staff to call 'good-night'.

She went out into the main store to make sure she was alone – she wanted no inquisitive person prying into what she was doing – and the great stillness filled her with an odd sense of awe. The goods on the counters – perfumery, hand-bags, jewellery – lay, like a beautiful woman, waiting to be admired, but they waited in vain. The admiring, covetous eyes had gone until morning. There was no hustle now, no chatter, no coming and going of people, and the place was all the lonelier for their absence.

But Juliet, her instincts sharpened by solitude and alert for the slightest sound, threw off her momentary apprehension and went back into the safety of the boutique like a bur-rowing animal making for cover.

She levered open the tins of emulsion paint, unwrapped one of the brushes and dipped it into a tin labelled 'orange glow'. She held her hand in mid-air, uncertain, inhibited by doubt – should she really be doing this without permission? – but the hesitation lasted no longer than a few seconds. The artist in her, the vision she carried in her mind of the walls transformed, overrode all rules and regulations. The paintbrush was lifted and applied and a great curve of orange swept over the insipid cream wash with which the partitions were covered.

Now she had started, she felt reassured. It looked better with every stroke of the brush. She followed no set pattern, applying the mixture of colours at random, guided all the time by her inborn feeling for design and the lessons in disciplined self-expression she had learned as a student.

She must have been painting for half an hour and had covered an entire wall when she began to feel the effects of a missed meal. But she was so carried away by her work that she pushed aside all thoughts of food.

A sound from the main store, soft though it was, stood out three-dimensionally from the intense silence. Oddly fright-ened, she stopped, brush poised, to listen. There were foot-steps stopping, moving, pausing, and – were they creeping? Fear had her skin prickling and trapped her breath in her throat.

Quietly she rested the brush across the top of a paint tin

and crept to the boutique entrance. A man stood a few yards away behind a counter, in the perfumery section, staring at her. He was wearing an overall and relief nearly made her faint.

' 'Evening, miss.' He was one of the caretakers. 'Workin' late, miss?'

She said, 'You gave me a terrible fright. I thought it was a thief, someone who'd broken in to rob the shop!'

'Just doing the rounds, miss, making sure all's well. Will you be staying much longer, miss? I'll have to lock up in half an hour or so.'

'I'll be through by then, I expect. Give me half an hour and I'll be off. All right?'

He raised a finger in a salute. 'Fair enough, miss. Good-night, now.'

Her heart had still not settled down to its normal beat, but she picked up the paintbrush, took a few deep breaths to steady her nerves and carried on. It must have been five minutes later that she heard footsteps again. Had the man come back? But these footsteps were different. They were decisive and fast, they knew where they were going. And they were coming straight towards the boutique. A different kind of fear had her heart thumping again, and a sickening feeling of guilt, of being caught in the act, spread through her body like the roots of a tree. She stepped back without turning her head and knocked over a tin of paint which, in toppling, knocked another flying.

'Oh,' she cried, almost in tears. 'Now look what's happened!'

'What the devil are you up to now, you little idiot?'

Only one person in the world could have spoken those words in that unpleasant tone, and she turned and faced him.

'What the blazes do you think I'm doing?' she cried, politeness and protocol flung aside like restricting bedclothes.

'Knowing you, I dare not think.' He looked around. 'You're *not* painting the walls?'

'What does it look like? And now the floor, too. It was all your fault, coming in so quickly, giving me another terrible fright. First the caretaker, now you . . .'

'Be careful what you're saying, Miss Bourne. You don't

speak to me in that tone. My name is not Malcolm Watling.'

'Oh, I'm sorry.' She dismissed his reprimand as though it was entirely irrelevant and stared horrified at the mass of paint merging into a rainbow of colours and creeping unchecked across the floor. She was tired, she was hungry and she was still suffering from the electrifying effect of two shocks each following the other in quick succession. 'Now what do I do? What a terrible mess! And all that money wasted.'

She crammed the tears back down her throat and looked at him. He saw the hopeless appeal in her eyes, heard the despair in her voice, and softened his tone a fraction. 'Obviously it must be cleared up, mustn't it? What paint is it and what's its solvent?'

'Water — it's emulsion paint. But where do I get water from at this time of night? And a mop and bucket?'

He tutted. 'And I've just sent the caretaker home. With you around, I must have been mad!'

'You saw him?'

'He came to see me. There was a young woman down here, he said, looking suspicious. Said he didn't entirely trust you and thought you were up to no good.'

She reddened indignantly. 'What did he think I was doing? Robbing the place? So you came down to catch me red-handed?'

'I had an idea who it was as soon as he described you, and when he said you were hiding, as he put it, in the boutique, I knew for certain.'

They looked down at the pools of paint inching across the floor. 'I'll get the necessary,' Drew said, 'while you put away what's left of your precious paint.' He looked round the walls. 'What a mad idea, staying after hours to slosh paint all over the place. Is this your idea of beauty? And at the firm's expense?'

His sarcastic comments, after all her efforts, unravelled the frayed edges of her temper. 'No. If you must know, I paid for the paint myself. And for the brushes. So it's cost the firm nothing. It's my money that's been wasted, not yours.'

She remembered the excitement she had felt all day and the enthusiasm with which she had started the work. She sank down on the floor and put a hand over her eyes, but his compassion was not stirred.

He said in a bored tone, 'If you must weep, Juliet, do it after we've cleared up the mess, will you?'

He went for some water and she mopped her tears and waited, kneeling and sitting back on her heels, staring helplessly at the sprawling stain the spilt paint had made. Would they ever wash it away? In his absence she felt contrite and when he returned with buckets of water, scrubbing brushes and cloths, she said,

'I'm sorry I was rude.'

He shrugged and rolled up his sleeves. 'Let's put it down to artistic temperament, shall we?'

'No, it is *not* artistic temperament! It was tiredness and disappointment and – and hunger.'

'Haven't you eaten?' She shook her head. 'Nothing since lunch? No wonder we had the histrionics. Nobody can be reasonable on an empty stomach. When we've cleared up this mess we'll have to do something about it.'

She said quickly, 'I'm not having dinner with you.'

'I haven't invited you to dine with me.' The coldness of his tone made her want to creep into a corner.

'Sorry,' she muttered, seizing a scrubbing brush and dipping it into a bucket of water. They worked in silence for a while. When the paint had gone, leaving only faint stains on the floor, Juliet sighed and Drew laughed.

'If the staff could see me now, the company manager on his knees helping to clear up the mess created by the most maddening and unruly employee in the firm!'

She protested, 'I may be maddening at times, but I'm certainly not unruly. How can you say that?'

He stood, pulling her up with him. 'How can I say that? Because you are unruly. You're an anarchist, my girl. You flagrantly disobey all rules, you refuse to acknowledge any form of control and believe in revolt for the sake of it. You're the most disobedient, undisciplined young woman I've ever come across.' He gripped her chin and a quantity of hair at the back of her head. 'There's a ruthless streak in me, so you'd better watch your step, because if you bring it out by going too far, I won't be able to help myself. I'll do something drastic to you.' His face came nearer, his eyes searched hers, his lips seemed to hover. He saw the tiredness and the touch of fear she could not hide. He dropped his hands.

Bitterly disappointed, longing for his kiss to ease away her tiredness and that haunting sense of failure which reared its head like a snake ready to hiss and bite at the slightest setback, she turned away.

'Would you like some food? I'll look for a sandwich or two in the canteen, if you like.'

'No, thanks. When I get home I expect my mother will have a meal waiting for me.'

He looked at his watch. 'I'll give you a lift.'

'No, thank you.' It came out a little too quickly for politeness. She didn't want to give him the impression that she was asking for a lift as she had assumed earlier that he was inviting her to dinner with him.

'All right, all right, I only offered. As a matter of fact, I am in rather a hurry.' He unrolled his shirt sleeves and buttoned them.

'Camille?' she asked, knowing as soon as it was out the question was impertinent.

'If you must know, yes,' he said, in a tone intended to squash her.

He reached for his jacket which he had hung on a hook, but put it back again saying 'Damn! I've got some paint on my sleeve.' He held it out as if asking her what to do about it.

She laughed and somehow it eased the tension. 'Just like a helpless male! I'll get it off for you. What would men do without women?'

'I wouldn't know,' he answered laconically. She picked up a rag and dipped it in some water. 'I'm hardly ever without one.'

She tightened up at once. With a cynical smile he offered her his wrist and she rubbed at the paint stain on his sleeve, holding the back of his hand in hers. Her eyes strayed to his slightly curled fingers and she fought with a crazy desire to lift the palm of his hand to her cheek, her lips, to feel it caressing her body. She stopped, horrified at where her thoughts were taking her.

She said, her tone deliberately flippant to keep at bay the powerful emotions clamouring, like an unruly mob, to have their demands met, 'Your girl-friend would disown you, wouldn't she, if you took her out to dinner with a paint-stained shirt?'

There was no reply and she looked up at him, smiling to meet his smile. But there was nothing there. His expression as his eyes met hers was more intensely serious than she had ever seen it and her smile died a slow, painful death. She held her breath. What was he going to say?

Nothing, it seemed. He frowned instead and pulled away his hand with some impatience. 'Thanks, that will do. I'll change when I get home.' He swung into his jacket, looked at his watch again and said, 'I must be off. You, too. I want to lock up.'

She tidied the tins of paint, put the brushes into water and picking up her belongings walked by his side through the silent store to the exit. Before he left her he said, 'Claim for those tins of paint you bought through petty cash. Go to the cashier, produce the receipts and she'll give you back your money. Goodnight.' Abruptly he left her.

She went to work next morning oddly happy. It wouldn't be long now before the boutique was ready. She had even decided on the name – *Girl Major*. She hoped Drew would approve. In a day or two the display stands would be placed in position. Some of the stands she had chosen were conventional racks, others shaped like swirling helter-skelters. A few would be suspended from the ceiling by long chains, so that the clothes hanging on them would swing and twirl. Others would hang low from flat, round table-like tops on which would sit dummy figures, displaying clothes.

As she entered the boutique she saw the stain left by the spilt paint the evening before. Her heart beat a little faster when she remembered how Drew had helped her clear away the mess. Then she thought about Camille and how he had spent the evening with her. She wondered if he intended to marry her one day and the idea hurt her like an untreated wound.

Her name being called out over the Tannoy, the internal public address system, gave her a shock. 'Miss Bourne,' the voice said, 'Miss Juliet Bourne to go to the company manager's office immediately.'

Her first reaction to the summons was one of pleasure that Drew should want to see her. But as she went up in the lift she wondered why he hadn't phoned. He must have been too busy. Of course, that was the answer.

When she knocked and entered he was seated at his desk. He raised his head and he might have been looking at a stranger for all the recognition there was in his eyes. His cold, evaluating scrutiny misted her vision like frost spread over a window pane.

'You – you sent for me, Mr. Major?' He motioned her to a seat.

She became aware that there was someone else in the room, a man she had never seen before. Drew indicated him. 'Mr. Cunningham, our chief security officer.'

Security officer? Why did he think she would be interested in meeting the security officer? Mr. Cunningham nodded but did not rise, nor did he proffer his hand. Instead he scrutinized her as closely as Drew had done. What was the matter with them? Did they think she was an escaped criminal? Was this an identity parade and she a suspect?

She knew the answer as soon as Drew spoke. 'Overnight,' he leaned back and fixed her eyes with his, 'an expensive transistor radio disappeared from the radio and electrical department.'

Juliet frowned. 'Did it? I'm sorry to hear it.' The trite expression sounded weak, but she could think of nothing else to say.

His next words, preposterous and bewildering though they were, revealed the direction of his thoughts. 'Since you stayed late last night, as I myself know, and since you were alone for a long time after everyone else had gone, I'm afraid that all the circumstances point to only one thing – that you are responsible for that radio's disappearance.'

It was a direct accusation. Her cheeks drained of colour. 'That *I* was responsible? Are you now saying, on top of all the other insulting things you've called me in the past, that I'm a *thief*?'

The security officer's gaze, intent, assessing, never left her face. His arms were folded, his thick glasses magnified his staring eyes to a frightening size – part of his stock-in-trade, Juliet assumed – and he had the look of a man who chose to believe the worst of anyone brought before him.

'My dear Miss Bourne,' Drew's cool, patronizing tones were harder to bear than the security officer's incriminating regard, 'what else are we to think? I'm merely saying that the situation is such that, try as we might, we cannot see how anyone else can possibly be blamed for the theft.'

'But you went out with me, Mr. Major. If I'd had the radio you would have seen me holding it, wouldn't you?'

'You were carrying a shopping bag. How do I know what you had in that?'

She tried again. 'But I wasn't the only one on the premises. There was the caretaker—'

'Mr. Robinson has been with us for many years. His character and his record are excellent. He's above suspicion.'

So Drew Major had put himself out of reach of all reason. Her cheeks flamed. 'And I'm not above suspicion. I'm a newcomer, an interloper, untried, therefore under no circumstances to be trusted.' Sarcastically, 'I must, *ergo*, be guilty.' She flung at the security officer, who did not react even by so much as the flicker of an eyelid, 'Hardly a considered and logical conclusion for a man to arrive at whose job it is to enforce the law fairly and without bias. If you're so sure I did it, why don't you march me along to the police station and have me arrested?'

Drew answered quietly, 'In this firm, Miss Bourne, we don't do things that way. Out of the kindness of our hearts, we try to make it as easy as possible for the culprit. As I told you once before, staff pilfering is a hazard every firm has to cope with. We take it in our stride. We don't go running to the police every time it happens. We have our own method of punishing those members of staff found guilty of stealing the firm's goods – instant dismissal.'

'And they get no chance to clear their names? You call that kind?' She cried passionately, 'What is this, a court of law? If so, I demand to see my solicitor – at least,' she corrected herself, 'my father's solicitor. But it's not a court of law, is it? It's not even as fair as that. Instant dismissal, made as quickly and unthinkingly as instant coffee. You call this justice? Prove that I took it,' she shouted, 'go on, *prove* it!'

'Prove that you didn't, Miss Bourne.'

'You know very well I can't prove anything. You've made an accusation. I deny that accusation. I tell you,' her voice was a mixture of outrage and appeal, '*I didn't do it!*'

'Miss Bourne,' Drew persisted, 'if you would produce the radio, return it to the department concerned, we might even, in your case, consider forgetting—'

'Produce it? Produce something I haven't got?'

'You haven't got it?' echoed the security officer sharply, speaking for the first time. 'Then where is it? Have you passed it on to someone else?'

'*Now* what are you implying?' she shrieked at him. 'That I'm a member of a gang dealing in stolen goods?'

'Don't be stupid, Miss Bourne. He means have you made a present of it to someone, a friend, a relative, perhaps? I myself am aware, by means which we both know, of your financial circumstances at home—'

She would not let him finish. 'Now you're telling me my family's so poor they couldn't afford to pay for a transistor radio? Just how insulting can you get?'

'It was an expensive radio, Miss Bourne.'

'I don't care,' she cried, 'if the thing cost a hundred pounds. I wouldn't dirty my hands, let alone my conscience, by stealing anything from anyone, let alone – let alone—' She couldn't get out the word 'you'. It stuck in her throat and choked her to tears.

By the expression on their faces, she knew her hesitation had cost a high price. If her passionate denial of guilt had made any impression at all, its effect was now receding fast. 'All right,' she began, but realized in time that if she had continued the sentence, had said as she had intended, 'I'll resign. There's no need for you to sack me,' it would have underlined her guilt even more. They were waiting for her to speak again, waiting like dogs eyeing a meaty bone for the confession they were sure was coming.

The door opened and Warren came in. 'Will someone kindly tell me what's going on in here? I heard her shouting and I'd like to know why.'

Drew explained irritably, 'A radio has been stolen from the electrical department.'

'Well?'

'Miss Bourne stayed late last night. She was alone for some time.' Warren froze as if he knew what was coming. 'We've arrived at the unfortunate conclusion, and you have to agree that we have no alternative, that Miss Bourne now has that radio in her possession.'

Warren said slowly, unbelievingly, 'In other words, she stole it?' He jabbed a finger in her direction. '*She* stole it? You must be crazy,' he looked disparagingly at Mr. Cunningham, 'both of you.'

She turned to Warren, crying, 'It's all based on circumstantial evidence, Mr. Major. I was there, I was alone, therefore I'm guilty.' She contracted the muscles of her throat. She was determined not to cry. 'I'm new, I'm untried, therefore my morals are suspect – all the more so because I was once an art student, and as everyone knows,' she flung her sarcasm at Drew, 'art students' morals are unspeakable.' She looked again at Warren. 'I'm being sacrificed at the altar of the System, with a capital "S". I'm innocent, but I can't prove it, so I must suffer the punishment of the guilty – instant dismissal. I have no chance to defend myself – the System being what it is, it can only accuse, never excuse, never listen to reason. I have no redress. So I'm to be summarily dismissed.' She rounded on Drew. 'You were right, so right, when you said you were ruthless. You're worse, much worse. You're cruel, you're merciless, you're unjust and you're – you're inhuman!' And because she realized she was abusing unforgivably the man she knew deep in her heart she loved above all others, she started to cry, she couldn't stop herself.

Warren's arm came round her and once again she sought solace at the shoulder of the man who, in very different circumstances, might have been her father.

He said over her head which was jerking with her violent sobs, 'Have a bit of compassion, son. Give her a chance to prove her innocence.'

'Thanks,' her voice was muffled against him, 'for your belief in my integrity, Mr. Major, but I can't prove I'm innocent, can I?'

There was a long silence, broken only by her intermittent sobbing. Then Warren said, 'At least commute the sentence into dismissal after a period of time. She's got to get another job. You know that as well as I do. Dismissal would prejudice her chances so much she might find it impossible to get one. There's the question of references for a start.'

'She could resign.'

'That wouldn't help, would it, son?' His voice was quiet in its appeal for clemency. 'Any future employer would want to know why.'

He was pleading with the man who, he had once claimed with pride, he had fashioned in his own image. He was now entreating him to show a mercy, a kindliness of which he, by his own hand and by careful and deliberate tuition, had 'gutted' him – his son's own words – from adolescence onwards. He looked now a little sad, a little pathetic, as if he would have given his all to undo the past and recreate this son of his in a more forgiving, more compassionate mould.

His appeal must have touched the company manager, whose eyes, although they did not lose their hardness, assumed a filial forbearance and he said, 'The dismissal stands, but she may stay until she has obtained other employment. If her stay here is extended too long, I shall be forced to use my prerogative and dismiss her at any time I think fit.'

Warren, without another word, led Juliet outside. He patted her shoulder. 'Go to the rest room, my dear. Don't go back to your work until you feel ready.' She nodded and thanked him. As she turned to go, Warren said, as if he could not hold back the question, 'Your mother? She's well?'

'Yes, thank you. And my father, for the moment.'

'Yes, yes, your father,' as if mention of him was irrelevant. 'With regard to this other business, Juliet,' he motioned towards Drew's closed door, 'you have an ally in me. Never forget it. I shall fight on your side.'

She gave him a weak smile, thanked him again and walked slowly towards the lift.

CHAPTER SIX

Girl Major was opened without prior announcement. No advertisement appeared in the press. Malcolm had said that even with the rather poor effort at a boutique which Curlews had made, they had at least taken space in the local paper to make its existence known. But because she was under notice, Juliet had not bothered to mention the matter of publicity. Her heart was not in the venture any more.

When she had told Malcolm the story of her dismissal, he had been furious. She had only just been able to restrain him from picking up the phone and having a violent quarrel with Drew Major.

'Get a job at Curlews,' he had urged her. 'They want a new assistant in the boutique. I know it would be a bit of a comedown going from buyer to junior assistant, but it would be better than nothing.'

But she told him she wanted to get right away from the area, even if it meant moving. She had no quarrel with Warren Major, none at all, but his son – she couldn't tell Malcolm, of all people, how she felt about Warren's son.

She had not told her parents about the missing radio. She had spared them the indignity of knowing that their daughter had been accused of theft and given notice by the company manager himself – the son of the man her mother had once nearly married, the man her father resented so fiercely and tolerated only because he knew it would upset his wife if he did not.

One morning *Girl Major* was not open, the next it was. It was as straightforward as that. Consequently, business was not brisk. Juliet stood around listlessly awaiting the first customer, feeling that all her efforts, the money spent on the fittings, the decor, the models had been in vain. A young girl, timid but inquiring, put her head round the entrance of the boutique, took a hasty look round, met Juliet's too-hopeful eyes and withdrew like a child afraid to go into a roomful of strangers.

An hour later, another young woman came in, a little bolder this time, wandered round, looked at nothing in particular, got the feel of the place – which somehow didn't seem to please her – and vanished as the other girl had done. Juliet began to fret.

The taped music, light pseudo-classical stuff, drifting innocuously out of the Tannoy, was putting over with a sugary efficiency the high-class image which the store had so painstakingly built up over the years, even in the face of fierce competition from its rivals.

Curlews had consistently levelled their sights at a different class of clientèle. Although its standards were undoubtedly lower than those of Major's, it had obtained and retained the unwavering loyalty of those who would not have allowed even their shadows to venture into the more superior air of the other store.

Perhaps that was what was wrong. The 'atmosphere', Juliet concluded, must be frightening away the shy young girls who, although the boutique had been designed and stocked specifically for them, were attracted to it, but at the same time felt hopelessly out of place in such an 'exclusive' establishment.

And all the time there was the music, that umbrella of pleasant, eminently orthodox sound which was twenty years behind the times. It was perhaps – although Juliet was reluctant to concede the point – the right kind of sound for the rest of the store, but it wouldn't do at all for the type of client *Girl Major* sought to attract.

The boutique, Juliet decided, should be provided with its own music. And, she thought with a delightful feeling of revenge, it should be loud enough to drown the insipid stuff which honeyed the air-conditioned atmosphere of the rest of the store. Should she bring her own transistor radio? But the very thought of the words made her wince. They reminded her of the scene in Drew's office when he had accused her of being a thief. No, music for the boutique would unfortunately have to wait.

Having nothing else to do, Juliet wandered out into the main store and saw with envy how busy her colleagues were, serving and smiling and wrapping customers' purchases. She felt bitter. Their jobs were secure. Hers was not. No threat of dismissal hung over their heads like Damocles' sword. She cursed her misplaced devotion to her cause when, over-zealous, she had stayed behind that unfortunate evening. She was the victim of her own enthusiasm and as a consequence was on her way out.

All those women in their high-necked black dresses – they were not rebels. They conformed, they worked set hours, went home and forgot about their jobs until next morning. She, with her burning desire to make the boutique succeed, had voluntarily worked overtime, and now she had been made the scapegoat for the real thief of that radio. It came to her with a shock that he – or she – was probably still working on the premises right now, undetected and uncaring.

She felt a resentment so strong it tasted bitter in her mouth. She put her hand to her throat and felt its bareness – she was still wearing the black dress – and another idea occurred to her for the failure of the boutique. She was wrongly dressed for the part. That was something which could easily be remedied, so remedied it would be.

Her spirits revived. Her anarchistic tendencies, as Drew had disparagingly called them, came into their own. She searched through the clothes on the racks, selected tight-fitting scarlet pants, an equally tight-fitting multi-coloured long-sleeved top and an imitation fur waistcoat, as long-haired and shaggy as Highland cattle. She went into one of her own fitting rooms, put on the new clothes, bundled her black dress into her shopping bag and emerged looking like one of her own customers. She draped herself against the entrance to the boutique and registered with a fierce kind of delight the gasps that came her way from other members of staff.

It took only ten minutes for her strategy to work. A young woman approached and pushed past Juliet as if willing to overcome all obstacles in order to get at the clothes *Girl Major* was displaying so enticingly. The coloured lights moved and halted, moved and stopped again, changing the colour of every object they settled on, even the girl raking feverishly through the racks. She selected three items and approached Juliet who was still leaning negligently against the entrance.

'Want to try them on?' Juliet asked, smiling encouragingly. The customer nodded. She went into a fitting-room and Juliet resumed her place at the door. Another girl hovered outside, peering past Juliet, who moved slowly to let her in.

The first customer emerged and said, 'I'll take all three,' paid and went out smiling. The second customer chose a long-sleeved ribbed dress, paid for it without trying it on and went away, smiling just as brightly.

From that moment on, *Girl Major* didn't look back. The rest of the morning brought a constant stream of customers, all of them young, although some were certainly past their teens. Juliet didn't even have time for morning coffee. During the lunch break business became even brisker. Having no assistant, Juliet worked on, thinking longingly of her sandwiches, but finding no opportunity to slip away.

She did think of asking one of the assistants from the main store to take over for ten minutes, but shrank from the thought. Heaven knew what damage might be done by one of those formally-dressed, tight-lipped women assistants.

It was during the afternoon that the general manager confronted her in a pause between customers.

'I've had complaints from other members of staff,' Mr. Havering said, 'that you are breaking one of the store rules by abandoning your uniform and wearing clothes totally unsuited to your position.' So someone had told tales. He eyed her with distaste. 'Will you kindly change back into your black dress at once!'

'But, Mr. Havering,' she pleaded, 'it would be disastrous if I did. I've proved by experience that it's absolutely essential for me to dress like this. It wasn't until I changed into these clothes that I started getting any customers at all. My black dress was frightening them away.'

He was unmoved. 'I'm sorry, Miss Bourne. Rules are made to be observed, not broken. If you don't agree I shall have to inform my superiors.' His superiors! His military bearing was coming through. He talked like a non-commissioned officer in the army. Major and Son had chosen the right man here to enforce the company's rules, with his unquestioning acceptance and rigid application of the regulations.

But Miss Bourne, like a mutinous private, refused, even at the risk of being confined to barracks, to obey orders. 'Then, Mr. Havering,' she said quietly spotting another customer wandering round, 'you'll just have to inform your superiors, because I'm not changing back into my store uniform.'

He made a short, sharp noise like the firing of a gun, turned on his heel and marched out.

Ten minutes later the extension telephone rang in her office. 'Mr. Drew Major,' the secretary announced, 'wishes to see Miss Bourne immediately.'

Juliet said, as slowly as if she were talking to a foreigner, 'Miss Bourne is very sorry, but she is unable to comply with Mr. Major's request. If Miss Bourne did, there would be no one, but no one, to serve all the customers who are queueing up for her to attend them.' She slammed down the phone and ran out to serve the girls grouped round the shop, money and purchases in hand, waiting patiently for attention.

The phone rang again. She let it ring until she couldn't stand it. 'Yes?' she asked into the receiver.

'Miss Bourne?' came the clipped, even tones of the company manager.

She didn't give him a chance to continue. 'I'm sorry, Mr. Major, but it's absolutely impossible for me to leave the boutique. I can't possibly come and see you now.' She rang off and ran back into the shop.

The phone rang again. She went into the office, removed the receiver and put it on the desk. Then she returned to her customers.

Three minutes later Drew Major strode in, looked bewildered at the crush, searched for the boutique buyer – it was difficult to distinguish anyone in that mass of highly coloured femininity – found her, stared as if he could not believe his eyes, turned on his heel as Mr. Havering had done and went out.

'Rounds one and two to me,' Juliet thought, enjoying herself. 'He can't sack me because I'm already under notice.' The thought delighted her.

The shop closed its doors at five-thirty. At five-forty the last customer departed. Five minutes later, when everyone else was preparing to leave, Juliet sat down to eat her lunch. An announcement over the Tannoy had everyone listening. It said, clearly and distinctly, three times over, 'Will Miss Juliet Bourne go to the company manager's office at once.'

Juliet munched on. She was going to finish her sandwiches even if it choked her. A young man put his head round her office door.

'Can't you hear, ducky? You're wanted by the big white chief.'

'I heard, thanks. I'll go in a minute.'

He gazed at the sandwich which was disappearing fast into her mouth, murmured, 'Everything stops for tea,' shrugged and went home.

When she did eventually make her way to the sixth floor and stood with Drew's door only a few inches from her face, her courage started to melt like ice cream left standing too long.

It hit her like a giant wave hurling itself against the rocks that she was guilty of disobedience of a high order, high enough, if she had not already been under notice, to get her fired on the spot.

But she had gone thus far, and there was no turning back now. She knocked, received the summons to enter and went in. His look fixed her to the spot as surely as if he were pointing a revolver at her head. One false move on her part and he would fire.

'I want to know,' he said, each word hitting her as if she were an object being used for target practise by an expert marksman, 'why, for the past hour and a half, you have resolutely and wilfully disobeyed my repeated instruction to come to my office. And,' through his teeth, 'since I feel at the moment as if I'd like to make mincemeat out of you, the explanation had better be good.'

'The explanation,' she said, her bravado forsaking her like a friend turned traitor, 'is simply that I couldn't leave the boutique unattended. I tried to tell your secretary that, but she can't have got the message.'

'The message was received all right, that Miss Juliet Bourne refused point blank to do as she was told and had no intention whatsoever of obeying my instructions.'

'If you want me to be free to run to heel at your command, then I'll have to be allocated an assistant.'

He swivelled sideways letting his arm hang over the back of his chair. 'Oh, will you? And where will the money come from to subsidize such a person?'

She shrugged. 'Out of the firm's pocket, I suppose. I'm sure once the boutique becomes established, the takings will justify an assistant for me. I haven't had time to calculate how much I've taken today – I handed the cash over on my way here – but when the total is known even you will be staggered at the amount.'

'After dealing with you, it would take a lot to stagger me.' He eyed her outfit derisively.

She saw where his thoughts were leading him. 'Mr. Major,' her voice had a pleading quality that would have moved the company chairman to give her anything, but the company manager appeared as unmoved as a range of mountains, 'I'm serious about the assistant. I've worked continuously all day – apart from an hour or so this morning when there was no custom at all.'

Despite the sandwiches she had swallowed before going to see him, hunger pangs caught her under her ribs. She looked round for a chair. 'Do you mind if I sit down?'

He nodded. 'Even if it is only a ruse to make me realize what a tired, harassed, hard-working girl you are.'

'My tiredness is genuine.' She sank down on to the chair opposite him. 'I couldn't come and see you straight away. You see, I had to eat my lunch.'

'Lunch? *Lunch*? At,' he looked at his watch, 'five-forty-five?'

She nodded. 'And that's why I should like an assistant.'

'I see no reason why you shouldn't have an assistant.' She was about to express her gratitude at his sudden change of heart when he added, 'We might as well start at once to train someone to take your place.'

She should have known there would be a sting in the tail. 'How can you be so cool,' she cried, 'about my leaving?'

'Have you forgotten the missing radio?'

'How could I forget? Anyone accused of doing something they didn't do and being punished for it could never forget the injustice being meted out to them. I promise you from the bottom of my heart that I'll never forget – or forgive you for mistrusting me.'

He frowned and studied the lines on the palms of his hands as if he were map-reading. He changed the subject, pointing. 'Those clothes – there will be no more of that nonsense.'

'This nonsense, as you call it,' she pulled at the furry waistcoat she was wearing, 'was the bait that brought the customers in. For two or three hours I was hanging round that boutique, very decent and nice in my black dress, and yet I sold not a single item. It wasn't until I changed into this outfit that the girls passing by – and I mean passing by – began to catch on. Then the real business of the day began.'

'Very plausible, Miss Bourne, and I compliment you on your efforts to sell yourself to me.' He smiled provocatively. 'Don't misunderstand me, I mean in the purely business sense of the word.' He seemed to enjoy the mutiny in her eyes. 'But you're pouring out your sales talk to deaf ears. That outfit, when seen within the context of the rest of the store, is as out of place as a mountain in the heart of London. From tomorrow onwards,' he pointed his finger for emphasis, 'and this is a directive from the top, from tomorrow onwards you return to wearing your black dress while on duty. If you disobey, and my father can intervene on your behalf as much as he likes, it will make no difference, you're out. Out, you understand?'

'But, Mr. Major,' she wailed, seeing her boutique, as she still thought of it, failing beyond resuscitation, 'I *must* wear clothes like these. That horror of a black dress I was wearing was frightening customers away. Go into any boutique and you'll see the sales assistants wearing clothes like the ones they're selling.'

His eyes darkened. 'That "horror of a black dress", Miss Bourne, as you so rudely call it, is official store uniform. And what is more, you're no ordinary sales assistant, you're a buyer – a considerable step above the status of an assistant. Therefore, like all the other buyers, and despite the fact that you've maltreated it almost beyond recognition, *you will wear that dress!*'

This was war. She rose and confronted him. 'I'm sorry, Mr. Major, but I will *not* wear that dress. If you try to force me to, job or no job, I'll walk out.' Her fingers, as they clutched the edge of the desk, turned white with the pressure she was putting on them. 'But before I go,' her efforts to contain her anger were draining her face of colour, 'with my own hands,' she held them up for him to see, 'I'll tear the boutique apart.'

He was standing now, breathing hard, lips compressed.

'I'll tear it apart,' she went on, 'as I tore up those pictures you wouldn't let me put up in the marking-off room, and as

I nearly tore up my black dress when you objected to it after I altered it.'

'So you're challenging me, are you? By threatening violence you think you'll win.' He moved slowly round the desk. 'If you aren't the most unscrupulous, unprincipled, shameless little bitch I've ever come across ...' His fingers clenched in his pockets as if he were trying to restrain them from acting disastrously on their own. 'You dare to challenge me?'

His eyes bore into hers, disregarding in his fury the whiteness of her face, seeing only her stubbornness, her defiance, her unbreakable spirit, and he raised his arms as though he could scarcely restrain himself from breaking that spirit with his own hands. She cowered away instinctively.

'You'd better get out, Miss Bourne,' his voice was dangerously controlled, 'you'd better get out while I still have control of myself.'

Still she defied him, making one last attempt to reason with him. 'Will you let me wear these clothes?'

At her question, his control snapped. '*Get out!*' he shouted. He took her by the arms and forced her backwards towards the door. She tripped and nearly fell. Without gentleness he righted her. She began to resist his pressure and his hands tightened, pressing into her flesh. She cried out with pain. He reached forward and opened the door, pushing her out into the corridor.

She was crying now with frustration and anger, misery and humiliation. Another door opened and Warren appeared. In her despair she turned to him. But he was staring at his son.

'What now, Drew?' It came out wearily, hopelessly.

But Juliet did not give the company manager a chance to answer. 'I hate your son, Mr. Major,' she said, her voice low and intense, 'I hate him as I've never hated any other human being in the whole of my life!'

Warren paled. 'What goes on, son? What have you done to her now?'

Drew replied, his face almost as pale as his father's, 'What have *I* done to *her*? My God, it's what she's done to *me*, not the other way round!'

Juliet ran away from them both.

Next morning she went to work in her black dress. She found on her desk an invitation, in the form of a duplicated memorandum from the company manager, addressed to all Major employees, advising them that the annual Major garden party would be held at the Major residence in a week's time. Everyone was cordially invited to attend, together with their husbands, wives or other partners.

She flung it down contemptuously. That was one invitation she had no intention of accepting. From the office cupboard she took out the clothes she had worn the day before. Dared she wear them? She returned the shaggy waistcoat to the racks, put into the till the money for the striped top and scarlet pants, then she went into a fitting room and put them on.

Stiff with defiance, she awaited her first customer, standing at the entrance as she had done the day before, to give the first one enough confidence to enter. Across the store she saw a tall, familiar figure wending his way in her direction. She withdrew speedily into the sanctuary of the boutique, and had to struggle with the desire to run away while she still had the chance.

He stood in the entrance and saw her outfit, his eyes lingering on the striped jumper which revealed her shape as only a tight-fitting garment could, lowering his eyes to the equally tight trousers hugging her hips and legs.

'I thought I told you,' he said quietly, 'not to wear those things.'

'I know, Mr. Major, but,' her eyes held his, pleading, moist, urging him to comprehend, 'I've just *got* to, can't you understand? Please,' she whispered, 'please let me.'

Her eyes were large with tiredness – she had slept badly and had left home without breakfast – her hands, palms upwards, in themselves pleading her case, and she gazed at him willing him to relent. She didn't know what she would do if he did not. Pack up and go home, she supposed.

He said, his voice hardly audible, 'I wish, I only wish, I could up-end you and put you across my knee. My word, I'd give you something to remember me by!' He turned and went away. She sat on the nearest chair, her legs oddly weak.

A sales representative called and all the while she was talking to him, she had to dash out of the office to serve customers. Word seemed to have got round at last that there was a new boutique at Majors. The passers-by had stopped passing and were coming in thick and fast.

When the salesman had gone, Juliet rushed into her office and dialled Drew's extension, asking to speak to him. His secretary went away, came back and said, 'I'm sorry, Miss Bourne, he's not available.'

So they weren't on speaking terms now. 'All right,' she said, endeavouring to keep calm, 'will you please give him a message? Will you tell him from me that I need the assistant he promised me right now, and if I'm not allocated one immediately, I shall either have to close the boutique, or go out into the store and pressgang a girl into helping me.'

The secretary went away, and in the distance through the receiver Juliet could hear something that sounded like a loud expletive. She supposed it was Drew reacting and she smiled, a shaft of sunlight penetrating her gloom.

The secretary returned. 'Mr. Major says that as long as you don't choose him, you can take your choice from every member of the staff in the building. He also says that if you asked his father to act as your assistant, he's sure he would be only too willing to oblige!'

Juliet made for the hardware department, keeping her fingers crossed. She knew the girl she wanted. She had seen her often behind the cash desk and had been struck by her flair for clothes, her taste and her looks, all of which added up to excellent potential for a boutique sales assistant.

She approached the girl, who was puzzled when Juliet asked her name. 'Selina Fawcett,' she replied.

As gently as she could, Juliet explained why she wanted her. The girl's eyes lit up. 'You'll have to get permission from the hardware manager.'

'I'll fix that,' said Juliet, and she did. The hardware manager was annoyed, but seeing Juliet's determination and hearing that she had the backing of the man in charge, gave in. He marched off to the staff manager in search of another assistant.

Selina proved a worthy choice. She had looked down at the regulation black dress she was wearing, then gazed enviously at Juliet's outfit. Juliet waved her arm towards the racks. 'Take your pick, as long as it's not too outrageous, and as long as you pay for what you take, even if it's only in instalments.'

Eagerly Selina searched for what she wanted and found it. She disappeared into the fitting room and came out transformed. Life became easier for Juliet after that. She was able to take her coffee and tea breaks at reasonable times and eat her sandwiches in peace while Selina served the customers.

It was while she was having her lunch that her mother put her head round the door. Juliet went to her, delighted. 'Don't tell me you've come to patronize the boutique, Mum?'

Cynthia laughed. 'No. I've been having a chat with Warren in his office. He phoned this morning and invited me to have a look at some washing machines which have just arrived. They're not on sale yet. They're upstairs being priced in some special place—'

'The marking-off room?' Juliet suggested.

'That's it. Ridiculous price they're selling at, and they've only got one or two scratches on them. I said I didn't mind scratches as long as they worked satisfactorily. Warren told me the wholesaler had guaranteed that, but had to slash the price because they were seconds.'

'Are you having one?'

'If your father doesn't mind.'

'But don't you think he might because of who's selling it to you?'

Cynthia sighed. 'I do hope not. It's so silly of him to be like that. It's not as though Warren means anything to me these days.' Juliet felt a spurt of joy and a tremendous release from the anxiety that had worried her so much lately. Her mother didn't return Warren's love – might not even be aware of it. But her mother's next words had her worried again.

'Warren's invited me to lunch.'

Juliet frowned. 'Are you going?'

'Why not? It's only in the store restaurant. It'll be a nice change not to have to cook for myself.' She bent down and kissed her daughter. 'See you this evening, darling.'

Cynthia went out, leaving a trace of perfume behind. It was something she rarely used, and the lingering scent disturbed Juliet, renewing her anxieties about her mother's relationship with her one-time fiancé.

When Malcolm called for her that evening, Juliet told him about the washing machine scoop which Majors had pulled off. She didn't bother to warn him to keep the fact to himself. She didn't care any more. She sensed his interest by the questions he asked.

'I couldn't tell you the name of the wholesaler. If you want to know, find out for yourself.'

'I will, darling, I will. Be prepared to see me some time wandering about like an interested customer in Major's precious store. I know I'm not in the electrical department at Curlews, but I'd give a lot to have our own back on that nasty so-and-so for giving you the push for something you didn't do.'

She shrugged. It was Malcolm's business what he did about the washing machines. 'I'll have to get another job soon. I've been scanning the ads in the local paper, but there's been nothing suitable for me yet. Everything I see that might be right for me carries a much lower salary than I'm getting at Majors. It'll be such a let-down for my parents if I have to take home less money. But it won't be long before Drew starts getting restive and asking me when I'm leaving. I can see the signs.'

As Juliet walked past the front of the store one morning she decided it was time she was allocated some window space. As soon as she arrived she changed and asked Selina to take charge for a while.

'I'm going to the fourth floor to the art section. I'm mixing with my own kind – as a certain acquaintance of mine would say.' She didn't name the acquaintance.

When she tapped on the art room door, there was no reply, so she walked in. Seated on high stools at benches, or sprawling over long tables, were an assortment of oddly dressed young men and women. She watched for a while as they ruled, measured and painted. They were working on direction signs, making sketches of new goods for press advertisements and ruling out elaborate lettering for the forthcoming sales.

She was completely ignored. Feeling strangely at home, despite the fact that she might have been a speck of dust as far as those dedicated artists were concerned, she crept round watching them work, experiencing a sharp stab of nostalgia for what she had left behind at the school of art. Her eyes wandered and she saw a small group working on some slogans, and she caught her breath.

Make Mine Majors, one of them said. *You get more for less at Majors,* said another. *Major Reductions,* announced a third. Her slogans, her ideas for bringing the store up to date! So her suggestions for giving the store a new image had not fallen on deaf ears. Drew had taken them to heart and soon a new store would be emerging from the old, one with greater popular appeal, playing and perhaps even beating Curlews at their own game!

'What's all this?' she asked one of the artists.

He shrugged. 'Directive from the top,' he muttered, without removing his eyes from his work. 'They dictate, we obey.' Then he raised his head and stared. It wasn't a friendly stare, nor were his words. 'What do you want?'

'To talk about being given some window space.'

He gestured towards the door with his thumb. 'Display, next door but two.'

Display was different. The occupants of the room were gathered in a circle, leaning on the nearest available support and talking. They noticed her as soon as she went in. They too were slightly belligerent. Again she was asked, what did she want?

'Some window space.'

Two of the young men roared with laughter. Another groaned.

'You're joking,' someone said. 'You have to take your place in the queue.'

'What's your line?' a girl asked.

'Boutique.'

'The one they've just opened? You haven't got a hope.' The girl counted on her fingers. 'There's about a dozen in front of you. Hardware for their special offer. Coats for their knock-down bargains of small sizes that wouldn't sell at the proper price. Underwear, shoes, furnishings ... Need I go on?'

'But,' Juliet said, frowning, 'I must have *some* publicity. How are people to know about the boutique if I'm not given any window space?'

'Oh, you'll get window space,' one of the lounging young

men said. 'In about three months' time.' Three months? She'd be gone by then.

'But that's ridiculous!'

'Couldn't agree more, but that's how it is.'

'I've got some good ideas I want to try out before – before—' She couldn't tell them she was under notice to leave. 'As soon as possible,' she finished lamely.

'Who hasn't got good ideas?' The girl sighed. 'Give it up, dear.' She took out a pad and pencil. 'We'll put your name on the list. We'll look you up in say, ten weeks and work out something between us. With any luck two or three weeks after that you might get your window space.'

'Thanks,' Juliet said shortly, going to the door. She nearly added, 'For nothing.'

She was sitting in the office at lunch-time finishing her sandwiches when Malcolm strolled into the boutique. She heard his voice and when she joined him he was eyeing Selina with as much dedicated interest as a judge eyes an entrant in a beauty contest.

'Hallo,' said Juliet and he jumped guiltily. 'I didn't know you had a roving eye, Malcolm.'

'You'd be surprised what I have got, darling,' he replied, addressing Juliet, but keeping his eyes on her assistant.

Selina, obviously taken with him, smiled and said, 'My name's Selina. What's yours?'

He looked at Juliet. 'Shall I tell her? Or is it a dark secret?'

Juliet shrugged. 'Tell her if you like. After all, we're just good friends, aren't we?'

Malcolm said to Selina, dipping his head in Juliet's direction, 'Don't take any notice of her. She's made it sound worse than it really is.' He held out his hand. 'The name's Malcolm. You new round here?'

'New to the boutique, not new to Majors. Miss Bourne got me moved from Hardware to here.'

Malcolm made a face. 'Miss Bourne, is it? On our dignity, aren't we, darling?'

She frowned, showing her irritation. 'I am supposed to be the buyer. Others show respect to buyers even if you don't.'

'Temporary buyers included?' Malcolm sat himself on a

chair and put his feet up on one of the circular display stands.

'What's the matter with you?' Juliet snapped. 'Showing off?'

Malcolm merely smiled and offered her a cigarette. 'You know I don't smoke,' she said. 'Nor does Selina, or any of Majors' staff, while on duty.'

'Implying that Curlews' staff do?' He shrugged, lighting his cigarette and releasing the smoke. 'So what if we do? Only when the management's not around, though.'

A girl came in trailing her boy-friend behind her. He hesitated at the door, saw Malcolm, and found the courage to go in with her. Malcolm stayed where he was, his feet still propped up, and watched the couple wandering round the racks. The young man took out a pair of trousers and held them against himself, asking his girl-friend what she thought of them.

Juliet was pleased. Was she going to have her first male customer? Apparently she was. The girl bought a long skirt, her young man the trousers. As they went out, Malcolm grinned.

'You owe me commission on that sale, Juliet. If I hadn't been here, her boy-friend would have been too scared to come in.'

'Why have you come, anyway?' Juliet's good-humour was only partially restored. 'To snoop around the electrical department, as you said?'

'That and,' he took her hand, 'to tell you I love you.' He winked broadly at Selina.

There were footsteps and Drew Major stood in the entrance. Malcolm didn't drop her hand, but put it to his lips instead.

Drew fixed her with his eyes. 'Miss Bourne, if you choose to allow your boy-friend to make love to you in the privacy of your office, that is your affair. But if you let him do it here, in this boutique, with customers in and out all the time, I shall have no alternative but to remove you from your position as a buyer and put someone else in your place for the rest of your time with us.'

Juliet tugged her hand from Malcolm's, started to apologize, but Malcolm cut in, 'You're exaggerating just a little, *sir*.' He lowered his feet to the floor and stubbed out his cigarette. 'When I make love to Juliet,' his eyes rose indolently to Drew's, 'I – er – go a little farther than holding her hand. I do it properly.'

His tone abrasive, Drew said, ignoring Malcolm as if he didn't exist, 'When your visitor has gone, Miss Bourne, I wish to see you in your office.'

Momentarily the loser, Malcolm turned, caught Juliet round the neck and kissed her full on the lips. ' 'Bye, darling, see you later.' He raised his hand to Selina. 'See you some time.' Selina nodded, smiling and not bothering to hide her admiration.

Malcolm turned at the door, knowing three pairs of eyes were watching him. He made the most of his exit. 'By the way, darling,' he said to Juliet, 'I got the information I wanted.' He saluted Drew insolently and left.

So now Malcolm knew the name of the wholesalers who had supplied those washing machines. Instead of the pleasure she had expected to feel at the prospect of getting even with Major and Son she felt afraid. Her standing in the eyes of Drew Major was bad enough. This could only make things worse.

She followed Drew into her office. She was on the defensive even before he could begin to speak. 'I'm sorry, Mr. Major, but I didn't invite him. He just walked in.' Drew sat on the only chair, leaving her standing. He crossed his legs and leaned back, his expression cynical. 'Anyway,' she was belligerent now, 'I don't see what harm he was doing.'

Drew raised his eyebrows. 'Just use your imagination, Miss Bourne. As an artist you're allegedly well endowed with it. What would happen if every girl on my staff allowed her boy-friend to visit her during store hours and sit as your boy-friend was doing, feet up, smoking and holding his lady love's hand?'

She frowned uncertainly. 'But, Mr. Major, the fact that he was there actually had a good effect on sales. A young man came in with his girl-friend, and he bought something, for himself.'

'A young *man*?'

'Haven't you heard of unisex clothes? I've got plenty in stock. If Malcolm hadn't been there, the young man would have run a mile. I could see that by the way he hesitated at the door.'

'Oh, good for you, Miss Bourne!' She could have hit him for his sarcasm. 'Perhaps you'd like Majors to adopt your boy-friend as a mascot and make him a permanent fixture in the boutique so as to encourage dozens of young men in?' He rose. 'My advice to you is to keep your boy-friend in his place – which is Curlews, not Majors.'

She sighed. 'Yes, Mr. Major. What did you want to see me about, Mr. Major?'

'The garden party. I take it you're coming?' She shook her head. He frowned. 'Why not?'

'I just don't want to. You can't make me. It's outside office hours.'

'But my father particularly wants you to go.'

'I can't see what difference it makes if I don't. No one will miss me, least of all you. So I thought I'd relieve you of my presence by staying away.'

'My feelings don't come into it. It's my father I'm thinking of. For some reason he – er – seems to be fond of you. He's the one who'll be disappointed.' He made for the door.

'Mr. Major?' He turned, eyebrows raised. 'This morning I asked Display for some window space. They said I couldn't have it for at least three months.'

'Well?'

'In three months I'll be gone, won't I?'

'Perhaps. So why should you worry whether you get window space or not?'

'Even if I'm leaving, I've still got the interests of the boutique at heart. I – I want to see it succeed. After all, I've been in on it from the start.'

'It's your baby, so you want to see it thrive, even if it is eventually taken from you and adopted by someone else?'

She dropped her eyes. 'That's rather a brutal way of putting it, but yes, I'd like to see it do well before I go – if there's time.'

There was a long silence. He said softly, 'You're not under sentence of death, Miss Bourne.'

'It seems like it to me, Mr. Major,' she whispered.

'Juliet?' She raised her eyes, devoid of hope. 'I—' He checked himself, went to the door again, then stood still as though a thought had struck him. When he turned back he was smiling. 'I'll do a deal with you. If I get you this window space, will you come to the garden party?'

Her spirits lifted like a released balloon. She smiled back. 'Are you blackmailing me, Mr. Major?'

'Never!' he answered. 'Let's say that it's one good turn deserving another. Agreed?'

She nodded. 'Agreed.'

She got her window space. Later in the afternoon she had a phone call from display. A disgruntled male voice said, 'Roy Hawkins here, Display. We've received a directive from the company manager to let Miss Bourne have the window space she wants. So we've got to give Miss Bourne her darned window space in front of all the other deserving cases. We can't tell you how much we love you for going behind out backs to get what you want.'

She ignored his ill temper, asking excitedly, 'When?'

'Next week. What are you, dear? Teacher's pet? Have you got – er – connections with the company manager? I've never known him put himself out like that for anyone else.'

'No,' she answered cheerfully, 'no connections at all. Just the old feminine magnetism, you know. It never fails!' A snort from the other end closed the conversation.

As she put down the phone she realized that she was committed. Drew had kept his word, now she must keep hers. She would have to go to the garden party after all.

CHAPTER SEVEN

JULIET was determined not to go to Majors' garden party alone, so she invited Malcolm to accompany her. He'd be delighted to oblige, he said. Anything Majors were giving away he'd accept with pleasure, whether it was food, drink – or information.

She did not bother to dress up. Selina, who had been to Major garden parties before, told her it was a very informal affair. 'We usually lounge about round the garden or, if the weather's fine, swim in the pool. If it rains, we gather in the large drawing-room and eat and drink and talk.'

The sun shone obligingly, rising to a crescendo of heat in the afternoon when even the tar on the road surfaces showed signs of melting.

'Who could ask for more?' Malcolm demanded of no one in particular as they took the bus across the town to the Major residence. 'The sun, a beautiful girl beside me and a garden party at Majors. Incidentally,' he hooked his arm in hers, 'watch the local paper on Monday for a splash advertisement by Curlews.' He grinned. 'Something about washing machines.'

'You haven't told them?' Malcolm looked smug. 'But, Malcolm, that's a breach of confidence.'

'I don't see that it is.' He seemed hurt as though she was deserting him. 'You wanted to get your own back on your boss, didn't you, for firing you for something you didn't do?'

'All the same, it was a pretty mean trick to let things get as far as that.'

He squeezed her arm. 'Competition, dear. It's what makes love and the business world go round. Life in either sphere would be dull without it.'

Someone had put daisy chains round the necks of the lions. Someone else had tied large pieces of paper to their tails bearing the words 'Going cheap.' So the inscrutable creatures looked a little more approachable as Juliet pulled Malcolm behind her and rang the doorbell.

It was answered by the housekeeper, Kate, but Mildred

Major hovered in the background. She failed to recognize Juliet and said, 'The garden party is in the gardens, not the house.' She eyed Juliet with as much joy as she would have eyed a dead mouse the cat had dropped on the mat. If Warren had not appeared behind his wife, Juliet would have been turned from the door like an unwelcome salesman.

Mildred and Kate melted away and Warren stretched out his hand, urging Juliet in. Because Malcolm's hand was still in her other one, he was pulled in behind her.

'My dear,' Warren kissed her on both cheeks, pretending Malcolm did not exist, just as he refused to acknowledge that Cedric Bourne existed, 'how nice of you to come.' The inevitable question followed. 'How's your mother?'

'Very well, thank you.' She looked at Malcolm, wondering whether to introduce him, but Warren simply wasn't interested.

'Come in, my dear, and have a drink.'

Feeling awkward and realizing that the invitation appeared to exclude her companion who couldn't be left standing in the hall while she drank the Major wine, she refused as gently as she could.

'I haven't long had lunch, Mr. Major. It's very kind of you, but—' She looked through the hall window, wishing she could smash the glass and dive out of it like a circus clown. It would at least get her out of her difficulties.

Warren, misinterpreting the glance said, 'Of course, you're wanting to join the others. I won't keep you, then. Get out there and enjoy yourself. I'll see you later, perhaps.'

'I like that!' Malcolm said as they walked away. 'So I'm the invisible man now.'

'He's got funny ways, Malcolm. He's like that about my father. He spends his time pretending I haven't got one and that my mother hasn't got a husband.' How much should she tell him? 'You see, a long time ago my mother was engaged to Warren Major.'

'Good grief, she had a lucky escape, didn't she? What did he do – break it off?'

'No, my mother did.'

Malcolm was muttering, 'Good for her,' when they turned the corner and found the garden party in full swing.

Girls in bikinis were sunbathing on the sacred Major

lawns, couples were sitting on the benches in the rose gardens, others, men mostly, were playing cricket. The tennis courts were in use and in the distance the swimming pool appeared to be highly popular.

Older members of the staff were strolling along the gravelled paths dressed stiffly in their best. They looked quite out of place in both mood and manner amongst the scantily clothed, relaxed equality of the younger set. Miss Skimpton had on her best hat. It was made of swathed blue satin with rosebuds peeping from the folds and it was perched on top of her head as precisely as if she had lowered it there with a crane. Mrs. Rouse of Separates was self-consciously overdressed in a bright pink trouser suit and was suffering from the heat.

As Juliet saw Drew, Malcolm saw Selina. Juliet's stomach muscles contracted with an odd sort of apprehension. Malcolm's facial muscles expanded into a grin and formed into an appreciative whistle.

He clutched Juliet's hand. 'Keep a tight hold of me, darling,' he murmured. 'Did you say her name was Selina?'

Juliet tore her eyes from Drew's – he had seen Malcolm's movement – and looked at Selina. She was certainly stunning in her pink and white check bikini, her long fair hair partly covered by a matching sun-hat. She saw Malcolm and took up an inviting pose.

Drew approached, his face as cold as his father's had been warm. Juliet wondered how soon she could slip away. She had done her duty, she had seen the man who had wanted her to come. Perhaps in half an hour or so she could plead a headache. Malcolm would probably be delighted. It would leave him a clear field for making up to Selina, who certainly wouldn't repulse his approaches.

Drew said, 'Nice of you to come, Miss Bourne.' His eyes took in her clinging purple low-cut top tucked into vivid yellow trousers. She could almost hear him thinking, 'Major boutique stock?'

She answered his unspoken query defiantly. 'Yes, it's from the Major racks, Mr. Major, but I haven't stolen it. I've paid the full price. I didn't even deduct my staff discount.'

Malcolm sniggered, but Drew, like his father, pretended he wasn't there.

'I don't doubt you for one moment, Miss Bourne. And I'm sure it's far more effective on a figure like yours than suspended uninvitingly from a hanger in the boutique.'

Malcolm's arm jerked up to her shoulders and pulled her close. She's my girl, the action said, hands off.

'Have you found the drinks table?' Drew's eyes shifted to Malcolm. 'It's on the house.'

Malcolm pulled Juliet towards it. 'Somehow I could do with one, especially if it's free. Come on, darling.'

Drew drifted away. Unreasonably disappointed, Juliet unhooked her arm from Malcolm's and told him, 'You go. I'm not thirsty.'

Malcolm shrugged and left her. She wandered among the roses, remembering the last time she had done so, with Drew at her side. He had been interviewing her for the job and her expectations had been so high she had actually looked forward to being an employee of his. Now the wheel had turned full circle and through no fault of her own, her time with them had almost run out.

She passed the fountain spurting from the middle of the pond and remembered how last time the wind had blown the spray all over her. Drew had stood and watched as she'd tried to dry herself. He hadn't offered to help and it had offended her, but she knew better now. Drew Major never helped anybody, unless it was to his advantage.

'Lost in thought?' She jumped as he appeared at her side. 'And all alone?' He looked round. 'Where's Romeo?'

'Drinking, probably.'

'You looked a hundred miles away. What were you thinking, Miss Bourne?'

She smiled up at him, his nearness making her bold. 'Bad thoughts about you.'

'My word,' he glanced down at her rear as if measuring it up for size, 'you're asking for trouble! Come on, out with it. What were these terrible thoughts about me?'

'I dare not tell you. You might throw me in the pond.'

He moved swiftly behind her and caught her under the armpits, jerking her backwards against him. 'You're provoking me, Miss Bourne, and that's dangerous. The outfit you're wearing's provocative enough without your words goading me still more.'

She struggled and he let her go. She faced him, her colour

high. 'Your girl-friend might be looking, Mr. Major.'

'My girl-friend isn't here, Miss Bourne.'

'Why not? Wouldn't she deign to mix with the Major and Son rabble?'

'How did you guess?'

'So you're on the prowl for someone to take her place — purely on a temporary basis, of course.'

He narrowed his eyes. 'Do you really want to be thrown into that pond?' She shook her head violently. 'Then behave yourself, Miss Bourne, *if* you can.'

'Yes, Mr. Major. *Sir*.'

He swung her round to face him, but after a few seconds controlled himself. 'Listen to me, young Juliet. My father asked me to be nice to you today. For heaven's sake help me by being nice back. Otherwise, I hate to think what I'll do to you before the party's over.'

'There's one way to be nice to me. Keep away from me.'

His arm dropped from her shoulders. 'Is that what you want me to do?'

Her heart was pounding, her pulses racing. She wanted him to pull her close again and . . . 'Yes,' she said.

He walked away. Well, she'd asked for it, hadn't she? She wandered disconsolately back to the lawns, searching for Malcolm. No need to conjure up a headache now. She had one, sitting on top of her head as if one of those stone lions had made a new home for itself there.

She glanced up at the house and saw Mildred Major through one of the windows arranging flowers in a pottery vase on the windowsill. She was as absorbed in her task as if she were alone in the world. With an infantile concentration, she was doing her best to forget that her gardens had been invaded by hundreds of strangers, all of whom, in her opinion, had no business to be there at all. She was pretending, as no doubt she pretended every night that she had no husband, that everything was normal. As a family, Juliet reflected, they were very good at pretending.

She looked for Selina, feeling sure that if she found her, she would also find Malcolm, and she was right. Selina was stretched out on the grass and Malcolm was reclining on his elbow admiring her from top to toe. If that's his loyalty to me, Juliet thought, then she's welcome to him. She pushed her way to the drinks table and helped herself to a glass of lemonade. Seeing all the other couples laughing together and walking hand in hand forced her to acknowledge just how lonely she felt.

She had sent Drew away and Selina had taken possession of Malcolm. She wished she had never brought him, she wished she'd never come. Warren wouldn't really have missed her, whatever Drew had said.

She felt Drew watching her and, putting down her empty glass, pushed her way into a group of laughing people. She didn't know who they were, but she had to do something to hide from his accusing, unsympathetic gaze.

'Well, well,' said one of the young men whom she identified as Roy Hawkins from Display, 'if it isn't the company manager's pet. All alone, dearie? Where's the boyfriend?' She knew he didn't mean Malcolm. Instinctively her eyes sought out Drew and Roy turned to follow her gaze. 'Yes, he's over there, isn't he? Keeping his distance, in case the staff start guessing things and putting rumours around about you and him?' He glanced at his friends. 'Hey, you lot, let's show this pretty little thing what we do to girls who use their – er – influence,' with his hands he fashioned the shape of a woman, 'to get what they want from the man at the top.'

Before she could utter a word of protest, he had scooped her up and run with her to the edge of the swimming pool. She screamed, 'No, *no*, I can't swim!' but he didn't believe her.

'One,' he said, swinging her tantalizingly over the edge, 'two,' he drew her back, '*three*!' He tossed her in. She screamed a second time and the moment before she hit the water she screamed 'No!' again.

She went under, her arms and legs flailing, trying to grab something, anything to keep her afloat. She surfaced and gasped, then down she went again. As she came up once more she was aware of shouts and screams from all directions.

She lashed out madly with her limbs again, but it was useless. She knew it was nearly over. She gasped agonizingly and the waters closed over her head again. A splash and a shout above her penetrated her consciousness for a few seconds. Hands seized her under the armpits and dragged her up, turning her on to her back. 'Drew, Drew,' she gasped, then everything went blank.

She didn't come round again until she stirred to find herself flat on her face on the ground, fighting for breath while someone seemed to be grasping her ribs, pressing and releasing them alternately. Water was coming from her throat and nostrils and slowly her breathing became more normal.

She heard someone say, 'I'm sorry, sir. I didn't realize she couldn't swim.'

'But she told you, you half-witted idiot!'

'I thought she was fooling.'

'Get away, all of you. Go on, enjoy yourselves. It's all over, she's safe, so for heaven's sake, go away!' She heard Malcolm's voice, then Drew's. 'I don't want you either, Watling. I'll deal with her. I don't need help.'

Arms came round her and gathered her up and she flopped against a man's hard body, feeling the hairs of his chest soft against her cheek. 'I've got you safely now, so hold on to me, Juliet,' the man said, and she did with the little strength she had left in her. It couldn't be Drew, she decided, because the voice was so tender. Drew would never speak to her like that.

He carried her into a room and lowered her gently on to a couch. She opened her eyes and caught him unawares. Drew was gazing down at her with an odd mixture of compassion and anxiety and his look didn't make sense. He was wearing only his swimming briefs and his shoulders were glistening with water.

As soon as he saw her eyes open his expression changed to an awareness of the need for action. 'What,' he asked, 'have you got on underneath that gear?' He didn't wait for her answer. He bent down and unhooked the waist band of her trousers and undid the slide fastener.

When she realized what he was doing, she started struggling. 'No,' she cried, 'no, no!' She gripped his hands and tried to stop him.

'Good grief, girl, what do you think I'm going to do, rape you? Nothing was farther from my mind. Come on, lift up, we've got to get these wet things off you.' He tugged off the trousers and saw the briefs of her bikini underneath. 'Why, in heaven's name, aren't you running around in next to nothing like all the other girls? You're wearing a two-piece swimsuit.'

'I can't swim—'

'As well I know,' he growled.

'So what was the use? I'd only be showing off if I did.'

'And what do you think all the others are doing, if not showing off their figures? And, my word, you could beat the lot of them at it if you tried. Come on,' his voice was brisk, 'let's take off that soaking wet top.'

She sat up and he helped her out of it. He disappeared into another room and emerged with a large soft bath towel. He threw it at her. 'Dry yourself with that.'

She looked down and said weakly, 'My bikini top's wet.'

'I'll give you one of my shirts to wear, then you can take that off, too.'

She heard a drawer open and close and a shirt came flying through the door. 'Put that on while I get myself dry and changed.'

When he returned he was wearing a pink open-necked shirt and fawn well-fitting trousers. He watched her drying her hair. The shirt he had lent her reached only to the lower edge of her briefs and he smiled at her efforts to pull it down.

'Where are we?' she asked.

'In my apartment. I had a wing of the house converted into a self-contained flat for my own exclusive use.' He sat on the couch beside her. 'I don't usually bring my employees here. You're an exception.'

She rubbed at her briefs under the shirt in an attempt to dry them. She started shivering. Reaction was setting in and with it, disillusion. His reminder that she was only an employee had started it off, like the first boulder that precipitated a landslide. 'I don't know why you bothered to save me.'

'I appreciate your gratitude to me for having saved your life.'

'I'm sorry, but it would have been so much easier for everyone if you'd let me drown.'

He gripped her shoulders and jerked her round. 'What the hell are you talking about? Let you drown? How could I let you drown?'

She tried to pull away. 'At least it would have got me out of your hair.'

He leaned towards her and exerting his strength, pulled her forward and against him. 'How do you know I want to get you out of my hair?' His voice had softened and she guessed his intention. She began to struggle. She mustn't let him kiss her. He had done it once before – to make his girl-friend jealous – and she had never forgotten the effect of his lips on hers. If he did it again, and in these circumstances . . .

'No!' she cried. 'You can't kiss me. You can't kiss a thief! That's what you call me, isn't it? To you I'm a thief,' she was twisting her face right and left away from his mouth, 'I steal transistor radios, I'm not to be trusted. You should have let me drown!'

Now his lips had nearly found their target. 'You're at it again, aren't you? Trying to destroy yourself, to tear yourself apart. Well, my girl, destruction may be your second name – it even seems to run in the family – but I swear you're not going to destroy me as your mother nearly destroyed my father.'

His arms forced her to be still and accept his kisses. They were devastating and the effect shattering. When at last she was submitting because she had neither the strength nor the will to do otherwise, he threw her back on to the cushions and walked about the room. She was drained of life and totally subdued.

'You should have let me drown,' she muttered again, her eyes closed, her lips stiff and painful, 'it would at least have put me out of my misery.'

He lifted his hand to his head. 'Heaven preserve me from the artistic temperament! *What* misery?' He stood in front of her, legs apart, hands in pockets. 'Come on, what misery? I want to know.' His voice was sharp.

How could she tell him? The misery of loving a man she knew would never love her?

Receiving no answer, he asked, 'You mean the loss of your job?' He wandered away and came back. 'Juliet, I want to tell you—'

'How sorry you are? Oh, don't apologize. That would only be rubbing salt into the wound.'

He caught her wrist and jerked her upright. 'Will you let

me talk and listen to me for a change?' He released her and she flopped back, rubbing her wrist. He resumed his walking. 'I want to tell you that last night we caught the thief. I knew all along that it wasn't you, but the security officer was not so easy to convince. He insisted on positive proof of your innocence.'

He sat beside her. 'You might not know that the television scanners – the cameras – are left on even when the store is shut and they remain on until midnight, when the store lights go out automatically.'

He walked about again. 'So every night, after the store closed, Mr. Cunningham, his assistant and I remained behind, watching the closed-circuit television monitor and keeping track of every move the cleaners and caretakers made around the building. Because Mr. Robinson was the one who had "found" you, as he said, hiding away, I suspected him most of all. Last night we were watching each floor – you may not know that we can "tune in" on the small monitor and watch any area of any floor and get the picture we most want to see on the larger screen – and Robinson did it again. He stole something else, quite unaware that three people upstairs could see what he was up to. We had parked our cars right away from the store and he thought we had all gone home. He was caught red-handed. When Mr. Cunningham challenged him with the theft of the radio too, he admitted it. So tomorrow we advertise for a new caretaker.'

He sat beside her again and smiled as relief transformed her face. 'Well,' he said invitingly, 'do you want to fling your arms round *my* neck now and kiss *me*?'

She laughed. 'So I keep my job?'

He nodded. 'Why do you think I've let you stay on all this time? If I'd really suspected you, I'd have thrown you out long ago.'

'It seems inadequate to say thank you.'

'I don't expect your thanks. I'm the one who really should apologize, for the agony and suspense you've been through. Did you ever tell your parents? No? Thank goodness for that.'

He became restless again. 'Where's Romeo?'

'Finding himself another Juliet.'

'Do you mind?'

'It would be all the same if I did, wouldn't it? He's chasing Selina, who isn't running very hard the other way.'

'You're letting her steal your boy-friend without putting up a fight? Surely that's out of character?'

'I only fight for what I really want.'

'Do you, Juliet? Always?'

She raised her eyes and met his for a few seconds, wondering what he was implying. She frowned and looked away. 'No, not always. For instance, you can't put up a fight, can you, when your two hands are tied behind your back?'

'What exactly do you mean by that?'

What did she mean? Make a man love her, fight for a man with a girl-friend like Camille, a man moreover who had vowed that if he ever married — 'if' being the important word — the woman he chose would have to be perfect, made to measure, as he had put it, in every respect?

'Those roses are beautiful.' She rose and walked across to a vase in the centre of a circular glass-topped table. She bent down to catch their scent.

'Don't change the subject.'

'The perfume's marvellous.'

He selected one from the vase and gave it to her. It was a deep red. She took it, and twirled it between her fingers. 'Now will you tell me what you mean?'

She continued to twist the rose around. 'Oh, damn! I've pricked my finger.' She put it to her lips to stop the bleeding. He pulled her into the bedroom, found a plaster in a drawer and applied it to the wound.

She thanked him and shivered, looking at the bed, the luxurious furnishings, the thick carpet. She felt genuinely cold now and returned to the living-room to look for her clothes.

He followed her. 'They're still wet,' he said.

The phone rang. It appeared to be an internal call from the housekeeper. He looked at Juliet. 'There's a young man making enquiries about you, name of Malcolm Watling. Interested?'

'No,' she answered defiantly.

He said into the receiver, 'Tell him politely to go away. Miss Bourne doesn't want to see him.'

He looked her up and down and laughed. 'You look a bit pathetic. But alluring at the same time.' His gaze lowered.

'Must be all that leg. Come on, I'll take you home. Unless you want to stay? The sun would dry your swimsuit.'

'No, thanks. I'll go home.' She picked up her wet clothes. 'What about this?' She plucked at his shirt.

He waved it away. 'Return it any time. Come through the house. That way we'll miss the crowd.' Still holding the rose, she followed him.

They met Warren in the hall. His eyes opened wide and he said, 'What happened to you?'

'She – er – fell in the pool. I rescued her and she's been drying out ever since.'

Warren was immediately concerned. 'Come in, my dear, and have a drink.'

'I think not, Father, thanks. She wants to get home.' He felt her hair. 'She's still a bit damp.'

'Well, Juliet,' Warren said, 'did you enjoy the garden party, the part before you fell in the pool?'

'Yes, thanks.' She wanted to say, 'But I've enjoyed the other part more.'

Warren looked at his son. 'Have you told her about Robinson? And that her job with us is quite safe now? And was she pleased?'

'Delighted.' Drew smiled. 'So delighted, in fact, that I invited her to throw her arms round my neck and kiss me.' Warren looked expectant. 'Unfortunately, she declined the invitation.' Warren looked disappointed.

'Have you been nice to her, son?'

'Yes, he has, Mr. Major. Nicer than I've been to him, I'm afraid.'

Drew gave her a playful spank. 'You should have heard her abusing me!' They smiled at each other.

Warren, his eyes watchful, shook his head. 'Just like her mother again. Right below the belt, dead on target.'

'Come on, girl.' Drew put his arm across her shoulders. 'One day I'll hit her dead on target, then she'll know how it feels!'

He took her home. Outside the house, she thanked him for saving her life. 'And for being nice to me.'

'My God, are relations between us normally so bad that you actually have to thank me for being nice to you?'

She put his rose against her mouth. 'We agreed once that we were incompatible. Our temperaments, our natures, our ways of life are so different I don't think they could ever be reconciled.'

'My dear Juliet,' he took her hand and his voice was misleadingly soft, 'you're talking as though I'd just proposed marriage. I haven't – yet. Is that what you want me to do, so that you can let me down and break my heart as your mother did my father's?'

She stared at him. Why the change of mood? What had she said to bring out the cynicism in him when all seemed well – if only temporarily – between them? Her lip trembled and she snatched her hand away and got out, slamming the door. His car moved on slowly, and she ran into the house.

Malcolm phoned that evening. 'What do you mean,' he demanded, 'by saying you didn't want to see me? I was your partner, wasn't I?'

'Were you?' she asked innocently. 'Selina's got something, hasn't she? Was she worth chasing?'

'Don't be an idiot, Juliet. You really think I'm serious about her? I was only having a bit of fun. After all, you left me high and dry.'

'That was hardly my fault. If you'd been with me, Roy Hawkins wouldn't have dared to do what he did. If it hadn't been for Drew—'

'Drew, Drew! That's all you can talk about. What was he doing when you were in there so long – making love to you?'

She coloured and was glad Malcolm couldn't see her.

'Now you're being an idiot,' she said, convincingly amused at the mere suggestion. 'He had just saved me from drowning, remember? I was in a state of shock.'

Malcolm was not fully convinced. 'I wouldn't put anything past him. Don't forget he's throwing you out of your job for something you didn't do.'

'No, he's not,' she told him joyfully. 'They've caught the man who did it. I've been reinstated.'

'So you're not on your way out?'

'No. You sound disappointed! Perhaps you were hoping that with me out of the way, it would leave you free to chase Selina some more.'

'If you're going to talk like that, I'm ringing off.'

'I'll save you the trouble,' she snapped. 'I'll ring off first.' And she did. He didn't ring back.

Cynthia washed and drip-dried Drew's shirt and first thing next morning Juliet returned it to him. She took the lift to the sixth floor and went into his secretary's office, asking if Mr. Major was free.

'No,' the secretary said, 'he's got Mr. Nolan, buyer of the electrical department, with him.'

Of course, Curlews' advertisement! How could she have forgotten? The secretary was ringing him. 'Miss Bourne is here, Mr. Major. Shall I tell her to wait or—'

'No, tell her to come in,' was the terse command. 'I was just going to send for her.' The words sounded ominous, but in the circumstances how could she expect otherwise?

Mr. Nolan, a tall, thin man with a friendly face, nodded and smiled, still in ignorance of the part she had played in the washing machine intrigue, as Drew probably regarded it. But as Drew started questioning her, Mr. Nolan's smile faded.

Juliet placed the shirt, which was in a paper bag, on Drew's desk. He didn't even notice it. 'You know about this, Miss Bourne?' he asked, pointing to the newspaper opened out in front of him. His voice was edged, like the blade of a bread knife. The look in his eyes showed that he had every intention of slicing through her, piece by piece, the thinner the better.

'I – well, yes, I knew something of the sort was appearing.'

'So you're at the bottom of it, you and your precious boy-friend? Have you seen it?' She shook her head. 'Come here and look.'

She went to his side. Curlews had taken a whole page advertisement in the local paper, setting out in the largest type the printers could produce that they had acquired a bargain purchase of washing machines – the word 'seconds' was in tiny print – and their prices were undercutting all rivals and competitors. 'Our sales representative has pulled off a mind-shattering deal and you, our loyal customers, will reap the benefit of his skill in talking the wholesalers into parting with these magnificent machines at throw-away prices.'

The advertisement went on to the end of the page, its language enticing, its persuasiveness irresistible to the gullible reader.

'Our rivals,' the advertisement concluded, 'think they're offering you a bargain. Don't listen to them – we're *giving* the machines away!'

He closed the paper and looked up at her. 'So, in spite of my warnings when first offering you employment with us, you betrayed our secrets to that unscrupulous boy-friend of yours.'

'It was pure accident, Mr. Major. Your father offered my mother one of the washing machines at a very low price and when Malcolm came one evening I told him about it. He took it from there. Somehow he got the wholesaler's name from the electrical sales staff.'

Mr. Nolan stirred uneasily.

'You call that accidental, Miss Bourne? I would call it outright disloyalty, deliberately passing on information with intent to damage Major's interests.' He turned to Mr. Nolan. 'Did you know about this?'

'Not a thing, sir. I've got one or two young assistants in my department who are still gullible enough to believe anyone who tells them a tale. That's probably how it happened. I'll have to investigate.'

Drew turned back to Juliet. 'I suppose you remember the penalty for passing on secret information to our rivals? I did warn you.'

She flagged. 'Yes, Mr. Major. Instant dismissal, Mr. Major.' So they were back to square one. She was on her way out. She moved to the door. 'I'll go now, Mr. Major. I couldn't stand hanging round again waiting for the axe to fall.'

'Miss Bourne!' he shouted. She stopped in her tracks. More quietly he said, 'I'll take over from here, Mr. Nolan. Thanks for drawing my attention to it.'

'Yes, sir,' Mr. Nolan said, lifting his finger in a salute and leaving the room.

'Sit down, Miss Bourne,' the company manager said wearily. She sat down. 'Tell me why you did this.'

'So you're giving me a chance to clear myself? I don't know why. It's an ideal opportunity for you to get rid of me, Mr. Major. Why don't you take it?'

'You're at it again, Miss Bourne, intent on self-destruction. Yesterday I should have let you drown. Today I should throw you out of your job. Tomorrow you'll be suggesting I marry you and give you hell for the rest of your life. Come on, out with it. Why did you do it?'

'Because at the time, I didn't care a damn about Major and Son. I was under notice. I was so angry with you for dismissing me for a crime I didn't commit—'

'You needn't go on. You were getting your own back. A perfectly normal reaction to be expected from anyone being unjustly punished. I'll forgive you – this time.' She went to the door. 'But, Juliet—' She turned and he smiled. 'It mustn't happen again. Understand?'

She nodded and opened the door. On the other side stood Camille Wyngard, her hand raised with the intention of knocking. Juliet stood aside to let her pass and she nodded condescendingly. Drew rose, looking not over-pleased with his visitor.

'Darling,' said Camille, 'why the scowl? I haven't seen you for three whole days. Haven't you missed me?' She stared at Juliet, as if wondering why she was still there.

'Haven't you any work to do, Miss Bourne?' Drew asked sharply.

'Plenty, Mr. Major, sir,' she answered, her tone insolent.

'Why don't you keep that girl in her place?' Camille's petulant voice drifted through the door.

Juliet's footsteps, quickening with jealousy, made tiny dents in the plastic floor tiles as she walked along the corridor to the stairs. She ran down the five flights without stopping, feeling the need to let off steam somehow.

Selina greeted her, her face all innocence, 'Did you enjoy the garden party? I think your Malcolm's a dish. He wouldn't leave me – I had to persuade him to go and see how you were getting on after they threw you in the swimming pool.'

'Oh, did you! Thanks for telling me.'

Selina smiled smugly and got on with the job of tidying the racks. Dermot Edmond, the Fresco fashions sales representative, wandered in. Juliet's heart sank.

'I don't remember giving you an appointment,' she said belligerently.

'You didn't, dearie. I took a chance on finding you free. Got some new stock I'd like you to have a look at.'

'All right,' she agreed reluctantly. 'Bring it into my office.'

He spread the clothes over her chair and desk and anywhere else he could drape them. Juliet used the method she had adopted in the past, putting the clothes into separate categories of 'certainties', 'possibles' and 'rejects'.

Then she argued over the price and having reached a certain figure, refused to budge from it. 'You're getting hard,' Dermot said, sitting in her chair, elbows on desk, and gazing into her face. 'Don't get like all your colleagues, sweetie. I like 'em soft and inviting, like you are now.'

'Miss Bourne?' Juliet turned swiftly. He was there again. It was almost as if he were spying on her, creeping up to her door and listening in on the conversation. It was plain by the look in his eyes that he had heard what Dermot Edmond had said.

Dermot rose lazily. 'Free tonight?' he whispered in her ear. 'You owe me a date. You let me down last time. I went – hungry all night.'

She looked uncomfortably at Drew, knowing he had overheard. 'Miss Bourne!' His tone held a warning.

'Sorry,' she said to the sales representative. 'I've got a date already – with my boy-friend.'

Dermot shrugged. 'Better luck next time.'

'Miss Bourne, if you would kindly tie up this transaction,' Drew indicated the clothes spread around her room, 'you have a customer waiting for you in the boutique. Miss Wyngard intends to patronize *Girl Major*. I want you to give her your personal attention.'

And Juliet's personal attention Camille undeniably received. She went to disproportionate lengths to please her customer, waited patiently while each selected garment was tried on and rejected, suggested others which might be more suitable and almost ransacked the boutique in an effort to find just what her very difficult customer wanted. Juliet felt her sufferance dying a slow, painful death. If the woman goes on much longer, she told herself, I'll be rude. I won't be able to stop myself.

The turning point came when Camille tried on a particularly becoming and expensive trouser suit, regarded herself in the mirror as though she was wearing a postman's delivery sack, took it off and threw it disdainfully on the floor. Juliet's patience uttered its last gasp and expired.

'If you don't want that, and you don't want this,' she held

up each rejected garment in turn, 'and this doesn't please you, and that one you hate, then what the blazes *do* you want?'

Camille opened her mouth and forgot to close it. 'I don't think,' Juliet stormed, 'you really know what you do want. I don't think you had any intention whatsoever of buying anything from the moment you set foot in here. And I don't think,' she threw caution to the winds, 'I want you in this boutique ever again. You can take your money and your custom elsewhere.'

Selina, who had been looking on, gasped. Camille snapped her mouth shut, clicking her teeth as she did so, seized her handbag and stalked out.

Juliet sank down on the customers' chair and surveyed the chaos of rejected garments. She also did a quick mental survey of her own position. She looked at her watch. 'Three minutes to get up there,' she said aloud, 'another three to tell him what happened, five minutes to tell him what she thinks of me and,' she calculated again, 'two minutes for him to recover and call me up there. That gives me thirteen minutes to find another job.' She looked at Selina. 'Not enough, really, is it?'

'You think he'll fire you?' Selina sounded really afraid.

'No doubt about it.' Juliet smiled. 'But it was worth it! She's been asking for it from the beginning. If I'm going to be shot at dawn, my goodness, it was a grand preliminary to the execution!'

She combed her hair and touched up her face with extra make-up. 'I might as well look my best for the executioner.'

On cue, the phone rang. Drew Major's secretary asked if Miss Bourne would kindly go to the company manager's office. Solemnly Juliet shook hands with Selina, who giggled, spoiling the dramatic effect. 'I'll remember you in my will,' Juliet promised, and obeyed the summons.

Camille was in there, of course, her eyes large with wrath, her cheeks blotched with temper.

'I understand,' Drew began at once, 'that you've been unbelievably rude to Miss Wyngard. I also understand that you said some unforgivable things to her, making accusations and insinuations and telling her never to darken the boutique doors again.'

Juliet looked at Drew. Was he being serious, or could she

detect an underlying touch of amusement in his voice? His expression gave nothing away. 'I'm sorry, Mr. Major,' she said, 'but there are times when one is goaded beyond control.'

'You, Miss Bourne,' he said through his teeth, 'are telling me!'

'I'm only human, Mr. Major. If a customer is given every possible attention, as I gave Miss Wyngard, bringing out almost the entire contents of the boutique in order to please her and satisfy her requirements, only to have them all rejected as "useless" and "rubbish", what am I expected to do? Grovel at her feet? Kiss the ground she walks on and tell her I'm always at her service?'

'Miss Bourne,' his voice was dangerously soft, 'may I remind you that in all the circumstances, it would be advisable for you to become just a little more, shall we say, penitent and even submissive?'

She swallowed her defiance and tried to look docile. 'I beg your pardon, Mr. Major.' She had meant it to sound sincere, but it came out as sarcasm, and his eyebrows rose. 'I shall have to cultivate the necessary subservience that customers – who are *always* right – seem to expect. I'll have to learn to pander to their every whim, and admit that my status is less than the dust. I'll have to learn to be self-effacing, obsequious, servile . . .'

'*You'll have to learn when to shut up, Miss Bourne!*'

Juliet recognized the extreme anger in his voice. Now she really had gone too far. She apologized to him, then she apologized to his girl-friend. 'I'm sorry, Miss Wyngard, for being rude to you. I had no right to speak to you like that. I'll be glad to see you in the boutique any time you'd like to come.' Had she prostrated herself enough?

Apparently she had. Camille Wyngard bowed her head graciously, and told Drew she would be going now.

'See Miss Wyngard to the lift, then come back here.'

He really was rubbing it in! She opened the door for Camille and walked by her side to the lift, pressing the button and willing the lift to appear quickly.

'My goodness,' said Camille, her eyes gleaming, 'Drew really does hate you, doesn't he?'

'The feeling, Miss Wyngard,' Juliet lied defiantly, 'is mutual.'

'You know,' Camille considered her, 'that time you were at his house and he kissed you goodbye, I really thought he had you in mind as my successor, but—'

The lift arrived and the doors opened. Camille stepped in.

'But,' Juliet finished for her, 'how wrong you were!' The lift doors closed and whisked Camille away. Juliet walked slowly back to Drew's office.

'Yes, Mr. Major?' she asked wearily.

'One more thing, Miss Bourne. I thought I told you no fraternizing with sales reps?'

'You did, Mr. Major. But I can't stop them if they pay me the compliment of fraternizing with me, can I?'

'You can at least put them in their place.'

She was about to answer back, thought better of it and decided on docility. 'Yes, Mr. Major.'

'Don't let it happen again, Miss Bourne.'

'No, Mr. Major.'

He was round the desk and facing her. 'And don't be so damned impudent!'

'I didn't intend to be, Mr. Major.' Her tone was tearful. 'Even when I'm polite you say I'm being rude. Whatever I do I can't seem to please you.' In spite of herself, her eyes filled with tears.

He looked at her oddly, pushing his hands into his pockets. 'I think you'd better go, Juliet.'

'Yes, Mr. Major,' she whispered, and went.

CHAPTER EIGHT

JULIET spent the evening committing to paper her ideas for the window display. She decided on the stock she wanted to promote, which included some of the slower-selling lines, then selected the most eye-catching colours.

Next morning she left Selina in charge while she joined the two members of the display staff who had been allocated to her – she was glad Roy Hawkins was not one of them – in the large shop window.

It took her a few minutes to adjust to being stared at by passers-by, then she became so absorbed in directing the others, a girl and a young man, that she forgot to feel like a goldfish in a bowl.

In the centre of the display, which, she told them, was to be arranged in the form of a 'room', she wanted several pairs of trousers in assorted colours, strung up like a giant lampshade. This they did, then at her suggestion they borrowed a small coffee table from the furniture department and searched the wine department for dummy bottles which they placed on the table. Beside them they stood wine glasses from china and glass. Grouped around it were four male and three female figures wearing 'party' clothes.

Across the 'room' was a record player borrowed from Radio and Electrical, and around it were a group of 'dancers' wearing casuals and separates. As a backcloth they pinned up shaggy waistcoats, pull-on hats and matching scarves.

'Right,' said Juliet, standing back and admiring the finished product, 'I think everything is there except the kitchen sink!'

They laughed and complimented her on her idea. 'We've got another couple of windows to dress after this,' one of them told her. 'Then we've had instructions to smother the windows with Major's new slogans. Rumour has it it's part of the store's new policy. You know, *Major Reductions, Money Means More at Majors*, and so on, to bring in new custom and make the place more approachable. They must have got some advertising firm working on it and they've come up with an "appeal to the people" angle.'

Juliet wanted to tell them, 'I was the brain behind it,' but modesty – or perhaps the feeling that they wouldn't have believed her anyway – held her back. But it didn't hold back her delight at the thought that Drew had taken her advice and put her suggestions into practice.

Someone tapped on the window and Juliet turned. Malcolm was outside grinning at her, his nose pressed against the window pane. He made a few faces, trying to get her to respond, but she maintained her disdainful expression. Good-humouredly he gave up, blew her two kisses, one with each hand, waved and passed on.

'Boy-friend?' asked the display girl.

'Ex,' Juliet answered offhandedly. 'He's got someone else in his sights.'

'If you want him, fight for him.'

'I don't particularly.' And she meant it.

The window display increased sales. All day long young girls and their boy-friends came in, inspected, bought and left clutching their purchases.

'I'm tired,' said Selina at the end of the afternoon, and sank down in the chair.

'For goodness' sake,' Juliet looked at her anxiously, 'don't go and be ill on me. Have an early night.'

But next day Selina was away. Her mother telephoned. 'Off colour,' she explained. 'I'm keeping her in bed.'

Juliet rang the staff manager and asked for a temporary assistant, but no one could be spared, he said. She had to face it, she was on her own. The window display continued to bring in the public in their dozens. There was no time for a mid-morning break and she even had to eat her lunch in between serving customers. She was interrupted so often she gave up and put the rest away untouched. The coffee from her flask grew cold in the cup, so she poured it back to take home and throw away. Unable to leave the boutique for the afternoon break, she worked on without a pause until closing time.

Then she sank down in the chair as Selina had done the evening before. Her face was flushed, her head was throbbing and her body ached with hunger. She thought of her sandwiches, but she had gone beyond food. There was still the till to be emptied, the money counted and handed to the cashier.

Long after everyone had gone she sat at her desk making up the accounts. Then the boutique had to be tidied, discarded clothes to be returned to hangers and put back on to the racks – work which was usually tackled by Selina as each customer left.

She was dragging on her coat when Drew came in. Her eyes opened wide. 'How did you know I was still here?'

'Television monitor.'

Fatigue soured her temper. 'Checking up on me, making sure I'm not stealing anything?'

His eyes narrowed. 'I could take offence at that, but something tells me you're tired out, so I'll overlook it.'

She sat down and put a hand to her head. 'Tired is hardly the right word. I've been on my own all day. Selina's ill.' She held her middle. 'I hardly had any lunch. I feel as though I've got an enormous, empty cave inside me.' She smiled weakly. 'Big enough for a potholer to get into!'

He considered her drooping figure, glanced at his watch and said, 'Come on, put on some make-up. I'm taking you out to dinner.'

She recoiled from the thought. 'Dinner? With you? Sorry. I've bowed and scraped to so many customers, I've got no small-talk left. I'd bore you stiff. You once told me you never took out dull-witted women, because they had nothing to say. Well, I'm dull-witted for once. Tonight I've got nothing to say. But thanks for suggesting it.' She hauled herself out of the chair and picked up her bag, but he took it from her.

'I'll ignore the speech of refusal to an invitation which was never given. It was a statement, not a question. You're coming out to a meal with me.' He put his arm round her waist as if he sensed her need for physical support.

She went a few paces and made him stop. 'What's the matter?' he asked. 'Got a date with Romeo? You can forget him.'

'No, but I must let them know at home.' He allowed her to do that and wandered round the racks while she explained to her mother that she was having a meal out. She rang off before the questions could begin.

She sat in his car and asked, 'Where are we going?'

'Where I took you before. So you needn't bother about the make-up if you don't want to.' He looked her over. 'As far as

I'm concerned you'll do as you are.'

But she took out her compact and lipstick. 'Would you object if I combed my hair?'

'Go ahead, as long as you don't comb it over me.'

'Don't worry,' she smiled, 'if any of my hair lands on your jacket, I'll remove it. I'd hate to get into trouble with Camille.'

He pulled out to overtake a parked car and said under his breath, 'At this point in time Camille can go to hell. She knows as well as I do there's no permanency about our relationship.'

Juliet put away her comb and closed her bag. 'I get the feeling she's dreading the end of your – relationship. She even said,' she knew she was treading on dangerous ground, 'she thought once that you had me in mind to take her place. You know, the next in the queue.'

'Did she now?' His voice was soft. 'And would Miss Juliet Bourne object if I made her my next girl-friend?'

She stared out of the window. 'Strongly. In any close relationship I had with a man I'd go for permanency. So count me out of your calculations.'

'That, as my father would say, is in character. You don't exactly pull your punches.'

The restaurant was in semi-darkness. All around them were couples too absorbed in themselves to care who came and went. A powerful longing for the love of the man beside her stirred her emotions like a stick pushed into the glowing embers of a fire. A flame leapt and threatened to burn her. But tiredness took over and damped it down.

She yawned, then apologized. 'I did warn you.'

'All right, no small talk. We can always converse in silence. Everyone else is doing it. They're just looking at each other.' His fingers held her chin and brought her face round. 'We can do that, too.'

His eyes gazed into hers and she was too tired to hold anything back. But her eyelids drooped, cutting off the communication between them.

He laughed. 'I wish I could decipher the message that was passing from you to me. Give me the key to the code and I'll unscramble it.'

'No message. Too tired.' She yawned again. 'Sorry.'

The food revived her temporarily. He watched her

brighten and said, 'I'll take you to a show. We might as well end the evening in style.' She made no objection.

Back in the car Juliet closed her eyes. She hoped it was not far to the theatre, because if it were, Drew would have to waken her.

'Sorry about the way I'm behaving,' she murmured. 'You must expect more of your women than this.'

'So you admit it! You're one of my women.'

She cursed herself for her slip, made only because of her exhausted state. 'Of course I'm not.' She felt herself drifting off. 'Never will be.'

It must have been hours later that she stirred. There was no movement of the car. No theatre, no show. Only arms round her and a comfortable shoulder under her head. She stirred, opened her eyes and looked up. Drew was gazing down at her and in the darkness she thought he was smiling.

'Had a good sleep?'

'I'm most terribly sorry.' She pulled herself out of his arms and smoothed her hair. She was horrified at what she had done. She looked at her watch. It wasn't as late as she had feared.

'What about the show? We've missed it, haven't we? And all my fault. I've ruined your evening.'

'I wouldn't say that. I could see it coming. You went flat out on me, so I drove a short way out of town and parked off a side road.' She saw the outline of hedges and trees. 'I'll take you for a coffee.'

He drove back into the town and they found a coffee bar still open. They sat side by side on high stools facing a mirror. 'I look terrible,' she said, touching her hair. 'I always do after a sleep. You should see me first thing in the morning.'

His reflection smiled mockingly. 'Should I? Is that an invitation?'

'Yes,' she grinned back. She could say things to his reflection that she couldn't say to him. He leaned closer. 'Come round one weekend just before breakfast,' she invited.

He drew away. 'Pity, I really thought I was getting somewhere.'

She yawned. 'You know, I'm so tired that if you tried

hard enough, you might even do that.'

'There's encouragement for you! Should I take you to a night club?'

'You mean in order to soften me up?'

'If you like to put it that way, yes. Ever been to one?'

'No.' She frowned deeply. 'On second thoughts, I don't think I will. You should take your girl-friend there. She's sophisticated and would fit in. But me,' she shook her head, drunk with tiredness, 'I wouldn't want to risk the consequences.'

He put his arm round her shoulders. 'Tell me, what are they? And what do you know about them?'

'A lot,' she grinned, fencing with him.

'Oh? From what sources? Personal experience? Romeo's tuition?'

'*Malcolm*? You must be joking! No, from films, books, television.'

He slipped from his stool, pulling her with him. 'We'd better go. You're too tempting in your present mood. I'd better get you home before you start seducing the chairman's son.'

Outside the house he reached across and gathered her into his arms. She went without resistance. 'I'm sorry,' she whispered, 'for passing out on you.'

'Apology accepted. You must do it again some time. I enjoyed the sensation.' His lips were tender at first, but as the seconds passed grew more demanding, seeking for a response she longed to give but did not dare.

At last he released her and she lay in her seat for a few moments lifeless and unwilling to move. His 'Goodnight, Juliet' was a little abrupt.

She left him with a final apology for spoiling his evening.

'I think it's high time,' Cynthia said a few evenings later, 'we returned Warren's hospitality and invited him to tea. And Mildred, of course. Drew, too, if he wants to come.'

Cedric decided to be awkward. 'I don't see why. With their money and position, it's a bit like royalty – they ask you there, but you don't have to ask them back.'

This annoyed his wife, as he knew it would. 'Warren's not a bit like that. He's too human.'

'Pity you didn't marry him, then,' Cedric snapped, and left the room.

Cynthia said to Juliet, 'I really don't know why your father always reacts so violently whenever I mention Warren. But don't you agree? We should ask them, shouldn't we? Warren's been so good in other ways, too.'

Juliet laughed. 'Dad's jealous. Yes, I agree, we should really. It would be bad manners not to, but,' her throat tightened, 'not Drew.'

'We'd have to ask him, dear. After all, they included you in their invitation.'

'That was different. I wanted a job. They had to ask me.' Her imagination shrank from contemplating Drew as a visitor to their simple, and by comparison, rather poverty-stricken home. It would be bad enough having to entertain Warren and his wife, feeling apologetic all the time about their surroundings. But to have Drew there, seeing for himself how stark their way of living was compared with the luxury he was used to – she couldn't bear to think about it.

But she need not have worried. When Cynthia phoned Warren next day to issue the invitation, she was told that Drew would almost certainly be tied up with his own affairs. Warren had added, laughing, 'And I don't mean "business".'

The night before Warren Major and his wife were due to visit them, Cedric was ill again. Cynthia sat up with him, listening in agony as he fought for breath. She insisted that, visitors or no visitors, he was not getting up. They argued, but he won – he was getting up, he said. They had royalty to entertain, remember. His wife said that if he hadn't been ill in the night, she would have been really angry with him for his sarcasm.

Warren and Mildred arrived in their large yellow car, leaving it parked outside the house. Neighbourly net curtains were twitched aside and neighbours' eyes looked their fill as the Bournes' well-to-do guests made their way to the front door.

There were handshakes and smiles, Mildred's strained and insincere, Warren's broad and buoyant. His large, expansive personality seemed to increase and the house grow proportionately smaller as he stepped inside.

He thrust out his hand towards Cedric with a disarming gesture of friendliness between rivals and as he eased himself on to the well-worn, shabby settee, he seemed to be trying to scale down his opulence to fit in with the modest surroundings. But he failed. His affluence spilled out of him like an overfull bucket and although he tried with his banter and determined good-humour to mop up the spilt contents, he could not rid himself of his air of wealth which he took with him wherever he went.

Cedric, still pale from the after-effects of his bad night, sat back and watched events with the knowing expectancy of a child watching a Punch and Judy show. Warren, with his joviality, was making a desperate attempt to show Cedric that he was not the only one with a claim on Cynthia Bourne. Once she had nearly belonged to him and now with his mind, if not with his body, he was reaching out towards her like a baby making frantic attempts to grasp something just out of reach.

Cedric stirred to life, perhaps moved by a forgiving pity, and went to sit beside Warren. It was not long before they were deep in conversation about the affairs of the business world. Cedric had relented with the beneficence of the victor – after all, he had had the prize in his possession for years and nothing could take her away from him now.

Juliet had to admire her mother for the way she forced Mildred to talk, mainly by talking herself first, then, having found a subject of interest to her guest, sitting back and letting the guest take over. From the snatches of conversation Juliet heard as she drifted restlessly round the room, it seemed to be about flower arranging, 'Clever Mother,' Juliet thought, 'to appear to be so interested in a subject which usually bores her to tears.'

Cynthia left the room to get the food, motioning to Juliet to take her place beside Mildred. She did so with reluctance. The subject of flower arranging had apparently been exhausted and Juliet floundered, until Mildred, eyeing with distaste her tangerine-coloured dress with its low neck and wrap-over skirt draped curtain-like into flowing folds, said, 'I suppose that dress you're wearing came from this wonderful boutique I keep hearing about from Warren.'

So Juliet talked boutique to Mildred who listened, stiff and bored, until the trolley trundled and bumped along the hall and Cynthia pushed open the door. With immense relief Juliet got up to help her. Mildred's eyes searched behind Cynthia's back and seemed to be looking for a non-existent 'Kate', housekeeper-cum-cook, trained to perfection by the mistress of the house, without whom, in Mildred's world, no woman could possibly manage.

Warren remarked on the excellence of the food, refraining from mentioning the past, as he had before, and Mildred lukewarmly agreed with him. A car pulled up behind Warren's and he half rose from the settee and exclaimed, 'I can't believe it! My son's arrived.'

Juliet, unbelieving too, went to the window. Yes, it was Drew, locking his car and strolling to the front door. Why had he come? And how was she going to hide from him her delight at his sudden appearance which was threatening to rob her of the ability to breathe?

Moving jerkily like a mechanical toy, she obeyed her mother's instruction to 'Let Drew in, dear, while I get a cup for him.'

'Hallo,' said Drew breezily, 'was I invited to the tea party?'

Cynthia, coming back from the kitchen, saved Juliet the necessity of answering. 'You're always welcome, Drew,' she said, joining the others.

'Am I, Juliet?' Drew asked.

Juliet, struggling to recover her poise, said, deliberately hesitant, 'Er – depends on the circumstances. At work, when I see your face, I want to run a mile. It usually means trouble.'

'The impudence of it!' he said, as she showed him into the sitting-room. 'It's the other way round. When I see *your* face, I *know* it means trouble.'

'You two at it again?' Warren asked. 'They can't meet for more than a few minutes without being at each other's throats.'

Drew, after being introduced to Cedric, accepted a plate and some sandwiches from Juliet. He smiled, answering Warren, 'Not entirely true, Father. We're on good terms now and then, especially when she's giving me something. A sandwich, for instance.' Their eyes met and she knew he was not really referring to that. 'But I must admit it's a rare occurrence.'

They laughed and Warren asked, 'What happened to Camille?'

'I put her off until this evening. We're dining together.'

That, thought Juliet, puts me in my place. Cedric had moved to his original seat and now Cynthia was beside Warren. His face was alight, his hands were restless as though he was having a struggle to keep them from touching her. There was a sparkle in her mother's eyes that was rare and Juliet wondered if Warren's nearness was affecting her, too.

She turned from them, refusing to acknowledge the unthinkable possibility that, after all these years, her mother still returned Warren's affection, and was now regretting the impulse that had made her, so long ago, break off her engagement to him.

Drew had finished his tea and caught Juliet's eye. He seemed restless, like his father, and Warren, watching them, said, 'Why don't you two go off and have a good fight? I can see Drew's spoiling for an argument. No doubt after a few minutes alone with Cynthia's daughter, a good subject for a quarrel will crop up!'

'Show him the garden,' Cedric suggested. 'If I didn't think my wife would throw something at me – she does the weeding – I'd say it was "all my own work".'

'We,' said Mildred, with studied simplicity, 'have three gardeners, full time.'

Cynthia intercepted the disgusted look Warren threw at his wife. She hurriedly glossed over Mildred's childish boasting by saying she could well believe it.

Drew held the door open for Juliet, who said to him as they passed through the kitchen, 'Shall I show you our estate?'

'No need for sarcasm, young woman. I get your not very subtle message.'

'I'm sorry there weren't any inscrutable lions at the front door to greet you.' She flashed a grin at him. 'No pond, complete with fountain, no rose gardens, no—'

'No swimming pool to throw you into, unfortunately, which at this moment I should dearly love to do.'

They walked round the garden and Juliet pointed to the vegetables and lettuces, saying that she thought Drew might at least admire them. He did.

'Shall I give you a lettuce to put in your buttonhole just as you gave me a rose?' she asked mischievously.

His hands settled playfully round her throat and she did not attempt to remove them, putting her hands over his instead. They looked at each other. 'What will the neighbours think?' she whispered.

'That I was about to throttle you.' He looked at her hands. 'And that you were helping me to do it.'

Confused by the emotions he could arouse simply by touching her, she pulled at his wrists and he removed his hands.

'Shall I,' she asked, when her pulse rate had slowed down, 'show you *my* apartment?' She smiled at him. 'It's a little smaller than yours and more modest. One room.'

'Lead the way, Miss Bourne.'

She took him upstairs and with pride showed him the paintings – her own work, she explained – with which she had decorated the walls. 'All part of my art training. Portraits, landscapes, still life . . .'

He looked at each of them in detail and commented, 'Pity you had to give it all up. You would have done well. If your – er– circumstances changed, would you ever consider going back to it?'

'Just give me the chance,' she answered wistfully, 'and I'd go back to art school tomorrow.'

There was a short silence. 'M'm,' he said, 'great pity you had to leave. A lot of talent there.' He turned. 'If I commissioned you to paint a portrait of me, would you do it?'

'Of course, but you would have to sit very still and not move a muscle even if I cursed loudly when I couldn't get the expression right. Now,' she considered him, 'what's your typical expression? A glower. Yes, you'd have to glower very nicely for me.'

He laughed and stretched out on her bed. 'What does Juliet Bourne see when she first wakes up in the morning?' He stared upwards. 'The ceiling.'

'Wrong. I see your face frowning at me and telling me what a bad, bad employee I am and how I ought to be dismissed and thrown to the wolves.'

He gripped her wrist and pulled her down until she was lying on top of him. 'Don't mention wolves. I might devour you myself.'

She struggled, trying to get up, but he held her still. 'I suppose,' she said, 'if I now called you "darling" like Camille, you'd really feel at home.'

'If that isn't provocation!' With a swift movement he had shifted off the bed and had her pinned face down and entirely at his mercy.

She glanced over her shoulder, saw his hand raised threateningly and shrieked, 'No, no! I'm sorry, I'm sorry.'

'So I should think.' He let her go.

She stood up and smoothed down her hair, to give herself time to regain her dignity. 'Now you've seen my living quarters,' she said at last. 'Hardly luxurious, but I call it my rabbit hole. I bolt into it when the world is too much for me.' She lifted her comb and ran it through her hair. She regarded herself in the dressing-table mirror. 'Perhaps now you've seen our house you understand what I mean by the difference between us – the sort of life you're used to and the completely different environment I live in.'

'You know,' he watched her reflection, arms folded, frowning, 'I think there's a sadistic streak in you that delights in dwelling on how different we are. Why?'

Because, she cried inside herself, I want you to refute it, that's why, but you never, never do. She said aloud, 'Can you think of any ways in which our thoughts and instincts do coincide?'

'Let me see.' He rubbed his chin, watching her powder her nose. 'Our thoughts, perhaps not. But our instincts—' His hand reached out for her, but she saw it coming in the mirror and evaded it, running from the room and down the stairs to the safety of the sitting-room and the others.

In the hall, as the visitors were leaving, there was the usual handshaking, thanks and good wishes. Warren watched his wife walk out to the car and on an impulse he seemed unable to resist, said to Cedric, 'Mind if I borrow your wife for a moment?' Without waiting for an answer he pulled Cynthia into his arms and kissed her.

Cedric grunted and said nothing.

Drew followed on with, 'Mind if I borrow your daughter for a moment?' and pulled Juliet towards him, but she evaded him again.

'Now, now, son,' came from Warren, 'you're not making her one of your women. She's different.'

'Don't I know it?' Drew muttered, walking down the path. He drove away without a smile or a lift of the hand.

Juliet did not see Drew for a few days. She missed him more than she dared to admit. Selina had soon returned to work and Juliet was able to attend to other things. The queue of salesmen with their wares was incessant and one or two invited her to visit their employers' factories and see the goods in the process of manufacture. One of them was a young man called Montague Weeks – 'call me Monty,' he had said – and together they fixed a date for her visit. It was a train journey away, so he warned her she would probably need most of the day for it. He said he would be there and would take her out to lunch.

Another sales representative showed her a caseful of accessories, which included belts and handbags, all designed to meet the needs of the type of customer who patronized the boutique. She was impressed by the range of goods and, since it would be a new line, wondered if she should get permission to stock them.

She contacted Mr. Havering, the general manager, but he turned the idea down straight away. 'It would overlap with the accessories section of conventional fashion. The management wouldn't allow it, Miss Bourne.'

But Miss Bourne refused to accept his ruling. She decided to ask Drew. 'What's the use of having contacts at the top,' she asked herself, 'if I don't use them?' Then she hated herself for adopting the 'back door' methods she would condemn in others.

But phone him she did. She asked if he could spare a few minutes. 'And I promise you it would only be a few minutes, because I'm going out for the day.'

He agreed to see her. Sitting at his desk he was all executive. Could he, she wondered, be the same man who only a few days before had held her down on her bed and threatened to spank her?

He greeted her with a smile that was a mixture of mockery and cynicism. 'I wondered how long it would be,' he said, 'before that bad, bad employee of mine would start pestering me again. It's been so peaceful these last few days. No irritant to drive me mad.' He pointed to a chair, which she occupied. 'What do you want, Miss Bourne?'

'To start an accessories section in the boutique, Mr. Major.'

'Just like that. What about the money?'

'I haven't spent all my allocation yet. It could come out of that.'

'What sort of merchandise did you have in mind?'

'Belts, jewellery, handbags, the sort of accessories which many boutiques stock in addition to clothes.'

His eyebrows rose. 'Empire building, Miss Bourne?' She flushed angrily. 'Because that's what the other members of staff would call it.' He thought for a moment or two. 'Sorry, can't be done. You would overlap with fashion accessories.'

'That's what Mr. Havering said. And that's why I decided to appeal to you.'

'Thinking you would use your influence with me and get me to overturn his decision?' She flushed at the truth his words contained. 'Well for once, Miss Bourne, you aren't going to get your own way. The answer's no.'

'But, Mr Major, all I want to do is expand a little, and surely expansion is a healthy sign? The demand for such products is there, I'm sure.'

'Have you been asked by the customers for these things?'

She had to be honest. 'Well, no, not yet, but the goods the sales rep has shown me are marvellous and—'

'So that's it! You've fallen for the patter of the reps. You're an infant where buying is concerned, aren't you? You can still be taken in by sales talk.'

'No, I wasn't taken in. You said once I had vision. Well, now I'm using that vision – I'm visualizing my boutique—'

'*Your* boutique?'

'Oh, I'm sorry, I suppose I should have said *your* boutique, providing an even better service to customers by giving them a greater variety of lines all under one roof.'

'Now you're trying your sales talk on me, and I'm sorry, but I'm proof against it. I'm hardened, as a result of living with it over the years. I appreciate your enthusiasm and your devotion to your cause. But the answer is still "no".'

She rose angrily, looking at her watch. 'If I had the time,' she said threateningly, 'I'd stay until I did get my own way.'

He smiled as if he knew better. 'But I've got to catch a train.'

'Where are you going?'

'To town, to visit a clothing factory. One of the reps invited me to go.'

'I've got a lunch appointment in town. I'll give you a lift.'

'A lift? No, thanks. I'm going by train.'

'You're going with me, Miss Bourne.' His tone had the stamp of authority about it and so did his expression. She had no alternative but to go with him.

'I'll get my coat, Mr. Major.'

'No, you won't. I don't trust you not to run out on me. You'll get your coat when I'm free to go with you, which will be in,' he consulted his watch, 'five minutes.'

She fretted away the five minutes which stretched into fifteen. At last he put the phone down. He informed his secretary that he was leaving, gathered a pile of papers and pushed them into his briefcase, then said, 'Right, we'll go.'

Back in her office he looked on quizzically while she made up her face. She put on her coat and told him she was ready.

In the car he asked, 'Where are you making for?'

'A firm called Trendmaker Fashions.' She gave him the address. 'If it's a bit out of your way, you needn't bother. I've still got time to catch the train.'

'It is out of my way, but I'm taking you there, all the same.'

Juliet took a chance on his annoyance and asked, 'Is it – is it Camille you're lunching with?'

'Camille? No, it is not. Camille belongs to my private affairs, not my business affairs.'

She said with an irritation she immediately regretted, 'There's no need to spell it out for me. I know exactly where Camille stands in your private life.'

'Stands?' he mocked. 'Camille *stands*?' She stared ahead, rigid with jealousy. He changed the subject. 'How's Romeo?'

'I haven't seen much of him lately. He comes round some evenings, but—'

'Quarrelled?'

'Not exactly. Since the garden party we've been – just friends.'

'A sad end to a promising romance. I can't say I'm sorry. I never did fancy your liaison with an employee of our rivals.'

'It *wasn't* a liaison, as you call it. And I told you, we're still friends.'

There was a long silence. He broke it by saying, 'You talked earlier of expansion.' He gave her a quick glance. 'How much can I trust you?'

'You should know by now.'

'If I tell you something, will you swear not to breathe a word to anyone?'

She held up her right hand as if in a court of law. 'I swear, on my honour.'

'All right, I'll take a chance. You know we have another branch of Majors?' He named a town some distance away.

'Are you thinking of opening another?'

'Not exactly. We've been looking round locally for a suitable piece of land for building an extension. We think we've found it. Negotiations as to price and so on are proceeding now. The man I'm lunching with today is the firm's solicitor.'

'It sounds exciting.' A thought occurred to her. 'You wouldn't – no, I suppose you wouldn't.' She found some courage and continued, 'You wouldn't consider transferring the boutique and giving it more space?'

He threw back his head and laughed. 'Opportunist to the core! We weren't thinking of that, no.'

'What I really want, of course,' she said cheekily, 'is a shop of my own.'

He laughed again. 'Now, if I set you up in a shop of your own,' she mistrusted his tone, 'what would you be prepared to give in return?'

Her smile faded. 'Sorry. Nothing doing. You heard what your father said. I'm different.'

'All the same,' he persisted, 'you know what people would say about us if I did, don't you?'

'Don't worry,' she muttered, 'some of them are saying that already. Roy Hawkins said as much when you got me that window space. That's why he threw me into the swimming pool.'

168

He frowned. 'Was it? I never knew. I'd like to teach him a lesson for that.' His good humour returned. 'They're so wrong, aren't they? Isn't it a pity to disappoint them?'

'I think we're nearly there,' she said shortly.

He drove through a maze of side streets, stopping once or twice to ask the way, and turned off into a rocky, unmade road. He pulled up outside a building that was little more than a series of shacks joined together and labelled in uneven hand-painted letters, Trendmaker Fashions.

'What do they call this?' he asked irritably. 'A factory? I don't like the look of this at all.'

'But, Drew,' in her anxiety to persuade him to change his opinion she forgot to be formal, 'some of their styles are fabulous.'

'Well,' he said reluctantly, 'I'll be fair. We'll go in and have a look.'

Inside he stared round disgustedly. Juliet pressed a bell at a desk marked 'Enquiries', but nothing happened. In the distance there was the noise of machinery, but no one appeared in answer to the summons. The atmosphere was grim and dreary, the windows little more than skylights, and the smell was stuffy and stale. After five minutes, Drew caught her arm. 'Come on, we're not staying in this foul atmosphere a moment longer.'

She resisted, pressing the bell again. 'I promised, Drew. They're expecting me. We can't go now.'

'Can't we?' He demonstrated that they were going and quickly. He almost carried her out and dumped her at the side of the car.

'How could you?' She was near to tears – of frustration, not sorrow.

'We're not dealing with a firm like that. Look how they operate – in a squalid backyard with an unattended back-room office. Shocking conditions of work. From the look of their premises, I wouldn't trust them an inch, any more than I'd trust their sales representative. If that's their method of manufacture, probably using cheap labour, and probably refusing to plough any of their profits back into the business to make improvements, then we're not dealing with them.'

He drove off. 'But,' she wailed, 'Monty Weeks, the sales rep, was going to take me out to lunch. He'll be waiting for me.'

'So that was the attraction! Now it's coming out. And that, even after I told you not to go out with any rep.'

'I can't see anything wrong with going out with a man as pleasant as Monty Weeks.' He gave a short, sardonic laugh.

'The trouble with you,' she said after staring through the window for some time, 'is that you won't let me grow up as a buyer. You've tied me to your apron strings as though I were a baby who can't walk straight without support. Every time I try to break free, you haul me back. It's well known that buyers are treated like royalty because of their power, the money they have at their disposal. Yet you object even if I'm only invited out to lunch. No wonder I'm rebelling against you all the time.'

'I happen to have slightly more than a professional interest in you.' She noted the word 'slightly'. 'Because of the friendship of our parents, if anything – regrettable were to happen to you as a result of your work, I should feel answerable to your family.'

'I don't see why. They haven't appointed you as guardian of my moral well-being. For some reason, you've set yourself up as a father figure where I'm concerned.'

He laughed softly. *'Father figure?'*

Juliet said accusingly into the silence, 'You don't treat other buyers in the firm as you treat me.'

'The other buyers are all a good deal older than you, and a lot more experienced. They aren't young, attractive – and vulnerable.'

'All the same, I don't need my hand held all the time.'

Drew flicked her a smile. 'Don't you?' He groped for her hand, his eyes on the road, but she clasped them together angrily.

'You see,' she cried, 'you still won't take me seriously. Anyway,' she said, knowing she would be provoking him to anger, too, 'not all men are like you with women. Not all men's morals are as questionable as yours.'

His lips thinned. 'You'd better take that statement back, my girl.' He drew up at some traffic lights. 'Otherwise on our return I shall take disciplinary action.'

'What will you do?' she cried, 'hold out that terrible threat again of dismissal? I'll save you the trouble.' She had worked herself up into an emotional state that was out of all proportion to the meaning of his words. She only knew that she could never talk on equal terms with this man, because it was within his power to slap her down whenever he felt like it. She knew, too, that with his taunts of so-called disciplinary action, history was repeating itself in a depressing, humiliating way and all she wanted to do at the moment was to get away from the threat that was constantly hanging over her like the roof of a partly demolished building. One day it would fall and trap her. And that, she knew, would be the end.

She gave way to an unmanageable impulse to get even with him somehow, and to get out of the range of his tongue. She wrenched open the car door and plunged into the road between the other vehicles which had congregated at the traffic lights and which were just preparing to move on as the lights changed.

'What are you doing?' he shouted. 'Trying to kill yourself, you crazy little fool?'

She ran round in front of his car, weaved her way between the cars which were already inching forward and reached the pavement just in time. He shouted again, but over the noise of the traffic she could not hear what he said.

He had no alternative but to drive on, trying to edge the car towards the kerb. But he was forced by the pressure of traffic behind him to turn left instead of going straight ahead as he had intended. He found a suitable place to park and slammed his door behind him. The traffic lights were in his favour and he sprinted across the road, catching up with her as she stood impatiently at the kerb in a crowd of people waiting to cross when the traffic had cleared.

He took her completely by surprise. He came up behind her and his technique was so subtle she did not realize what was happening until she found herself, arm linked in his, walking back with him to his car. 'Hallo, darling,' he said softly and apologetically, but loudly enough for others to hear, 'sorry I was late. Did you think I'd forgotten?'

When she realized what he had done she wrenched her arm away and turned to run, but he had been expecting an attempt to escape and caught her almost at once. She was back, arm linked in his, and he was saying, 'If you make a scene, I'll lift you bodily and carry you, if necessary screaming and kicking, back to the car.'

He did not let her go until he had forced her into her seat and fastened the safety belt across her to make escape more difficult. He drove on, and by a series of right turns, got himself back on his original route.

'This,' she muttered, 'is nothing less than abduction!'

'And what you did,' he snapped, 'was nothing less than a suicide attempt.'

'I'd do it again to get away from you and the awful things you say to me.' Tears of frustration splashed on to her handbag like someone stamping their foot in a puddle. She said thickly, 'The only way you could make me stay with you is if you carried a pair of handcuffs around with you.'

'Thanks for the hint,' he said acidly. 'One day I'll do just that, and use them, too. Good grief, there are times when you need to be physically restrained from doing yourself an injury!'

She stared dully out of the window. 'Where are we going?'

'To keep my lunch date.'

'I'm not going with you. You can't force me.'

'But you are coming with me, my *sweet*. And if necessary, I could force you, very easily, simply by using my physical strength.'

'Have you booked lunch for two?'

'I have.'

She smiled triumphantly. 'Then there won't be a place for me at a table for two.'

'I can alter the booking. It's a large hotel and I'm a fairly regular customer.'

'But you'll be talking business. You won't want me in on that, will you? I might tell tales.'

'You'll tell tales at your peril, my girl. I'm trusting you, and if you fail me in this, it will be the end, and I mean the irrevocable end between you and me, and you and the firm and you and your job. So you have been warned.'

She could do nothing but sulk after that, but when eventually she was ushered into the smooth silence of the hotel, and was handled with the professional deference of the staff into the condescending acquiescence they so cleverly evoked in their patrons, she found she had been wooed, quite against her will, into a more amenable state of mind.

She was therefore able to greet Drew's guest, a sharp-eyed, quick-witted but not over-young solicitor, with tolerable calmness and even a welcoming smile. The thought that she had been manoeuvred into the position of hostess to Drew's host did flit in and out of her mind like a bee finding its way into a room and immediately flying out again, but she was so becalmed by the soft carpeting, subtle lighting and persuasive atmosphere of the hotel that she had by that time passed the point of caring.

Throughout the meal her thoughts wandered. She caught snatches of the discussion about the vendors, the price of the land and the legalities involved in buying it, but she took in very little of what the two men were saying.

'She's a friend of yours?' drifted into her consciousness and brought her mind back to her surroundings.

'Juliet?' Her eyes swivelled round to Drew's, catching his sardonic expression, 'Mr. Finlay asks if we're friends. Are we?'

She smiled. 'I think the best answer to that,' she told the solicitor, 'is sometimes.' She looked doubtfully at Drew. 'I don't think we are at the moment.'

Drew laughed, leaning back in his chair and holding his drink, which rested on the table, at arm's length. 'Oh, I wouldn't say that. To be honest, she and her parents are friends of the family. There are times when the two of us are – er—' he raised his eyebrows, 'shall we say more than friendly?'

Juliet blushed as he had meant her to, and Mr. Finlay smiled knowingly. 'It's not like that at all,' Juliet blurted out, annoyed at what the solicitor must be thinking. 'There are times when we hate each other.'

'Don't all couples?' murmured Mr. Finlay, worldly-wise.

Drew moved his hand from his glass to her hand and held it firmly. 'We lead a cat and dog life, don't we, Juliet?'

'Yes, we do,' she admitted grudgingly, 'but that's not because of any personal relationship.' To Mr. Finlay, 'He's my employer, that's all.'

Mr. Finlay's eyes dropped to their linked hands. 'I must indeed admit that it looks like it!' he laughed.

'It's true what she says. She is an employee of mine, but with a difference.' Drew leaned forward and rested on his elbows, lifting her hand to imprison it between both of his. He parted her fingers and inspected them closely one by one. The action was almost a caress. 'There are times, Mr. Finlay, when this girl almost drives me crazy. She's just about broken every rule in the book. She's been more trouble to me in the short time she's been working for me than the whole of my department store staff put together. I've threatened her with dismissal more times than I can remember, yet she's still with us. Every time she comes bouncing back, like a ball thrown into a neighbour's garden.' He touched her fingers with his lips, like a lover, and said, 'I can't get this girl out of my hair, no matter what I do.'

'It doesn't look,' said Mr. Finlay, 'as though you want to, very much.'

'Don't let appearances fool you, Mr. Finlay,' Juliet said, tugging at her hand and managing to disengage it from Drew's. 'The day I walk out of Major's store for the last time, Drew, I mean Mr. Major, will throw a celebration party.'

'The day Juliet Bourne walks out on me,' Drew smiled mockingly, 'my heart will break.'

'There's always one way a man can prevent a woman from running away,' said Mr. Finlay, moving back his chair as the waiter presented Drew with the bill, 'and that's to marry her.'

'No good,' murmured Drew, settling the account, 'Juliet has a Romeo.'

'And you,' muttered Juliet, 'have got a Camille.'

'Ah, yes,' Drew agreed, as they made their way to the door, 'let us never forget Camille.'

After a few more words of business, they left the solicitor with handshakes and a promise of action on his part.

On the way back, in the car, Drew's provocative mood disappeared. He said a little sharply, 'I rely on you implicitly not to breathe a word to anyone,' he emphasized the word, 'about what you've heard today. My discussion with the solicitor was completely private and confidential and you can consider yourself privileged to have been allowed to be present. It shows how much I trust you. I hope you'll fulfil that trust.'

'Of course I will,' she snapped. 'In any case, I didn't take in a word of what you were saying.'

'That I can't believe.'

'If you can't believe what I'm saying now, then how on earth can you say you trust me?'

'Point taken, and I apologize. All right, so you didn't "hear" what we were saying. Very diplomatic, very discreet, and I'm glad to know it.'

'It also happens to be true. All legal matters bore me silly.'

'So when you marry Malcolm, you'll either dispense with the legal side altogether,' he paused for her reaction, but there was none, 'or you'll leave it all to him.'

'I'm not going to marry Malcolm,' she answered calmly. 'I told you, we're only friends. Not even that sometimes.' She glared at him, daring him to dispute her statement. 'So you needn't worry about my divulging any of your secrets about expansion to him.'

'Glad to hear it. In any case, I've already warned you of the consequences if anything of the kind should occur.'

Before they parted at the staff entrance she thanked him for the lunch. 'And I'm sorry about running away from you.'

He nodded. 'Next time at your own suggestion it'll be handcuffs and no nonsense. So I'm warning you.' He raised his hand and shut himself in the lift.

CHAPTER NINE

WHEN Juliet returned home one evening her mother told her, 'Warren phoned. He's invited me to lunch again.'

'Are you going?'

'Of course. Why not?'

'Just that – well, Dad might not like it. You know how he feels about Warren.'

'My goodness,' she was indignant, 'will I never live that engagement down? First Cedric, now you. Don't either of you understand that was thirty years ago?'

'Sorry, Mum. You go out to lunch and have a nice time.' Her tone was pacifying, but misleadingly so. She couldn't tell her mother about the niggling anxiety at the back of her mind that she might one day succumb to Warren's un-doubted charm and the feelings she must once have felt for him return.

Malcolm called at the boutique next day while Juliet was eating her sandwiches. He looked round ostentatiously and Juliet said, 'Selina's gone to lunch. You're out of luck.'

'It wasn't her I came to see, ducky. It's you I love.'

Juliet laughed and offered him some of her coffee. He refused, taking out a cigarette instead. 'You love me,' she said, 'as much as you love this flask of mine.'

'Darling, I can't kiss a flask.'

'Be honest and admit it was Selina you were after.'

'No, truly, this time it was you. Business. Curlews need someone to run their boutique. Their buyer's walked out on them. How about it? To get you, now you've got more ex-perience, they'd pay double the money you're getting here, if only to get their own back on Majors.'

Juliet had to admit the idea was tempting, but – leave Majors? Leave Drew and never see him again? The thought appalled her. He could threaten to fire her every other day if he liked, but she knew she would never voluntarily walk out on him.

'Sorry, Malcolm. Good of you to think of me, but I couldn't do it.'

He shrugged. 'Let me know if you change your mind.' He

looked out into the boutique. 'That girl has a long lunch hour, doesn't she?'

'I thought it wasn't true when you said you didn't want to see Selina. I can't blame you. She's got a lot to offer.' She saw the appreciative gleam in his eyes. 'I set you free to run after her.'

'Thanks, darling. I'll kiss you for that.' He did. 'But I rather think running after her won't be necessary. She's the sort who stands still while you catch up.' He lifted a hand. 'I'll leave the offer with you. If you should change your mind contact Personnel. They'll snap you up.' He went out.

It was when she had just served a customer and was putting her flask away that she first smelled the smoke. It was faint at first, but grew stronger as the minutes passed. A fire? It couldn't be a fire! Not at Majors! Should she tell somebody? She looked out into the store. Others were getting worried, too. Someone was using the phone, saying the words, 'Smoke, is the place on fire?'

Over the Tannoy came the message, the voice calm but firm, 'Will everyone leave the store, please? The store must be evacuated. There must be no panic. Will everyone leave the store in an orderly fashion?'

Over and over again the message came. Juliet thought, terrified, Drew? What about Drew? He might not know. She tried dialling his extension. No reply. She tried again, but still no answer. She had to get to him, to warn him. Someone must tell him the store was on fire.

The caretakers were showing the customers out. The fire bell began to ring. 'Staff,' the caretakers were shouting, 'staff out, too. Everybody out! You heard the message.'

Juliet went in the opposite direction, towards the stairs. She knew better than to use the lift in a fire. A hand shot out and caught her. The caretaker said, 'Wrong way, miss. That way to the exit.'

But she shook herself free. 'I'm just going upstairs for a minute. Forgotten something.'

He dived after her, but she evaded him and was up the stairs before he could follow. But his shouts followed, if not his feet. She ignored his warnings. She must get to Drew. By the time she had reached the sixth floor, pushing against the tide of people coming down, resisting all efforts to stop her, deaf to their urgent warnings, she was gasping for breath and felt that her very lungs had collapsed. She fell into Drew's office. He wasn't there. She looked along the corridor, now nearly empty, and he was striding towards her.

'What the hell are you doing up here? You heard the message. Get out with the others.'

'Drew,' she gasped, 'I had to warn you . . .'

'Warn *me*? I can hear the fire alarm as well as you can. Anyway, I was the first to know.' They were in his office now. 'Get out, girl!'

'You come, Drew, then I'll go.'

'I've got to stay until the place is empty. Don't you understand?'

Like the captain of a ship, he wanted to go down with it? No, she couldn't let it happen. Now the corridors were silent and the smoke was beginning to choke her.

There was the sound of sirens. The fire brigade had arrived.

'Drew, now you must come.' She held on to his arms, pulling at him, using all her strength to make him move. But he shook himself free and half-lifted her from his office. He put her outside. '*Get out*, Juliet! My God, you'll be overcome by smoke if nothing else. I *order* you to go.'

She flung her arms round his neck. 'If you're going to stay here, Drew, I'm staying with you.' She whispered, 'If you're going to die, I'll die with you.'

He wrenched her arms from his neck. 'Don't be a crazy, melodramatic fool! What is this? Another act? Another attempt at self-destruction?'

But her arms found him again and there was terror in her grasp, terror that she would lose him if she left him. 'I'm not going,' she said hoarsely, 'I'm staying with you.'

'You're demented, girl. What do you mean you'd rather die with me than—' The internal phone rang. He took her hand and pulled her with him. 'Yes?' into the phone. 'False alarm?' He listened, relief making him sag. 'What happened?' He listened again. 'I see. Yes, yes. So he's been found now? All's well, then.'

He put down the phone and his hand was shaking. He found his chair, using his hands as a blind man feels his way. He sank into it, holding his head. She put her arms round his neck, drooping with relief. He felt the pressure of her body against his and pulled her on to his knee.

His arms came round her and she lay against him shaking. 'My sweet, crazy girl, what did you think you were doing?'

'I don't know, Drew, I don't know.'

'I've heard of staff loyalty, but my word, I've never known an employee want to die with her boss before!'

She hid her face against him. 'Don't make fun of me, Drew.'

'My dearest girl, I wasn't making fun of you.' He rested his cheek against her hair. 'But this instinct for self-destruction you seem to have in such abundance terrifies me. Look at what you did the other day when you dived amongst the traffic. This is just another example, isn't it?' He said softly, 'Juliet? Thank you for coming to find me.'

She raised her head and his lips came down and rested tenderly against hers. Then their pressure increased and she clung to him giving kiss for kiss.

He put her from him with a strange reluctance and she sat in the visitors' chair. 'I think,' he said at last, 'we're both a little crazy. Suffering from reaction, I suppose.'

'Drew?' He looked up. 'Wasn't it a fire?'

'No. Apparently some passer-by threw a match into the rubbish cage we keep in the sideway for scrap, unwanted boxes and wrappings. The stuff caught alight and the smoke got drawn into the air-conditioning system. You may not know that there's a very large air intake grille in the sideway near the rubbish cage. This took in the smoke and the fan drove it round the building. Since the electrician was at lunch no one else seemed to know where to switch off the fan. Hence the "fire" and the false alarm. Seems incredible when you look back on it, but not so funny if it had been real.'

He came round to stand in front of her. 'Feeling better, or would you like a drink?'

'No, thanks. I'll get back to work.' He pulled her to her feet. 'Sorry, Drew, to have been so stupid. You'd better forget it ever happened.'

He held up her hands and inspected them like an archaeologist examining a rare find. 'Artistic hands,' he murmured, 'and the temperament to go with them.' He smiled.

'I wish you weren't so impetuous. There are times when you have me really worried.'

She shook her head. 'I can't help it. It's just me.' She tried to remove her hands from his. 'Please, Drew. I must get back to work.'

But he had not finished with her. 'With your precipitate nature, a man who loved you would be afraid of letting you out of his sight. He might turn away, turn back and find you'd gone. Tell me, if you loved a man, would you do to him what your mother did to my father – walk out on him?'

She stiffened. 'Let's face it, my mother did what she did because she didn't love your father. If she'd loved him, she would have stuck to him come what may, as she's stuck to my father, come what may, ill at times though he is.'

He let her go then. 'I'm sorry. I had no right to talk of your mother like that.' He sat down as though his legs were tired. 'You'd better go.'

She left him without another word.

At home, she found her mother alone and a little pale.

'Dad not back from work yet?' Juliet asked, washing her hands at the sink and drying them.

'No. Had a good day?'

There was something about her mother's voice that made her turn. It was brittle and determinedly bright. But she looked as calm as usual, so Juliet chatted to her about the false alarm and how the building had been evacuated. She said nothing about her interlude with Drew.

'So all in all you've had quite a day.' Her mother's voice was still a little odd.

'Something wrong, Mum?' She expected a laughing denial, but to her horror her mother collapsed on to a chair and burst into tears. 'Mother, what's happened? Is it – is it Dad?'

'No no, dear. Nothing like that.' She dried her eyes. 'Silly of me. It's just—' She looked up, her voice urgent. 'Promise you won't tell your father?'

'Of course I promise.'

'Well, I had lunch with Warren today. Juliet, he's – he's going away.' So that was it. Her mother loved him after all! 'He's going abroad somewhere. South America, I think. He said he's got to get away. He's at the end of his tether. It's his wife mostly. Things are terrible between them. Juliet,' she looked up and there was a childish disbelief in her eyes, 'he asked me to go away with him. He said he still loved me – more than ever, he said. He told me he was desperately unhappy. He had no interest in the business, no interest in anything. Without me, life had no meaning.' She wiped her eyes again. 'Darling, what could I say to him?'

'Mother,' Juliet whispered, drawing up a chair and sitting beside her, 'you're not going? Father, what about him?'

'Darling, how could you doubt me? Of course I'm not going. I told Warren, and it shattered him, that I loved my husband. I was tied to Cedric, I said, by the past, the present and all that was to come. He offered me money, position, whatever I wished for he'd give me. But I said it wouldn't make any difference.' She paused, as if trying to remember what had passed between them.

'I told him,' she went on, 'that I had a high regard for him, was fond of him even, and wished him well in every way. I wished he'd had a happier life, but he couldn't blame anyone else for his choice of wife. He said after I'd left him all those years ago, nothing mattered any more. He'd married the first woman who had come along. I said he couldn't really blame me, because that was life. He couldn't grumble, he'd had all that money could buy. Except, he said, the one woman he had ever really wanted – me.'

'So now he's going away?'

'Yes. I told him to forget me, put me out of his mind. He said that would only happen on the day he died.' She caught at her daughter's hand. 'I was so sorry for him, Juliet. It was terrible sitting there watching his misery. But there was nothing I could do, nothing.'

They sat, mother and daughter, silent and still, the one thinking of the man who loved her, the other thinking of his son, the man she loved. The irony of the situation struck Juliet, but she didn't want to laugh. She wanted to cry – for Warren and for herself.

The key turned in the lock. Her father had come home.

'Thank you for listening, darling,' Cynthia whispered. 'I feel better now I've shared it with you.' They embraced.

Cedric came in and Cynthia greeted her husband with a smile and a kiss.

A few days later, Warren went away. Juliet heard it on the grapevine. 'Business abroad,' the rumour said.

It was almost the end of a particularly long and tiring day. Juliet was in her office, Selina was putting away the iron she had been using to freshen some of the customer-handled stock.

The phone rang. It was Drew Major's secretary. 'Mr. Major,' she said, 'wishes to see Miss Bourne as soon as the store closes.'

'Can't it wait?' Juliet asked. 'I'll come as soon as I've cashed up and put things in order.'

The mouthpiece was covered, a question asked. 'Mr. Major says he'll give you ten minutes.'

Juliet was puzzled. What was the mystery? She hadn't seen Drew for some days. She told herself it was better that way. What was the use of seeing him, talking to him but never being able to touch him? The kisses he had given her in the past he must have forgotten long ago. She wondered, as she counted the day's takings, if Camille was still in favour, or whether he had yet passed on to another woman.

When at the end of the stipulated ten minutes she went upstairs to Drew's office the store was almost deserted. The last customer had gone, the staff had drifted home and the doors had been bolted. Soon the cleaners would come with their mops and their chatter, but until then there was an uncanny peace hanging over the store, like the breath-holding stillness of trees in advance of a storm.

The peace was shattered as soon as she saw Drew's face. The storm broke directly over her head. He was standing, his eyes were blazing and his mouth a taut and furious line.

'So you've done it again.'

'Done what again?' She was stupefied.

'Don't turn on the Little Miss Innocent act. It doesn't wash with me any more.'

'I wish,' she said faintly, 'you'd tell me what I'm supposed to have done.'

'Do I need to? Not content with betraying our scoop purchase of washing machines to Curlews' number one spy, your boy-friend Malcolm Watling, you had to go and blab to him about our current negotiations for a site on which we wanted to build our extension store. I knew I shouldn't have trusted you, although you touchingly swore on your honour to tell no one.'

'And I kept that promise.'

He smiled contemptuously. 'You did, didn't you? And I believe you – of *course*. Especially when I hear from the estate agents with whom we were negotiating that the deal has fallen through, that Curlews have beaten us to it by offering more money, in excess even of what was actually being asked for the land by the owners, and have therefore scooped the lot. Which leaves Majors right out in the cold.'

'I'm – I'm sorry,' was all she could find to say, but she knew that those two apologetic, innocuous words would condemn her in the eyes of this man as surely as if she had actually admitted to the crime of which he was accusing her.

He rounded on her and she flinched at the violence in his face. 'So you're sorry, are you, *after* the event, after giving away to that traitor of a boy-friend of yours the firm's most important secret?'

She had to make some attempt to defend herself. 'But, Mr. Major, I swear I didn't breathe a word of it to anyone. You *must* believe me.'

'Believe you? When this is simply a repeat performance of what has gone before? I'm sorry, but I'll never believe you again, never trust you again, do you hear?'

That she could not take. Her voice rose. 'What evidence have you that I passed the information on? How can you prove it?' Her voice wavered. 'After all that's happened, how can you doubt my loyalty?'

'Your loyalty? I don't give that,' he snapped his fingers. 'for your loyalty.'

'No, you wouldn't.' Now her anger equalled his. 'How can you talk about loyalty? You don't know the meaning of the word. You and your legion of women, and your take-them-and-leave-them attitude. You wouldn't understand,' she breathed deeply to steady her voice, 'the sort of love and loyalty that someone could feel for another person which would endure for a lifetime.'

'And what do you know about love that lasts a life-time?'

'A lot,' she cried, 'more than you'll ever know. I have the

example of my mother and father. I might be mad, in fact, in saying what I'm going to say, I know I'm mad, but – but,' she was determined to get it out whatever the cost to herself, whatever the humiliation it would bring in its trail, 'I wouldn't just die *with* you, as I said the other day, I'd die *for* you. That's how deep my loyalty is to you. Now do you believe me when I say I did not betray any secret of yours to anyone – anyone at all?'

He paled. 'No,' she rushed on, crying now, 'I can see you don't. When I've gone – and I'm going for good this time – you can laugh and laugh at how you've enslaved another woman, made yet another conquest to add to your list.' She ran to the door.

'Juliet!' He was after her and caught her arms, swinging her round. 'Do you realize what you're saying?'

She tugged her arms away and ran, blinded by tears, down the six flights of stairs. He didn't follow. When she reached the boutique, she was quite alone.

'So that's that,' she sobbed, 'exit me, Juliet Bourne, from Major and Son. Curlews, here I come.'

She glared at herself in the mirror. She had to stop crying. She scrubbed at her face with her handkerchief and with a shaking hand put on some make-up, but the tears kept coming and smudged it all and she had to rub it off and start again. The telephone rang.

Automatically she stretched out her hand and answered. 'Why are you crying, Juliet?'

'I'm n-not c-crying. You're imagining it.'

'I'm not. I know you're crying.'

'H-how do you know?'

'I can see you on the television monitor.'

'That's all you can do, make f-fun of me. I'm going.'

'You're not going. You're staying right there. I'm coming down.'

'You're n-not. You'll be too late.' But she was talking to herself. He had gone. She crashed down the receiver and started feverishly on her face again. It was no good, it would have to stay like that. She'd just have to hope no one looked at her. She grabbed her coat and her bag and flung herself at the entrance. He was there and her momentum made her hit him squarely on the chest. She was momentarily winded but recovered and tried to push past him. But his body, hard and unyielding, prevented her escape.

He edged her back into the boutique. She struggled. 'It's no good trying to stop me. I'm leaving. I'm going to work for Curlews. Their boutique buyer's left and they're prepared to offer me twice the salary—'

He shook her to make her stop. 'You, work for Curlews? Over my dead body! You think I'm going to let you go now, after what you told me upstairs?'

'You can't stop me!'

'Oh, but I can. Like this.' His arms came out and secured her as surely as a rope tied round her. His mouth fastened on hers, pressing back her head and forcing her to respond.

But she struggled to get away. 'It's no good. I'm not going to be one of your women. I'm not going to have an affair with you, so—'

'My darling,' his voice was urgent, 'I'm asking you to have an affair with me. A life-long affair, until death do us part.'

She held back and looked at him, suspicious even now of his motives.

'I'm proposing to you, sweetheart. I'm asking you to marry me, Juliet.'

'But – but if I accepted,' she still could not bring herself to believe that what he was saying was sincere and genuine, 'how would I know you wouldn't be unfaithful to me, like your father to your mother? You told me he taught you to be like him—'

'You've forgotten one vital fact. He chose the wrong woman to be his wife. I'm choosing the right woman from the start. And,' he whispered, drawing her now acquiescent body to his, 'I'm not going to make the terrible mistake he made. I'm not letting you run away from me, as he allowed your mother to do. We, my darling, are not even going to be engaged. We're going to be married. At once.'

'But I haven't said,' she whispered faintly, 'that I'll marry you.'

'You have no choice, my sweet. I know you love me. No woman would say to a man what you said to me in my office without loving him. Am I right?'

She nodded and this time there was no resistance to his kisses, and afterwards she rested against him, needing the support of his body to keep her upright.

'My darling,' he said, lifting her face and cupping it with

his hands, 'my father's in South America.'

'I know. My mother told me.'

'I want us to do something. I want us to contact him now and tell him the news. I know the name of his hotel. He left it in case of emergencies.' They walked, arms round each other, towards the lift.

She smiled up at him. 'And this is an emergency?'

'It most certainly is. If he doesn't come home at once, he'll miss our wedding!'

In the lift he held her in his arms as if he was afraid to let her go. He told her, 'I've discovered the answer to the mystery about the sale of the land. When you left me upstairs, I phoned Curlews' manager – I caught him just before he went home. He told me it was the estate agent's double dealing that was the cause of the trouble. Apparently, Curlews were contacted by the agents, who told them we wanted the land, and if they were interested they could have it, provided they offered more money than we were offering. They did and they got the land. I told the man exactly what I thought of Curlews for such a miserable piece of deception, that we might even take them to law. He said that if Majors felt that strongly about it, we could have the perishing land back as he put it, and good luck to us.'

They got out of the lift and strolled along to his room. 'Will you ever forgive me for those accusations I made against you and for saying you were to blame?'

She pulled his head down and whispered in his ear, 'If you tell me you love me, which you haven't done yet, I'll forgive you anything.'

He unlocked his door and took her inside and proceeded to convince her in a most satisfactory way of his love for her. So she forgave him.

He sat in his chair and pulled her on to his knee. She asked, touching his cheeks with her fingers, 'How long have you loved me, Drew?'

His hands covered hers. 'How long does it take for an avalanche to hit you after the first rock falls? The first one hit me the day I met you. The rest followed almost at once. That,' he whispered, against her lips, 'is how long I've loved you.' They drew apart.

'But, darling, why didn't you tell me?'

'Why? Because when a woman tells a man she hates him

more than she's ever hated anyone else in her whole life, what is that man to do, except what I did – keep silent?'

'I didn't tell you, I told your father. Anyway, I did hate you – for being so horrible to me and for not loving me back when I loved you so desperately.'

'What,' he said, kissing her again, 'a lot of time we've wasted.'

It took Drew some minutes to contact his father's hotel and even more before they found him. But at last his voice came loud and clear over the thousands of miles and when he heard the news, the voice became even louder. The joy in it was unmistakable.

'He wants to speak to you,' Drew said, handing her the receiver. 'Don't worry about the cost. The call's on the firm.'

'Juliet?' Warren said. 'Words can't tell you how delighted I am. My dear, will you do something for me? Just once—' his voice cracked and recovered, 'will you call me Dad? After that you can call me Warren, or anything else you like, rude or otherwise. Go on, I'm listening.'

She answered, shyly, smiling at Drew who had heard what his father had said, 'Hallo, Dad. I'm – I'm glad you're pleased about us.'

There was a brief silence. Then, 'Thank you, my dear. Put my son back, will you?' Drew took the phone from her. 'Drew? Marry her quick, son, don't let her get away like I let her mother.'

'Don't worry, Father. A few days at the most. We're not even going to be engaged. Coming home for the wedding?'

'You just try to stop me! I'm on my way. But before I go, just tell your girl one thing, will you? Tell her thank God I'm going to be related to her mother in some way, even if it's only distantly. Tell her that, will you?' He rang off.

'You heard?' asked Drew.

There were tears in her eyes as she nodded.

'Come on,' Drew said 'I'm taking you home to your parents. Then we're going to celebrate.'

'I must get my things from the boutique. And do something to my face.'

'Why bother? It's beautiful as it is.'

In the boutique she combed her hair, but make-up was

187

unnecessary. Her face was transformed. 'You once told me,' she said, as she gathered her things together, 'that the woman you married would have to be perfect.'

'I did not. I said "made to measure", which is a very different thing. You're certainly not perfect, my darling, and I wouldn't be marrying you if you were. Who wants a perfect woman? But, my word, as far as I'm concerned, you're certainly made to measure – my measure.'

They kissed again then made their way, his arm round her waist, to the car park, leaving the building by the rear entrance. The caretaker was standing beside it and as they approached he smiled and wished them every happiness.

Overwhelmed, they asked him, 'How did you know?'

He laughed. 'I saw you on the television monitor in the security room. My goodness, it was just like a film!'

'Keep it to yourself,' Drew urged him, 'don't tell anyone yet, will you?'

'Not a soul, sir, I promise. Except my wife. She can't resist a happy ending!'

Mills & Boon Classics

The very best of Mills & Boon
romances, brought back for those of you
who missed reading them when they
were first published.

There are three other Classics for you to collect this
June

ONE MAN'S HEART
by Mary Burchell

A harmless — well, fairly harmless — escapade took an
unexpected and horrifying turn that nearly landed Hilma in
serious trouble. But fortunately there was a handsome and
chivalrous stranger at hand to help her.

THE KISSES AND THE WINE
by Violet Winspear

Lise supposed she ought to be grateful to the imperious
Conde Leandro de Marcos Reyes for helping her out of an
awkward situation — but not so grateful that she was willing
to repay him as he suggested, by pretending to be his fiancée.
A domineering Spanish nobleman was not her idea of a comfortable husband. However, she reluctantly agreed to the
deception, just for a short time . . .

THE WATERFALLS OF THE MOON
by Anne Mather

'He's allergic to emotional entanglements,' Ruth declared
after she encountered the disturbing Patrick Hardy. But it
was an allergy that Ruth unfortunately didn't share and she
tricked Patrick into marriage and accompanied him to Venezuela.
Would her husband ever forgive the deception?

Mills & Boon Classics

The very best of Mills & Boon
romances, brought back for those of you
who missed reading them when they
were first published.

In
July
we bring back the following four
great romantic titles.

SONG IN MY HEART
by Rachel Lindsay

When Sara's brother got into serious trouble, she first gave up
her training as an opera singer to help him and then persuaded
his employer in the Combined Television Company to give
him another chance. Her unselfishness had its reward — for it
led her to a new, glittering career, and at last to the love of
her life.

THE GLASS CASTLE
by Violet Winspear

'Out in the East they say that the mind of a woman is a
jungle, and it is the one jungle in which a man should never get
lost.' That was the code by which the arrogant Edwin Trequair
lived — or so he told Heron. Why then did he ask her to marry
him?

INTERLUDE IN ARCADY
by Margery Hilton

When Nicola agreed to accompany Marcus Hillary to his hide-
out on the Yorkshire moors, she had no illusions. Marcus was
only using her as a means of warding off certain predatory
females while he finished writing his new play. So, when they
began to descend on Arcady, why should she find herself
beginning to mind?

THE INNOCENT INVADER
by Anne Mather

Sarah, straight from a convent, went out wide-eyed with
excitement to the West Indies to a job as governess to the
small wards of Jason de Cordova. And had the bad luck to fall
in love with her employer — who was not only married but
had every intention of staying married! How could she cope
with the heartbreak?

If you have difficulty in obtaining any of these books through
your local paperback retailer, write to:
Mills & Boon Reader Service
P.O. Box 236, Thornton Road, Croydon, Surrey, CR9 3RU.

Doctor Nurse Romances

and June's
stories of romantic relationships behind the scenes
of modern medical life are:

STAFF NURSE AT ST. MILDRED'S
by Janet Ferguson

Staff Nurse Jill Thompson was not used to feeling
unsure of herself. She liked things to be well organised,
like her future with Clive Farmer. But perhaps she was
only clinging to Clive because Dr Guy Ferring, her boss
at St. Mildred's, disturbed her so ...

THE RUSTLE OF BAMBOO
by Celine Conway

Inexperienced as she was, Nurse Pat Millay found it
hard going at the little hospital on the Burmese island
of Pelonga. And that was before she had experienced
the abrasive effect of Dr Mark Bradlaw's personality —
or fallen in love with him ...